If I Never Remember

If I Never Remember

MEAGAN WILLIAMSON

IF I NEVER REMEMBER
Copyright © 2024 by Meagan Williamson

Cover design by Nysha Lilly
Editing by Britt Tayler

authormeaganwilliamson.com

*To my husband and all the memories we've made in Bear Lake.
Our life together is the greatest love story I could ever write.*

CHAPTER ONE

NOW

I float. Nothing but a woven knot beneath my feet and a ten-foot drop below me. A thick jute rope chafes a trail of exposed skin running down my breastbone and between my thighs, skipping the only section covered by a pair of high-waisted bottoms and a bikini top. An expanse of water waits beneath, settling into the cracks of inky shadows and steep rocky cliffs. Here, suspended in the air, miles from our cozy cabin on Bear Lake, is the last place the daughter of Archie and Birdie Fletcher should be.

I close my eyes and drift back to last night's conversation over dinner.

"Teddy, you aren't eating," my mom commented as I shuffled this week's vegetable hash around the center of my plate with a fork. "Did I cook it too long?"

"No, it's fine, Mom," I assured her.

I tracked the movement of my dad's hand out of the corner of my eye. When it met his mouth, he grimaced but let the wet, pulpy bite mash between his teeth.

"Really, honey. I can make you something else. Maybe avocado toast?" she offered.

I jammed my fork against the ceramic plate, excavating a bite of my own and scrutinizing it as it dripped from the sides. I'd need a levitation charm to will it to my mouth.

"I had avocado toast for breakfast," I reminded her.

Although, anything would have been better than this.

"Oh." Her eyebrows bunched, and then she leapt from her seat, sending the straw fedora toppling off her crown. "Well, I'll just fill your water then!"

Before she could close her hand around the rim of my seven-eighths-full glass, I jerked it off the table. "You know what, no!" I screamed in defiance. "I don't need any more water. I don't want avocado toast. I don't need anything from you!"

The wooden legs of the dining nook table rattled as I shoved away from it. Two pairs of stunned eyes followed me as I marched up the stairs leading to the third-story loft.

"Teddy, wait..." I heard her falter and move to hustle after me, but still I took the steps two at a time and slammed the door shut.

My body trembles against the rope, snapping back to the present. I refuse to believe it has to do with anything other than my nervous system's reaction to swimwear before the sun has risen. I should have worn a wetsuit for this.

Bloomington Lake is a crater of melted snow so clear I can see the bottom from my bird's eye view. Lush green grass grows around the water's edge, and droves of wildflowers pucker open, even at five in the morning in the beginning of June. It won't be long before a sea of cars overflows the gravel parking lot near the mouth of the trail, so I close my eyes and savor the single sound of a robin's song.

Like clockwork, my mind perceives the moment of calm as an opportunity to intrude, and the memories seep back in...

A soft tap, tap, tap *sounded from the other side of my bedroom door, and I already knew what she was going to say:*

"Please, tell me what I'm doing wrong. You know I just want to help."

When I didn't respond, she pushed the door open anyway.

"I'm coming in."

It was a column of wooden slats on an old frame. There wasn't much stopping her.

"I see that."

I knew I was being unfair. I was lucky to have two parents who cherished me. They'd already proved they'd do anything to help me through this, but it was the one thing they didn't give me that I needed the most.

My mom tiptoed toward me like the floor was made up of broken glass fragments. She perched on the edge of my bed and sighed. "Was it something I said?"

I lifted my head where it rested against my knees, tucked up close to my chest.

I wanted to tell her, "It's everything. The nutrient-dense diet and strict routines. The constant emphasis on hydration. Daily meditation and sleep hygiene. The two La-Z-Boy recliners you donated so you could make space for an elliptical machine right in the middle of the damn living room. Most of all, it's the way you and Dad treat me like a porcelain doll, poised to shatter at the slightest touch."

But I couldn't do that, because to them, I was. I almost died nine months ago, and their world hadn't been the same since.

"I'm just tired," I said.

A half-dozen charms jingled as my mom read the watch fastened around her wrist. "It's only seven o'clock. Are you feeling okay?"

"Mom, I'm not physically tired, I'm emotionally tired. We've been at this for months. I've done everything Dr. Spalding suggested, everything you and Dad requested. I'm tired of *pushing for something that has clearly disappeared. I need you to let it go."*

I flung myself backward, my strawberry blonde bob fanning across my lumpy pillow. I mapped the textured ceiling, searching for any direction other than the eyes of the woman I couldn't meet. They housed nothing but pain and disappointment.

It was impossible to miss the tears that pooled in them as she pleaded, "Can we just try one last thing? PLEASE. And then I promise I'll stop."

I groaned, stretching out my five-foot-two frame like a starfish. I already knew my parents would look at my choice as giving up rather than moving on, but I also knew we were heading into uncharted territory. I had to give her this. "You promise?"

"I do."

She sprang up and scurried for the old wooden vanity tucked against my bedroom wall. The drawer gave way on a tug, and she extracted a book with spiraled bindings from its confines. She cradled it between her hands like a newborn baby. I sat up cross-legged as she laid it in my lap.

"What's this?" I scrubbed my hand over the dusty worn cover before meeting her mossy green eyes that matched my own.

"You used to sketch." A far-off look and a hint of a smile haunted her face with the memory. "By the time you were out of diapers and starting preschool, it was your thing. You never left home without some kind of bound paper. Everything you've ever loved, you've drawn in those pages. I just thought..."

She didn't finish her sentence. She didn't have to. We both knew that anytime we tried something new like this, it planted a seed of hope.

I flipped open the cover to the first page. A pencil-drawn sketch of our cabin on Bear Lake rested in the center. Charcoal strokes mapped the water on the next one, but the view was from *above, like I hung from a tree branch when I drew it. I brushed my palm over the flat surface, expecting to feel the ripples beneath my fingertips.*

The next twenty minutes were consumed with page-turning. Each drawing growing more vivid in detail than the last. When I got to the final sketch, my mom propped herself up a little taller. An outline of a heart-shaped locket rested open in the center, a silhouette of a different boy on either side. A deep dimple carved the cheek of the one on the right, while the other boy's smile tipped up on one side.

I studied their hair next. Memorized the way one curled up over his eyes, and the other's hid beneath a baseball cap. Even in black and white, they were both nice to look at. Both striking and strong. Both... figments of my imagination.

"Well?" my mom started.

How was I supposed to tell her that her last resort failed? As much as she wanted me to remember, I couldn't give that to her. I didn't know how to break her heart.

"It's... beautiful," I chose to say instead.

Tears tumbled down her cheeks. I'd seen them a hundred times before, but this time they were a firm and brutal reminder that I was disappointing the people I loved.

The frown of my reflection, no longer distorted in undulations, shifts my focus back to the present moment, back to what I determined this morning. I can't stay in Bear Lake.

I may not know who I am anymore, but I know I won't figure it out here. No matter how bad I feel about it, I meant what I said to my mom last night.

I just need to survive the summer, I convince myself. Three months of saving money at my new job and, somewhere along the way, I'll confess my plan to my parents. I can do that.

As I stare out over the water, a soft glow nudges against the horizon. It's too low in the sky to feel its warmth yet, and the shiver that snakes its way up my spine is getting harder to ignore. Goose bumps prick against my skin at the thought of dunking my whole body in this glacier, but no one is here to stop me. No one is here to tell me it's unsafe, or that I'm not ready.

Taking a deep breath, I rock my hips in one final arc.

Snap.

The sound of a stick splitting in two jolts my body rigid. My grip falters and my feet slip below the knot that anchored me in the air. I yelp and scramble for purchase, my right hand sliding in a nasty wake of razor burn until my feet crash against the earth.

"Woah, are you okay?"

I startle and whip around at the sound of a deep timbre voice. My gaze catches on a pair of hazel eyes, on an outstretched hand, as if this guy planned to catch me from several feet away.

I squint, drawing details from beneath the brim of his ball cap. There's something familiar about the way his jaw angles in a sharp slope toward his chin.

When he tips his head to the side, jerking a pair of headphones out of his ears, I see it. The dark shading of his hairline. The rounded fullness of his lips. There's no denying that he looks an awful lot like a sketch from my past. One that I shoved away in the depths of a drawer for a reason. And he's standing right in front of me.

"I can't wait to see this place!" My dad drums his hands against the wooden steering wheel to the beat of "The Boys are Back in Town" streaming through the radio speakers.

My mom adjusts the volume down a handful of notches.

"Do you think we're jumping the gun, Arch? Maybe we should have opted for an inspection before we arrived." She draws the purple frames of her glasses down the bridge of her nose, revealing a pair of worried eyes.

"Nah." He shakes his tousled hair. It curls at the ends just before meeting the collar of his AC/DC T-shirt. "I've seen enough of these; I know what to look for."

That's what he thinks, Mr. Architect. He may design custom homes for a living, but if it doesn't have door handles that stick and floorboards that creak, then it's not for him.

I choose to agree with my mom. Not because a ten-year-old has any worthwhile knowledge on the subject, but because I wasn't given any stake in this decision. I thought I'd be spending my summer playing night games with Cozy and Baker at the park, not living in Timbuktu with my parents.

In fact, it never even crossed my mind they might consider

this. But here we are—one real estate auction site and fully furnished cabin in Bear Lake later. Forty miles into a five-hour and three-minute drive away from our roomy suburban home in Boise, Idaho—I can't imagine this place is any better than that.

I tug a chunk off a Nerds Rope with my teeth, elbowing a wall of cardboard boxes. I groan and nurse the tip with my hand. If it weren't for the brand-new sketchbook in my lap, I'd be sulking right about now.

"I packed mouse traps," my mom warns him, and I cringe.

It's mouse-infested too? What has he done.

She pushes her glasses back into place and drops her gaze to the *Better Homes and Gardens: Summer Edition* magazine draped across her lap. I watch the trimmed salt-and-pepper whiskers of my dad's five o'clock shadow lift in the rearview mirror.

"Sure, hon. And I brought the cheese." He weaves his hand through the pile of belongings heaped in the center console and squeezes her bare knee.

My face must be frozen in a grimace because he asks, "What's wrong, Teddy Bear?"

"Nothing," I say, forcing my feelings down. I may be moping inside, but I can't show it.

"Don't worry, ladies, it will be the perfect adventure!" he says. Then he turns the radio back up four notches and continues his drumming, while I lose myself to a portrait of the summer I was hoping to have.

As an only child, I've learned to entertain myself by drawing. I carry a sketchbook like an organ I can't live without. I guess exploring your creative talents comes naturally when you have an acrylic painter for a mom.

When an update from Siri tracks forty-one miles to our destination, I peel my eyes from my sketch to peer out the window. My jaw hinges open.

I don't actually know what Timbuktu looks like, but the image I conjured up in my brain is not this. Steep rocky cliffs wind a trail through the Logan Canyon Scenic Byway. Countless evergreens stretch to touch puffy clouds scattered across the palest of blue skies.

I roll down my window, letting my hair tornado around me. The contrast of the sunshine's warmth blankets my skin. Between the scents of pine and damp earth, I fight the urge to close my eyes and revel in my overloaded senses. We're not in Boise anymore, that's for sure, but maybe this won't be so bad after all.

We pull onto a narrow road that curves like a centipede around a large body of turquoise water. Cabins of every shape, size, and color come into view, stamping the shoreline.

"Do you ladies mind if we make a pit stop before the cabin? I've heard of this place that makes incredible raspberry milkshakes," he says, turning over his shoulder at the stop light to look at me.

My eyes brighten and I nod, sitting a little taller in my seat. If there's one thing I can get on board for, it's dessert.

A hand-painted sign welcomes us to the town of Garden City, population 600—home to a marina, safety station, ATV rental shop, and a handful of family-owned restaurants.

My dad drifts our car into a grassy parking lot tucked behind a small shack. Bright blue umbrella-covered picnic tables circle the building, and an oversized sign in the shape of a shake cup advertises LaBeau's down the front of it.

The line to the takeout window snakes a good ten families deep as my parents rattle off the options from the menu. But I'm too distracted by the family in front of us to notice. A short woman in a neon pink coverup, her hair piled in a bun on top of her head, fields a twelve-way thumb war between six boys. They look like they just stepped straight off a speedboat with hair dried backward, wind-chapped cheeks, and all sporting matching fluorescent-patterned boardshorts.

"Stop it, right this instant," she demands.

I stare in fascination as every boy ignores their mother's request. My head tips forward as if my shrunken eyelids can shield me from witnessing the entire scene. I can't recall a single time I've ever disobeyed my parents. But these boys wrestle and mock each other like they don't have a care in the world.

When their mother fails to break them apart, she herds them out of line to the side of the building like a pack of wolves, leaving her very flustered husband to order alone. I crane my neck to see what will happen next and am struck by a twinge of jealousy.

I wish Cozy were here.

She may not be the built-in best friend that a sibling would be, but living down the street where I can walk to her house is much better than miles apart for the summer.

When the dad in front of us finishes ordering an army of food, the teenage waiter ushers my family forward and takes our order (three cheeseburgers, two raspberry shakes, and a large fry to share).

As luck would have it, the only vacant table sits next to the family I've come to know simply by observing their behavior. In the time it's taken us to gather Ketchup packets and napkins, their kids have launched a french fry–throwing contest to see who can catch the most in their mouth.

"Going out to eat with kids is always fun, huh?" my mom says to their mother.

"Oh, I'm so sorry. Are they bothering you?" She shields her forehead with her hand.

"No, not at all! I was just remembering when we took this one"—she points to where I'm sitting, eyes wide as I wonder what she's about to share—"to a Wingers once, and she spit out a piece of meat on the aisle floor screaming, 'It's too hot!' I think the only thing in that entire restaurant hotter than those wings was the color of my face." My mom chuckles, shaking her head.

The woman joins in on her laugh, the tension in her shoulders easing. "Yeah, kids can be so fun. You're lucky you only have one. There's no one around to fight with."

My mom gets a soft, glassy look in her eye before she leans over and squeezes me by the shoulders.

"I am lucky. No need for more when you put all your eggs in one *perfec*t basket," she says, and I offer the lady a small smile.

It's *a lot* of pressure being the only child sometimes. I'd give anything for our family to grow. I'd even be okay sharing their attention, but I'd never tell my mom that. I want them to always believe I'm happy with things just the way they are. After all, it was a miracle they even had me.

The family leaves long before we do. I'm the first to finish my raspberry milkshake, slurping the bottom clean with every pull of my straw. I can see why it's world famous—it's creamy and smooth and is the sweetest thing I've ever tasted.

"Why don't we head out and finish this back at the new cabin. I'm anxious to see it," my dad comments, already packaging up his half-eaten burger.

A short five minutes later, he guides the hatchback down a sloping driveway. It's patchy in most places, unsure of whether to give way to the lawn's growth or keep the pebbly terrain. Near the bottom, tire tracks have worn two paths clear down to the dirt, but plush grass grows everywhere else on the property. Then there's... the lake.

It's the color of green sea glass and— *Wow*. The entire surface is glittering like a disco ball. It's *so* much better than I ever expected.

I scramble for my sketch pad and unbuckle my seat belt.

"Hey, Mom, do you think I could go draw from that dock over there?"

The sun's just about to go down, and I don't want to miss it.

She pushes open her door and steps out, leaning her slender frame against the car as she scrutinizes the safety of the situation. When she tucks her head back inside, she says, "Just don't go in the water, and watch out for snakes, okay?"

Snakes too?

I gulp as she turns away and tiptoes after my dad, crossing the cabin's threshold. But as I pad out onto the lawn, every concern I might've had rushes away like a tidal wave. I don't know what she thinks she's going to find in there with a place looking like this.

From where I stand rooted to the spot, a slender three-story tower with a wraparound patio and brick firepit opens up before me. A bunkhouse addition with a sliding glass door juts off to one side. The roof's made of tin, the siding coated in dark green paint, and at least a half dozen windows stack like dominos across the front, facing the lake. From here, I think it's safe to say we can throw away those mouse traps. It looks perfect.

Besides our cabin, two additional properties bracket the place. The one situated on the right is framed in construction tape but resembles the makings of a traditional log cabin. With two decks, a private dock ten yards out into the water, and a massive water trampoline floating just beyond that, it's the most expansive of the three lots.

Maybe they're almost finished with it, I hope. It might be my best chance at a neighbor friend to play with this summer. Because there's not much hope with the opposite property.

On a sea of dandelions sits a lone 1979 Prowler camp trailer. It's rusting near the hitch with brown paint chipped off the sides, and it's untethered. Curtains drape closed over the windows, but the stairs have been left extended from the front door. A shed half the size of the trailer runs parallel to it. Also humble in size, dated, and latched with a deadbolt. A dinged-up Ford Ranger with blue and white stripes down the sides hugs a red Toyota Camry. The two vehicles are the only clue that anyone might live there.

I notice the sun dipping lower in the sky, and I sprint to the end of a long stretch of wooden planks floating on top of the water to take it in.

When I sit and dangle my feet off the ledge, I let the foam bottoms of my flip flops float on the surface like boats. The horizon shifts from bubblegum hues to gradients of purple until it's solid black. Crickets chirp all around me, and the moon casts a soft, bouncing shadow across the surface of the water like a white pool ball.

I don't know how much time has passed when the gradual darkness announces an orange glow coming from the trailer window. A duet of dark shapes crosses the drawn curtains and a single voice escalates, angry and female.

"Theadora, is everything okay?" my mother's floating head hollers from the doorway.

She's worried about me.

The only other time she calls me by my full name is when she's sentimental. I can almost feel the bristles of a round brush tunneling through my hair as she said to me, "Theadora, did you know your name means 'gift from God'?"

It was five years ago—the night before my first day of kindergarten—and I was prolonging bedtime because I was afraid to leave her the next morning. I knew after she dropped me off at school, we'd spend the whole day apart, and that seemed like a very long time.

Even though the tangles had long since unwound from my hair, she resumed her short, soothing strokes through the silky strands.

I shook my head and sat a little taller. She'd never told me how she and my dad came up with my name. I hadn't ever thought to ask, but now I wanted to know more than anything.

"Before you were born, I was sick. I had something called cancer. Have you heard of that before?"

I shook my head a second time.

"It's when bad cells in your body stop the good ones from doing their job. For mommy, those bad cells were growing in a place called my uterus, and they were keeping me from having you."

"What did you do?" I remember asking her with wide eyes.

I knew what it was like to have bad germs in your body, and there was nothing more miserable than being sick.

"Well, first, I had three rounds of medicine to make the bad cells go away, and then we tried to have you," she said.

I turned over my shoulder to look up at her.

"Did it work?"

The edges of my mom's smile slipped.

"Not at first, no. It was hard to get you here. Because of my cancer and losing something called a fallopian tube from a pregnancy that wasn't quite right, my doctor told me I might not have a baby at all."

Her brush strokes slowed when she saw me frown, and she pulled me close to her chest.

"But then, a year later, a miracle happened."

My eyes brightened.

"You were born! Our gift."

She draped her arms around my neck.

"And you were beautiful and strong—just like I know you'll be for your first day of school tomorrow."

When I turned away from her, she lifted my chin with her forefinger.

"But if you need me, I'll always be here to protect to you, my Theadora."

Unlike the softness she used that day, the pitch of her voice now suggests fear.

"I'm okay," I assure her, pointing to the neighbor's camp trailer.

Even from the dock, the light off the kitchen highlights her profile. Her mouth hangs open and her brow furrows. When she ducks back inside, I track the moon's shadow.

Whack.

The sound of a screen door slamming has me plunging my feet into the icy lake water, and I jerk around.

Someone from the trailer is running right for me.

CHAPTER THREE

NOW

The guy from the sketch's eyes widen when he sees my face.

"I'm... so sorry... are you hurt?" he stutters.

"Um..."

I stare at him at first as I pat my body up and down before dropping my eyes to follow the pattern of my palms. I half expect to find a gaping hole where the rope burned a stretch of skin on my right hand and a patch the size of a quarter by my navel. It stings, but it's my heart that's in worse shape, threatening to beat right out of my chest.

"I'm... yeah. I mean, no. I'm fine," I finish, sounding like I don't believe a single word coming out of my mouth.

"Okay... good."

He drops his gaze to his feet.

"I should go then."

He lifts his headphones to his ears and starts jogging back the way he came.

"No, wait!" I shout.

He doesn't make it more than five feet before coming to a

halt. The muscles in his back bunch with tension but he doesn't turn around.

What am I doing?

If I thought rope swinging in the pitch black by myself was risky, striking up a conversation with a complete stranger is ten times worse. He could be a serial killer for all I know. This is how those *Dateline* shows start. *Nineteen-year-old girl wanders into wooded canyon alone... doesn't make it out alive.*

Not to mention, it was mere minutes ago when I settled on leaving the past behind me. Now here I am, playing tennis with it. It doesn't help that I can't shake the feeling I'm supposed to know him, and I need the ball in his court to find out if I'm right.

The stiff wind against my small frame has me wrapping my arms around my torso like a shield, but I know it can't possibly be strong enough to keep this six-foot male from turning his shoulder and looking at me. I don't know what else to do to get his attention but to introduce myself.

"I'm Teddy," I say, balancing the weight of my body on my tiptoes.

He pivots, a flash of grief passing over his expression. It's something I'm sure I would have missed without the memory of a similar silhouette drawn with a smile.

By the time he's facing me, he's a blank canvas.

With a polite nod, he says, "It was nice to meet you, Teddy."

Was? He's supposed to say *I know*, like everyone else in this town. Maybe I'm wrong. Maybe we've never met before this moment. Maybe I just want him to stay because I could use a friend. It's isolating being stuck in a cabin with no one but your parents for months on end.

"What are you doing out here all alone?" he asks.

For most women, a thousand alarm bells would be sounding in their head with a question like that.

Stranger danger, stranger danger.

But he lifts his hat, his dark ruffled hair falling along his forehead, and my idiotic brain repeats a single word on a chronic loop...

Handsome handsome, handsome handsome.

I swallow, searching for my voice.

"Wasn't it obvious?" I lift my palms in the air to show off my sandpapered hands, only to notice how raw they look and swiftly jerking them behind my back.

"Not at this time of day, no," he says, looking at me like I need to be admitted to a psychiatric facility.

And who am I to disagree? I look unhinged. *I have literally lost my mind*, I want to offer in explanation, but even people you know on an intimate level don't understand that form of early-life crisis.

"Good point." I chuckle, trying to keep the conversation as lighthearted as possible. The last thing I want is for this guy—who has still not offered up his name, by the way—to be another person on my lengthy list of individuals who know I've suffered a brain injury. Yet I'm struggling *not* to be transparent with him.

"I just wanted to feel free," I admit.

I hadn't noticed how tense he was until his shoulders soften.

"Yeah, I get that," he says.

In the ten seconds he takes searching for a place to land his gaze, he notices his undone shoelace and bends at the waist to tie it. I use the moment to study him.

Everything about him is dark. From the locks of his hair to the full eyebrows resting over a set of eyelashes that curl at the tips. His long, lean lines are more pronounced by his olive skin.

When he stands, stretching to his full height, his shadow dwarfs mine. Which is not difficult to do with at least a foot's height difference between us.

Perspiration beads across his abdomen, and I clear my

throat. Sweat cascades toward the waist of his black workout shorts, and I blink a handful of times before getting ahold of myself and finding his face. Even then, it's a struggle to think straight beneath his gaze.

"Like I said, I should get going," he reminds me, taking a few backward steps.

And what do I do?

I stop him. Yet again.

"You never told me your name," I blurt.

Our eyes meet one last time.

"It's Miles," he says.

A smile pulls at the edges of my lips.

Miles.

"See you around, Miles."

But he doesn't smile back at me. He just vanishes in a jog like he was a figment of my imagination.

It's almost seven o'clock by the time I park the hatchback at the cabin. I slip through the backdoor that opens into a mudroom. A mudroom that also serves as the downstairs bathroom and laundry room combined. I poke my head through the opening to a silent home and sigh in relief.

They're not awake yet.

I was just cleared to drive solo days ago. Had they known I snuck out with the car before the sun was up, I'm certain those privileges would be revoked.

I shut the door and start the shower, stripping off my dry swimsuit as the room fills with steam. If I wasn't worried about tipping off my parents, I'd go look at the sketch that's been haunting me ever since Miles and I parted ways.

Ignoring that thought for now, I lather my hair with Pantene shampoo. It stings against the rug burn on my hand, but I have no choice but to rinse, run conditioner through the strands, and rinse again. I shut off the water just in time to hear the familiar creak of the second stair before the landing. Had I been awake in my room, a knock on the door would have sounded. But the bathroom is the one place they give me complete privacy.

I blot the moisture from my skin with a fluffy bath towel, then reach for the khaki shorts and baby-blue polo draped on top of the dryer. As I pull the soft cotton over my head, I notice *Bear Shore* embossed in white thread above the left breast.

If I thought this day was off to an interesting start... it's about to get even more so wearing a uniform like this. I haven't so much as strayed from my daily routine in months, and a full-time job is the definition of a change of pace.

Once I have it fitted, I lift the fabric of my shirt, wincing slightly. The skin is raw and sensitive, and the reminder of that constant aching sensation has me glimpsing at my face in the mirror. I run the pads of my fingertips over the invisible lacerations that once marked my right cheek. I know if those can heal, these will too.

I lather a topical cream along my navel and hand. It burns just as bad as the shampoo did, but it's my best chance of quick healing. I don't need my parents finding out I sneak out to Bloomington Lake in the mornings.

I reach for the blow dryer next. After experiencing both lengths, I can say that the greatest thing about having a bob is the drying time. I don't have to hold my arm above my head and fan it until the limb feels like it's going to dismember from my body. The whole thing dries in less than four minutes. Given my stick-straight hair, it also means I don't have to do a single thing to it if I don't want to. Or in today's case, if I don't have the time.

When I push open the bathroom door, I'm hit with a smoky smell drifting through the air. The overactive gurgle of my stomach carries me straight to the kitchen before my brain has the chance to remind me that I never mended things with my parents last night.

"Oh good, you're awake!" my mom squeaks.

She's wrapped in her signature hand-painted apron, and her curly auburn hair is pulled back with a head scarf.

"You made bacon?" I question in disbelief, saddling up on a barstool.

She tops a piece of jelly toast with blueberry eyes and a bacon smile. Then she leans across the counter and deposits it in front of me.

"It's a peace offering," she says. "I can't promise I won't still get lost a time or two to what I feel like I *should* be doing as your mother, but I made you a promise last night that I intend to keep. Starting with bacon."

I want to believe her, I do. But I think it will take a lot more than a change in the breakfast menu to convince me.

I flash her a smile though and take a bite, the crispy strip crumbling beneath my teeth. An explosion of flavor hits my tongue from the sugar-filled jelly I've been deprived of, and I cover my mouth with the back of my hand, groaning, "So good."

She grins. "Good."

"Holy shit. Is that bacon I'm smelling?" my dad hollers as he rounds the corner into the kitchen.

His flannel pajama bottoms come into view first, followed by his favorite T-shirt with the words *I arted* screen-printed across the front. It was a gift he bought himself at Art in the Park the summer he met my mom. She sells her paintings there once a year. Or at least she did, before the end of last summer when we left Boise for the last time.

I may have forgotten a lot of things, but my parents' origin tale is not one of them.

As the story goes, my dad wandered by her booth and overheard a narcissistic balding man arguing with her over the authenticity of her hand-painted landscape of ocean tides. The man held her canvas up to the sun's light, scrutinizing her talent, and then proceeded to barter with her over its worth.

I have no doubt my five-foot-nothing mother could have taken this guy with her words alone, but she wasn't given the chance. My dad slid on in and hip-checked him to the ground. When the man landed on his arrogant ass, a foghorn sounded from his rear end. He scurried off faster than a toddler with a foreign object in their mouth.

My dad purchased her painting at full price, but that shirt from three booths down? That was his ultimate prize.

"Arch," my mom warns as he puts four burnt pieces on an empty plate.

My mom might love to monitor his cholesterol levels per his doctor's recommendation, but he loves his bacon more.

"Oh, come on," he grumbles. "Teddy gets some." He nudges my shoulder and smirks.

"Very funny," she says. "Can I at least make you some toast to go with it?"

"Not today, Birdie. Today, I indulge."

He winks at me, and it feels good to see this playful side of him again. He's been on board with all of this, but he looks just as relieved as I am to take a break.

"So, first day at the big new job, huh, Teddy Bear?"

"Yep. Don't miss me too much," I tease, knowing full well they'll both stake out the parking lot with a set of binoculars.

He stands from his barstool, rounds the counter, and circles my mom's waist, kissing her neck.

"Oh, we won't. We've got big plans today."

She giggles and swats him on the arm with a spatula. "Archie!"

I groan. "Okay, too much."

No one enjoys their parents' blatant displays of affection. But there are times when it doesn't bother me. Like when he tucks her hair behind her ear while she's reading. Or when he squeezes her thigh to distract her as she flusters in five o'clock traffic. I catch them paving an example of what lasting love looks like, and I'm not ashamed to admit I want what they have someday.

He nuzzles her neck as he squeezes her waist, and she yelps.

"And I've lost my appetite," I say, dropping my half-eaten piece of toast on the plate in front of me and escaping to my bedroom.

I listen for the familiar echo of someone following me or begging me to finish my food, but it's only their laughter that travels up the staircase.

The real reason I left breakfast wasn't their PDA. I've tried and failed to quiet the incessant thoughts about that sketch. I want to know if it's him. I *need* to know.

I close the slatted door to my room for privacy. Like true vintage furniture, the center drawer of my vanity threatens to remain superglued shut unless you give it a good shuffle. I rock it back and forth until it gives way and lurches open.

There, resting in the middle, waits the book my mom showed me last night. I flip it open to the last page and gasp, taking a handful of steps until I feel the backs of my legs collide with my bed. When I fall, the mattress dips with my weight. My heart does this weird stuttering thing in my chest like a hummingbird that's learning to fly.

I trace the tip of my index finger over the bill of a Dodgers baseball cap, down the sloping jawline, and pause at the square of his chin. Just when my finger is about to brush his lips, my breath hitches. Everything I believed to be true is staring back at me.

It's him.

It's Miles.

He wasn't a figment of my imagination at all.

He was someone pretending not to know me.

CHAPTER FOUR

SUMMER, NINE YEARS AGO

The hard lines of a body—a *boy's* body?—flash through the darkness, running straight for the dock.

Maybe if I hold still, they won't notice me, I try to convince myself.

I bunch my knees up to my chest in an attempt to make myself smaller. The constellations in the sky illuminate the space between us, but no matter how hard I squint, I can't make out more than a faceless form about three feet tall.

The person with a cropped hairline comes to a sudden stop at the edge of the grass.

It must be a boy.

He looks about my age too, but it's hard to tell. He's not my height.

Jerking his head from side to side, he scours the yard for somewhere else to go.

I swallow. He must have detected me. But my hands aren't shaking like his, and my heart isn't racing in my chest. I don't feel all the things I thought I would feel, alone in a moment with a stranger like this, and that's when I realize that *I'm* the intruder in this situation.

It's not as if I can stand my ground and claim that this is my dock. I just moved here. Our properties share it, or he wouldn't be using it to seek refuge.

There's no way back to my cabin except right at him, so I remain motionless to see what he'll do next.

He takes his first hesitant step from the grass onto the wood planks, then another, inching closer to me. The beady blacks of his eyes scrutinize me with every movement. With only a yard separating us, I'm sure it's a boy.

Now feet apart, it's his eyes I make out first, and they're not black at all. Flecks of gold in a rich hazel brown glow against the moon's light. They're rimmed with dark lashes that crinkle at the corners.

He looks scared. Sad, even. But harmless.

"You can sit with me if you want?" I offer into the darkness.

He falters, waiting to see if I'll move. I don't. I let him close the rest of the gap.

When he sits down next to me, we both face the lake. I'm far too nervous to look at him.

The shades of dark swirl together—the midnight of the water, the espresso of the mountains, the charcoal of the sky.

It's quiet when I say, "My name's Teddy."

He doesn't answer right away, but it's okay. I don't want him to be scared, and I have time.

"Miles," he whispers back.

A voice escalates into a scream from the trailer. When the screen door slams behind us, we both flinch.

Miles twists his hands in his lap like a pretzel, refusing to turn around. But I can't help it. Someone moves toward the red car.

The engine hums, followed by a pair of tires peeling out of the dusty driveway behind our cabins.

Before I turn back around, I catch a frail-looking man with a fishing hat watching from behind the screen of the doorway. His eyes scan the yard until they land on us, and it's plain to see all over his face; he looks even sadder than Miles does.

When I look back at Miles, he's drawing a never-ending circle in the palm of his hand—over and over like he's wearing a hole right through it.

"Miles?" I whisper.

When he looks at me, there's nothing but heartbreak in his eyes.

How can someone so young be so sad?

I'm not sure I've ever known a sadness like his. Maybe Miles just needs a friend.

Right then and there, I make it my mission to become his friend so I can see him smile.

"How old are you?" I ask.

"Ten," he says.

"Hey, I'm ten too! Do you like tadpoles?"

"Yes," he says.

"So, we're both ten, and we both like tadpoles."

I declare it as if that's enough to bond the two of us for life, but Miles doesn't seem to make the same connection, so I try something else.

"I was thinking about bringing a bucket down here tomorrow and hunting for tadpoles. Do you want to come with me?"

"Okay," he says.

"Okay!" I grin.

I was hoping for this. I just didn't think I'd find it from the empty-looking trailer next door. He's not Cozy, but I could make a new friend. A summer cabin friend.

Gosh, maybe I need this friendship even more than he does, I think to myself.

But then, out of the corner of my eye, I see the edges of his mouth tilt toward the moon in the sky, and I change my mind.

I made Miles smile.

⁓

I find him on the dock the next morning. He's shirtless, peering over the edge into the crystal-clear water, his oversized swim trunks sunken low on his hips. He's wearing a bucket hat that says *Bear Lake* with a canoe stitched below it. His scrawny arm holds up a red bucket with a white plastic handle.

"Miles!" I yell, running with my yellow pail down the grassy slope. "Have you spotted anything yet?"

He's squatting now, hanging over the side of the dock, inspecting something. One degree forward and his body would tip right into the lake.

"Look," he whispers.

I squat too, just as a pod of tadpoles drifts by a foot below the water's surface.

"Wow!"

I examine them up close. There's maybe ten all together with long, squiggly tails.

"Can tadpoles hear?" I ask him.

He gives me a quizzical look beneath the rim of his hat. "I don't know, why?"

"Because you're whispering," I say.

He drops his gaze back to the water.

"Sorry," he mutters.

Then I whisper too. "So, how do you think we catch one?"

His smile widens. "With patience."

He says it like he knows that's the very character trait I do not possess.

"They keep swimming toward the shade, so if we put one

bucket in to create a shadow, maybe we can both scoop at the same time and get lucky."

"Miles, you're a genius!" I say, smiling so wide I show off my missing bottom tooth. I dunk my bucket in the water. It catches on the bottom of the lake, and all the tadpoles scamper away just as the water paints itself into a murky shade of sludge.

"Oops, sorry," I cringe.

"It's okay," Miles says. "We'll try again."

And we do. We try for the next eight hours, stopping once for lunch—peanut butter and jelly sandwiches in the shape of a sandcastle—courtesy of my mom.

When I introduced her to Miles, she seemed thrilled for me that I made a new friend. Or maybe it was because he told her he liked her fedora. He must have a thing for hats.

After lunch, we relocated from the dock to the shell-covered shore. We waded out knee-deep until our arms were buried up to our elbows, and it's where we've been for the past two hours—buckets circling just above the bottom.

Miles's brow is pinched and I'm standing rooted in the sand when my mom interrupts us.

"Teddy, it's time to head in, sweetie. Say good night."

I let out a disappointed sigh. We haven't caught anything yet, but that doesn't mean we're ready to give up. When I look over at Miles, he's already lifted his bucket from the water and is trudging back toward the grass. A sadness ghosts his eyes again. I don't think he wants to go in either.

I stop him, resting my hand on his shoulder.

"Hey, same time tomorrow?"

He turns his chin and smiles right at me.

I love his smile.

"Yeah. Same time tomorrow," he says.

An obnoxious whirring sound, followed by a *thump, thump, thump*, wakes me the next morning. The source of the noise is the second thing I think about after opening my eyes.

I yank the Hudson Bay throw from where it's tucked beneath my chin and exchange my Rapunzel nightgown for the first swimsuit I find in my closet.

When I round the corner at the bottom of the stairs, I'm greeted by my dad's toolbelt-covered butt high in the air, his head buried as he drills into the inside of our kitchen cabinets. A collage of weathered paper resembling the ones on his office desk cover the countertop. When his drill comes to a stop, I lean in close and inspect his handywork.

"Whatcha doin'?"

He cracks his head against the top of the surface, sending one of the battered documents floating to the floor, and hollers, "Shit!"

I giggle as he begins backpedaling, pulling his head out from beneath the frame and rubbing the top of it.

"I mean, *shoot*. You scared me, Teddy Bear."

I squat to retrieve the fallen paper and notice faint rectangular drawings marked with measurements around the outer edge, the word "kitchen" scrawled at the top.

Yep. They look exactly like his clients' blueprints.

I hold it out to him.

"Thanks, kiddo. I was trying to get a good idea of the bones of this place when I got distracted by these wobbly hinges. Turns out they're a lost cause because the screws are stripped."

He returns the sketch from where it fell.

"That sounds exciting! Can I go play with Miles?" I ask, edging my way to the front door.

"Now hold up." He halts me with an outstretched palm. "I'm glad to see you've perked up at the idea of living here this summer, but who's this Miles I'm hearing so much about? Mom said he's replaced me as your adventure partner, and I'm not sure I like the sound of that."

"Oh, he's the *best* at adventuring, Dad! He knows everything there is to know about tadpoles and he wears this awesome fishing hat and he doesn't even wear a shirt!" I ramble.

My dad's eyebrows perk at that last part, but then his face splits into a grin. He folds his arms over his chest and drops to a squat right in front of me.

"I have a feeling there will come a day when I'll need to be concerned about this Miles character, but if you say he's the best, then I guess I can let him pass me up as the greatest adventurer of all time." He says it with a haughty look on his face.

"You're cool too, Dad! Does that mean I can go now?" I plead.

"Right after we run a quick errand," he promises, and I try not to frown. Patience really isn't my thing. "I was just waiting on... Oh, look! Here she is now! And dressed for... the Kentucky Derby?"

My dad's amused eyes scan my mom in her paint-splattered overalls and oversized straw hat.

"Is there some new hat trend I'm not aware of?" he asks.

"What? I like it," she says, tipping the feather-adorned brim back and fanning her eyelashes.

He tries to lean in and kiss her on her cheek, but his forehead ricochets off the brim.

"What's not to like," he gripes, trying the same maneuver on the right, then back to the left, over and over until he gives up altogether.

"Do you think the three of us and that hat of yours could stop at this little tackle shop in town?"

My dad holds up his phone, showing her a picture of a small shop with a green-and-white-striped awning over the door.

"Google says they have a hardware section, and I need to replace some of the hinges on these cabinet doors."

He gestures to the nearest one hanging by a single screw.

"Yes. I think we'd better do that," my mom teases on a hiccup as he smirks back at her.

"Who knows, you might find yourself one of those boonie hats with a neck shade to try out," he says.

She swats him on the arm, and we follow him out the back door.

All Caught Up is about as quaint as a small-town shop could be. Just like the Google picture, the awning shades the hand-carved sign, and when you pull on the door handle, a little gold bell chimes above it.

"Well, isn't this cute," my mom comments as we stop and take in the store's three short aisles and single checkout counter.

"It's smaller than I expected," my dad admits, scratching his mop of hair.

A man in a cotton canvas fishing hat stands with his back to us behind the counter. He's bent over at the waist and talking to someone half his size.

My dad gets right to work, stalking up and down the aisles and scanning the rows of lures, rods, and tackleboxes for a set of screws.

A pair of light-purple water socks catches my eye, and I pull on my mom's hand, pointing to them.

"Are these my size?"

She wanders her gaze from a pair of magnifying glasses to my outstretched finger and reaches inside the shoe. Lifting up on the white tab that's sewn against the back with a *Two* written on it, she says, "They're a little big for you, sweetie."

"I don't mind. I can grow into them," I convince her, thinking about how much better they'd be for tadpole-hunting than my bare feet. Those seashells feel like stepping on a thousand Legos. I know, because Cozy has a little brother, and I've done it before at her house.

My mom swivels her head ninety degrees, as if she's looking for the rest of the sizes, and frowns. Then she looks back at my pleading green eyes.

"Yes. Okay. You can get them."

"Thank you!" I squeal, squeezing her around the middle and bunching the back of her overall straps.

The man behind the counter turns around, and I study his face. His lips angle down at the corners, and his eye don't hold the usual shine you'd find in someone who says, "Can I help you find anything?"

He looks familiar, but I can't place him until his three-foot-tall coworker emerges from behind his wader-covered legs.

"Miles!" I exclaim, running over to where he stands.

He looks like a mini version of his dad from his long, lanky body to his matching fishing gear.

"I thought I was going to miss you this morning. Look what I'm getting for tadpole-hunting." I dangle the water shoes from the string they're held together by with the tip of my pointer finger.

"I forgot to tell you I have to work with my dad at his shop sometimes. And you aren't going to want to get those. They stick to the bottom of the lake," Miles says.

"Oh," I say, caught by surprise.

I think it over and then turn to put them back. If my mom thinks they'll be too big, and Miles thinks they aren't any good for the lake, then they're not for me.

The man slaps a hand on Miles's shoulder.

"Well, that's not how we get a sale, son. I guess I haven't been doing as good of a job teaching you as I thought."

He chuckles, and it's the first time I'm seeing this man's eyes smile. They're warm and inviting and make me wonder why this side of him got hidden away until now. He wanders over to where my dad is hunched over, thumbing the tags of an empty display case, his eyebrows morphed into one solid shape.

"Can I help you find something, sir?" Miles's dad asks.

"Google told me you had a hardware section," my dad starts to say, holding up his phone to show him just like he did with my mom. Like the guy doesn't have a clue what he sells in his own shop.

"Oh yeah, don't believe everything you read on the internet." He chuckles.

My dad's a smart guy, but the only technology-adjacent thing he can claim to be good at is his architecture software. He likes technology, but technology doesn't exactly like him. I had to help him turn on the satellite TV last night at the cabin. Cozy has one back at home, and you press the *Sat* button first before the *On* one.

"I guess not." My dad chuckles again, tucking his phone back in his cargo pants pocket.

"How about you tell me what you're looking for, and I can help you out," the man suggests.

"Oh, just a few hinges and three-inch screws. The screws are stripped on the kitchen cabinets at our new cabin."

"Ah." He nods his understanding. "I take it we're neighbors, given our kids are already fast friends."

His eyes roam to where Miles and I stand together, then he offers his outstretched hand to my dad, who straightens and shakes it.

"Welcome to Bear Lake. Shepard Bishop, owner of the not-hardware store."

"Nice to meet you, Shepard. We're the Fletchers. I'm Archie. This is my wife, Birdie"—he wraps his arm around her shoulders and squeezes—"the one who keeps me in line. And yes. It seems our daughter, Teddy, has become quite fond of your *adventurous* son in the last twenty-four hours."

What? The color drains from my face.

Why did he have to say that?

"Seems like the perfect place you got here." My dad changes the subject. "Even if it doesn't have a hardware section."

"My father always told me, if you do something you love, you'll never have to work a day in your life. It's what got this business off the ground. And now, I think I have something that might help you, if you want to follow me behind the counter," Shepard says, leading the way.

My dad trails after him, and they crouch down where I can't see them, the whirring sound of a drill buzzing against the wall between us.

"No wonder you're good at hunting tadpoles. You work in a fishing store," I comment to Miles.

His mouth tips up on one side as if he appreciated my compliment, and it's the most heartwarming smile I've ever seen.

"Want to see something?" he asks.

"Yeah!"

I follow him a couple of aisles over while my mom leans over the check-out counter to inspect what the guys are doing. Miles stops near a row of Styrofoam cups. I peer at the lid as if it's translucent and I'll find minestrone soup inside. They're the same ones my mom sends in my school lunch. He peels back the edge, revealing a packed brown circle.

"You sell dirt?"

Miles snorts. "Of course not."

He fishes through the crumbly mess and grips the head of something slimy, unearthing it and letting it squirm between his fingertips.

"We sell these!" He grins, holding up a wriggling invertebrate with pride.

"Cool!"

He transfers the squiggly thing to my open hand, and it swivels in an S shape against my palm, tickling it and making me fight off a giggle.

"What do people do with worms?" I ask.

"Use them for fishing bait," Miles says.

"All right, that's everything," my dad interrupts, carrying a small plastic bag the size of his hand with a fishing hook on the front of it.

I cradle the worm until it drops into its dirt home once more. Miles covers it back up with the lid.

"You have the coolest job, Miles. I want to work at your fishing shop one day. Maybe instead of tadpoles, we can try fishing sometime?" I propose, even though he probably already has.

"I like fishing," Miles says.

I'm pretty sure I could do anything with Miles, and it would be the best day ever.

I wave goodbye as my dad holds open the chiming door for my mom and me.

He's through the threshold when he says, "Can you believe he just took the hinges straight off his cabinets and didn't charge me a thing? Where do guys like him come from?"

As my mom draws me by the hand through the door, I look back at Miles. He's waiting behind the counter, waving and smiling at me like I'm someone he hasn't seen in forever, and I think I have my dad's answer.

I'm pretty sure the good ones come from Bear Lake.

CHAPTER FIVE

NOW

It's just past 8 o'clock when I slip out and begin my two-mile walk to work. Starting my day with twenty questions courtesy of my parents is not all it's cracked up to be.

I need to clear my head.

The last thing Emmett Morgan deserves is a distracted employee at his brand-new restaurant. He's taking a chance on me, and I need this job.

I pick up my pace until I stop short in front of a renovated brick building sitting to the right of the marina. Above the entrance, two beveled iron bars support a rectangular sign, its black aluminum letters welded in a scripted font that reads: *Bear Shore.*

How this place was ever the old safety station my parents described is a mystery to me. Nothing about the freshly painted garage doors and wraparound patio addition looks like a police station or a fire department.

I scan the building, conscious of the fact that I'm early. All of the doors appear locked except for a single one propped open along the back wall. Light shines through the crack and reflects off the glossy front of an industrial-grade stove. Wedged in the door frame is a lone leather loafer.

I peek through the opening and discover an empty kitchen.

"Hello," I call to the silence.

There's a metallic-blue Ford F-150 in the parking lot. Someone must be here.

"Mr. Morgan?"

I wind my way through the kitchen until a U-shaped bar lit with floating lanterns opens up. Just beyond that, upholstered leather booths frame floor-to-ceiling windows, and a giant sign near the hostess stand reads *Don't Feed the Bears*. With mini lamps on each table and beams decorating the ceiling, it's the perfect mix of rustic yet sophisticated.

That must be why the Morgan family chose to buy this building when it went up for sale last fall, I decide. With this view of the lake, it'll draw one hell of a crowd.

"Teddy?" an unfamiliar voice calls from behind me, and I spin around on the heels of my Saltwater sandals to greet its owner.

A guy with a head of sandy brown curls waits with his hands stuffed in his pockets. He's wearing the same branded polo as me. *Must be another server.*

When he sees my face, a dimple sinks into his right cheek, and I panic.

He said my name.

He said my name, and I don't know who he is.

But... that's not exactly true. I do know where I've seen him before, I just don't know how I'm facing two pieces of my past in the same day.

I take a deep breath before acknowledging him, doing my best to avoid his eyes.

"I'm so sorry... I think I'm supposed to know you, but..." I wince and feel my cheeks darkening to a deep cherry red.

His eyebrows lift for a moment, then melt back into that dimpled smile.

"Oh, no, it's fine," he says, waving his hand at me. "I mean, it's not like we kissed or anything."

He lets out a relaxed chuckle, shoving his hands back into the pockets of his khaki shorts.

I blush and drop my gaze to the floor, tracking his body on the way down. He's not only wearing the same uniform as me but missing one loafer.

"So, you're the culprit of the shoe-cracked door."

He looks down at his feet as if he's forgotten they exist on his body.

"Oh, that. Yeah, my dad can be a real piece of work about these garage doors," he says, hiking his thumb over his shoulder.

My attention follows to a series of glass-paned frames surrounded in black metal and latched to the floor.

"I told him to just open them, but he's convinced people are going to stampede in here like a crash of rhinos."

"Ah." I laugh softly, nodding in recognition.

Then I freeze.

"Wait, Emmett Morgan is your *father?*"

He chuckles like I just made an unfortunate joke.

"That's the one."

"That would make you—"

"Your neighbor." He finishes the sentence for me. "Reed Morgan."

Reed—a guy with midnight blue eyes rich enough to mirror the lake at dark. A very *attractive* guy with a megawatt smile.

"Reed." I nod as if I remember, but my face contorts. "I'm sorry... I was in an accident last August, and—"

"I know," he interrupts. "I mean, I didn't know you'd lost your memory, but it makes sense now."

He tugs a hand from his pocket and grips the back of his neck, clearing his throat.

"I came and visited you in the hospital once, but my parents wouldn't let me stay."

My brain short-circuits.

Forget not remembering, how have my own parents not told me about this part?

Come to think of it, the accident itself and the hellish week in a medically induced coma following it are the *only* parts they never talk about with me.

I guess I should have asked more questions when I had the opportunity last night.

It's killing me not to have some kind of processing time in this situation. A chance to hear the information without a guy standing right in front of me waiting for me to say something. It's humiliating when all I can manage in response is an "Oh."

I always do this—crumble under the weight of everything I can't remember.

Change the subject, Teddy. Say something, anyth—

"Are you ready for your first day of work?" Reed interrupts my internal battle, and relief washes over me, however short-lived.

He gestures around the empty room, and I feel myself start to sweat just looking at it.

What was I *thinking* saying I was ready for something like this? I don't know the first thing about waitressing, and if this morning with Miles was any indication, I'm bound to be terrible at this job.

"Not even a little bit," I admit. "I think I might be socially stunted after being stuck in a cabin for the last nine months with the same two people."

"You seem to be doing just fine to me." He flashes a grin.

"But just in case, I'll give you the *Get to know a stranger* crash course."

He holds his hand out between us, and I consider making a run for the door. A good fifty strides and I could pretend I didn't even show up today. But that would be a one-way ticket to losing this job before it's even begun.

You have to do this.

I extend a hand with the reach of a T. rex arm, and Reed leans forward, wrapping his fingers around my palm. His hand is smoother than I imagine most guys' hands to be. He scans my reaction before jerking it up and down.

"Hi, I'm Reed Morgan. Captain of the thrill seekers, future wildland firefighter, and son of the cranky man who owns this restaurant. I'm in love with golden retrievers, but have never owned one, and wear a single shoe when the situation warrants it. I'd choose a romantic comedy over a horror movie any day and scream at the sight of a bee. I'm obsessed with pickles and hate those sticky things people use to hang picture frames."

I laugh out loud. "Command strips?"

"YES! Those. Loathe them and the toenail they lost me," he says, letting go of my hand and cupping his in a prayer toward the beams across the ceiling. Then he reaches for my hand again and holds it between us.

"I would rather wrestle a man o' war jellyfish than mow a lawn," he continues, "and some might say, I'm attracted to freak-ishly short girls."

He winks at me, and I melt inside.

"Well, that was oddly specific," I tease as I check his foot on instinct. It must have been the loafer-covered one that got impaled. All five of his toenails on the shoeless foot are still intact.

"I have a lot to live up to," I say.

He lets go of my hand and waves for me to go next, folding his arms over his broad chest.

"Me?" I point to my face, as if I have to single myself out in an empty room.

"You don't think I just poured my heart out to you to get nothing in return, do you?"

I scrunch my nose. "I don't know if I'd call admitting your love for pickles and disdain for Command strips as *pouring out your heart.*"

The corners of his mouth twitch in amusement.

"All right, you've got a point. Let's call it a list of endearing character traits then. No heart pouring involved. After all, I wouldn't want you to have to reveal why you've looked like you're in pain since the moment you walked in this place."

I swallow.

No, I do not want to have to do that.

"What if I don't... have a list of charming ways to describe myself to you?" I cast my eyes down to the floor.

I could tell him I have a habit of sneaking out of my house at four in the morning. Part of me thinks he'd appreciate that. But the other, more sensible part of me believes a *neighbor* should not know that kind of information.

"Wait!" I shout, thrusting a finger in the air. "The sound of gum chewing repulses me!"

It's not until the words tumble out of my mouth that I hear how stupid they sound.

"Wow, that's not charming," I say, shrinking my neck toward my shoulders.

"Oh, believe me, it is," he says. "But how about you tell me who you *want* to be instead."

Who I want to be?

Not the kind of girl who squirms under his comfortable and

confident stare, that's for sure. It's hard to think with him looking at me like that.

"I want to be..."

"I'm listening," he encourages.

I suck in a gust of air, then let it out as a confession: "Someone who skinny dips."

My hand lifts to cover my mouth as if I can snatch my words from the air and stuff them back in. Tuck them in a box and lock it with a deadbolt.

Holy crap, I can't believe I just told him that. You don't divulge your private desires of swimming in the nude to guys you just met.

His eyebrows lift and then dissolve into a pleased grin that spreads across his whole face.

Or maybe you do? I think he liked it.

Sweat gathers on my palms, and I clench my fists to my sides, praying he can't see. Then I start spewing the rest of my thoughts like a *Price is Right* contestant.

"I want to be someone who slow dances in the middle of a crowded room because she can't help but move to the music. Who eats an ice cream cone with her teeth even if it causes an instant brain freeze. Who jumps from a rope swing into ice-cold waters and doesn't build her life around other people's expectations. Someone who *feels* everything, all at once."

I take a deep breath as Reed drops into the nearest chair, covering his heart with his hand.

"Teddy Fletcher, you might be the most interesting girl who has ever lived."

CHAPTER SIX

SUMMARY, NINE YEARS AGO

SUMMER, NINE YEARS AGO

"Are you kids having a good summer?" my dad asks Miles and me one night as we sit together around the patio. He reclines against the back of his Adirondack chair, his flip flops inches from the brick campfire's open flame. My mom sits in the complete opposite position—perched on the arm of her chair, glasses pushed up high on the bridge of her nose, and studying the amber glow of the coals as she swirls the tip of a marshmallow-trio stick.

"The best," I mumble.

"Me too," Miles says.

We both giggle when our lips stick together from gooey s'mores.

My sketchbook lies open in my lap, and I shove the rest of my dessert in my mouth just as a pelican soars toward the water out past our dock. I jerk to an upright position and yank my charcoal pencil from where it's tucked in the binding. I chew on the tip of my tongue, working the fine point of the pencil with flicks of my wrist to get the snowy feathers just right.

In its majesty, the bird swoops down and skims the surface

of the water until it's drifting along in a buoyant dance that matches the rhythm of the lake.

"I knew this was going to be our place," my dad sighs.

"Do we get to come back here every summer?" I ask.

"Every summer," he breathes, his eyes scanning the fruit smoothie–colored sky as it swirls with brilliant oranges and pinks.

Miles and I share banana split grins.

"I got you guys something," Mom says as she tips her head toward a box wrapped in craft paper painted with tiny suns all over it.

I hadn't noticed it nestled between our chairs.

Miles and I lunge for it at the same time, ripping her artwork to shreds and uncovering a two-person pineapple floatie. We both gasp.

"Your dad bought a new air compressor that I think he'd like to try out."

He topples out of his chair and runs for the trunk of the hatchback as she chuckles, shaking her head. Miles and I unfold the rectangular floatie while she lays out three open-faced graham crackers on the edge of the brick surround. She covers each one with a bronzed marshmallow and tears open a Hershey's chocolate bar wrapper with her teeth. Splitting it in unequal thirds, she adds the largest sections to the ones she hands to me and Miles.

With a s'more in one hand and one end of the pineapple floatie in the other, we take off running together toward my dad, yelling, "Best summer of our lives!"

The last two days of summer break are the longest in the worst way. My parents force me stay inside the cabin all day playing Uno with them while a storm rages outside.

I knew, as the summer days dwindled, I was going to miss this place. But I didn't realize just how much until my very last morning.

I press my face against the dining nook window. No rainfall!

I skip breakfast and barrel down the dock with my bucket in hand. When I find the dock empty, I think he didn't show up, until I see him, squatting on the edge of the shore, his face planted inside his bucket.

"Miles! Caught anything yet?" I call.

After our fair share of misses this summer, we *finally* figured out the secret to catching tadpoles. A fine mesh net. We always release them back into the lake before the sun goes down.

Some days we collect shells or hunt for rocks in the shape of hearts. One time, we found a cracked crab claw on the shore. It was a real relief when my parents convinced us that it was from a cookout, and that freshwater crabs did not exist in Bear Lake.

But today, I can tell Miles has something new in his bucket in the way he lifts his head and grins at me.

I jump off the edge of the dock, rushing right for him, and gasp when I peer inside. There's a small green-as-a-lime frog bouncing around in the bottom. I squeal at the sight of it.

"You found a frog!"

"I think I'm going to name it Miley," he says.

Miley? For a *frog?*

"That's kind of a weird frog name," I admit.

"I don't know, I kind of like it," he says.

"How did you come up with it anyway?"

"It's Miles and Teddy put together."

I grin so wide I think my nose and eyes, even my hair, grow a smile.

Never mind. It's not weird at all, it's perfect.

"I love it!"

"You just said you thought it was weird," he counters.

"Well, that was before I knew what it meant."

Miles seems pleased with my answer, and we leave his bucket on the shore for a while, not wanting to let go of Miley while we hunt for tadpoles one last time.

As the hours pass, a blanket of grey clouds starts to filter in, growing thicker until there's a complete patchwork quilt over our heads. When a sudden crack lights up the whole sky, Miles hurls himself out of the water for the grass and toward his trailer.

"Miles, wait!" I call, rushing after him, knocking his discarded bucket sideways. Miley leaps to freedom as the first wave of drops falls from the sky.

I plunge toward him, trying to catch up, but my short legs remain sixteen steps behind his. The dam breaks, and in seconds, we are both drenched from the sky's reservoir. My eyes dart around the yard for a place where we can take cover. I don't want to leave him yet. I'm desperate for our day not to end when I remember…

The bunkhouse.

It sat vacant all summer long, the twin beds still made, the glass door untouched. But when I reach for the handle and find the latch unlocked, my eyebrows lift.

"Miles! In here!" I call.

He's only a few feet from his trailer when he spins around, terror etching his face. He hesitates. He ping-pongs between both places before racing after me. When he crosses the threshold, I yank the door shut.

By the time I turn around, Miles is nowhere in sight. I climb the ladder to check the top bunk, expecting to find him there, but it's empty. There's only one other place he could possibly be.

The wind whips against the glass, rattling the door. I make sure it's latched tight, locking the storm outside before dropping to the floor. Miles has scrambled under the bunkbed and is huddled in a heap in the far corner. I crawl underneath to hide with him too.

"Well, that was crazy," I whisper.

My eyes adjust to the darkness, and Miles's face comes into view. His pupils are the size of marbles, his lower lip's trembling, and his breathing is coming out strangled. My vision adjusts even more as I see that he's huddled in a tight ball, his legs bunched up beneath him. I don't know what's happening to him, but I know I won't leave him until he's no longer shaking the way that he is.

"It's okay, Miles. I'll take care of you," I say, holding my hand out to him. Because that's what friends do. They take care of each other.

The crinkled worry softens a bit at the bridge of his eyebrows and he reaches for me. His fingers lace with mine. We stay like that for a while, waiting out the rain. When his breathing begins to even and I can tell he feels safe again, I work up the courage to ask him what I've wanted to all summer.

"Miles, what happened that first day we met? You know... that night on the dock, when..."

I can't finish that sentence because I need Miles to. I don't know what came next, but I could guess. The way those long dark locks that matched his slipped out of view. A woman driving away in the red car. The same car that hasn't been back since, not once.

A sadness knits his eyebrows back together, and I almost regret asking. I wouldn't want to do anything to make him not want to hunt tadpoles with me anymore or be my friend. I just want him to be okay.

"You promise you won't tell anyone?" he whispers.

"I promise."

It's a long minute before he says anything else. Like he's trying to arrange the words in an order that won't hurt as much. He starts to shake again when his eyes well with tears. It makes me feel sad inside.

Miles's sadness is my sadness.

"She left," he confesses.

I let him take all the time he needs because he's having a hard time saying the rest. I can tell he's never told anyone else.

"My mom... she left me and my dad."

My faces pinches with confusion. I ask myself at least a hundred silent questions I'm hoping Miles can't hear.

Parents leave?

When?

Will my mom leave too?

The next one I ask out loud.

"She's coming back, right?"

Because that's what moms do. They come back. They drop you off at school, and they come back to pick you up at the end of the day.

Miles's head swings side to side. Tears fall down his cheeks in ripples, much like the lake in a storm.

I grip his hand tighter. I think he needs it. I want to show him he still has me. That even though I'm leaving tomorrow, I'll come back. That I'll never leave him forever like she did. I'll be back next summer, and we can tadpole-hunt and catch frogs named Miley and swim in the water and find rocks that look like hearts. We'll always be best friends.

But I don't know how to say all those things out loud to someone who is this sad. So, I just dip my forehead against his like a silent promise, and he presses into mine like he understands.

Please don't let my mom leave me like Miles's mom did, I pray in my heart.

If only that heavenly being could have answered me. Maybe I would have heard the warning. That I *would* almost lose her, in a different way, but that I'd be okay. Maybe then I would have been more prepared for the fact that it would be four years before I ever saw Miles again.

CHAPTER SEVEN

NOW

"I see the two of you are getting reacquainted," Mr. Morgan intrudes between smacks of his gum that send me spinning on my heels to face him.

"We sure are," Reed remarks with a grin so wide it could lift him in the air like a sail. "Teddy here was just informing me about how much she finds gum chewing repulsive."

Mr. Morgan's jaw stills. "Very funny. I take it you two haven't gotten to the tour part yet?"

"We were just waiting for you, Captain." Reed salutes his dad.

"Right." Mr. Morgan rolls his eyes while smiling at me. "Good to see you again, Teddy! Let's get started then."

He waves for us to follow him.

"The menus are kept on the shelf beneath the hostess desk. Empty pitchers, ice machine, and the tap are on the far side of the bar. As servers, you'll relay the special. It rotates daily. Today's special is the crab cake sliders with a side of coleslaw. At the beginning and end of every shift, you'll clock out the old-fashioned way. The timecard slot is in the file folder beside my office door. Since you both are doing the opening shift, we'll stagger your breaks at 3:00 and 3:30. We're expecting a full house for the grand opening, so anticipate fast-paced work. Here's an apron," he rattles on, "and you'll find a notepad and pen in the front pocket. Any questions?"

"I've got a question!" Reed jumps in.

"Something tells me it's a question I'm not gonna like."

"Can we open the garage doors now? It's a little stuffy in here, don't you think, Teddy?"

Reed nudges my foot with his bare one, catching me off guard.

"Um... I..."

"Don't worry, you'll get used to him." Mr. Morgan smirks at me before backing away. "And the answer's no, Reed."

"Okay!" Reed hollers. "Just thought I'd check."

"What you need to check is that bare foot of yours. Get your damn loafer back on!" he shouts from out of sight, and I hear what must be the latch of his office door shutting.

I follow Reed as he makes his way to the back door.

"Do you always goad him like that?"

"The man's uptight. Someone's got to do it." He winks at me over his shoulder.

"You're a flirt, aren't you?" I say, my hands planted on my hips.

"With you, yes," he says, taking giant backward strides toward the cracked door and slipping his foot into his shoe without ever looking at it.

I'm thinking he's the kind of trouble I should stay away from.

By the time my shift ends at six, my feet are throbbing. Saltwater sandals were the worst idea I've ever had. As Mr. Morgan predicted, the place crawled with people. A consistent thirty-minute wait proved it.

I hand off my section to a girl named Gloria, then make quick work of yanking at the ties on my apron. I reach into one of the pockets and pull out my wad of tips, fanning it between my fingers with wide eyes.

Holy crap. Three hundred dollars?

Well worth the drink mishap at table nine.

I catch Mr. Morgan leaning against the bar, surveying the shuffle. From the giddy tap of his loafers to the drumming of his fingertips against his trousers, he's glowing.

Folding my apron in thirds, I hand it to him.

"Pretty good turn out," I say.

He shakes his head in astonishment, and a boyish grin lights his eyes when he looks my way.

"Amazing. I mean, I hoped bringing something new to Bear Lake would be just what this town needed, but I didn't realize how many people would show up. One couple even came back an hour after having lunch just so they could experience drinks by the lake."

"I'm not surprised," I say, remembering my own first impression of the patio view this morning.

"You did great work out there," he says, and I hide my face behind my hands.

"I stained that woman's white pants with Diet Coke."

A deep, hearty laugh tumbles out of him. "Could have happened to anyone."

"Thank you for saying that."

"We only agreed to a trial run..."

Oh, great. Here it comes.

I feel the beat of my heart start to accelerate in my chest.

He's going to let me go and that compliment was just his way of making the blow less painful.

My throat threatens to close off, but I round my shoulders, determined not to show how deflated I feel.

"I just don't want to overwhelm you," he continues. "I'm sure this level of busy wasn't what you expected."

No, it wasn't what I expected, I want to tell him, *but it doesn't matter because I need that tip money.*

"I'm ready. I promise," I plead.

The curls that frame Mr. Morgan's part bounce with his boisterous nod. "Well, good then. It turns out, I could use the help."

He reaches into the back pocket of his ironed slacks and pulls out a slip of paper, holding it in mid-air between his pointer and middle finger.

I snatch it from his grasp before he has the chance to change his mind about me. When I unfold the centered crease, I catalog two weeks' worth of shifts as if he planned on me staying all along.

I could hug him! But I won't. Because that would be weird.

"Thanks, Mr. Morgan," I say, bolting for the back door.

The hallway is cramped with servers, so I slow to a speed walk before my spill count for the day increases by an entire tray of food. With my new work schedule waving in my hand like a flag, I wonder just how many shifts I'll share with the owner's son. Aside from our small talk during my rapid-fire training session this morning, Reed and I served on opposite sides of the restaurant where we barely shared a look, much less a conversation.

It's good, I think. *Better this way.* It makes leaving a hell of a lot easier the less friends I make.

I stuff the schedule in my pocket.

"Hey, you're in a hurry! Are you leaving?"

Reed snags my arm before I reach the back door, and I whirl around to face him.

"Yeah, my shift ended at six. Are you headed out too?"

"Aw man, I wish. I'd offer you a ride home, but I told my dad I'd stay late to make sure the first day goes smoothly, so..."

"Well, that was kind of you. I can tell he places a lot of trust in you."

He smirks. "You got THAT from his *Don't open the garage doors a minute early* speech?"

"It's more of a feeling, I guess."

We both laugh at how ridiculous that sounds. But I do think Mr. Morgan trusts Reed. He wouldn't have him showing up early and working a double shift if he couldn't rely on him.

"Hey, listen, I was wondering if you wanted to get together tomorrow night? Maybe we can hang out?"

"Oh, um—" I drag my eyes from Reed to the back door as if the answer to his question is written on it.

"I can pick you up at your cabin around seven... I do live right next door." He winks at me.

I clasp my hands behind my back so they have somewhere to fidget other than beneath his nerve-wracking stare.

"What, like a date?"

A smile splits across his face. "If you want it to be."

Don't get me wrong, I'm curious about him, but I can just see it now. It starts out all innocent at first—the occasional get together after work, the subtle references to our shared history. We'll spend every weekend together, forge inside jokes that only the two of us get, work together, eat together, *sleep together*, until I'm hopelessly devoted to discovering who Reed is and what he meant to me.

Nope. There's a three-month sand timer. I have no time to give.

"I don't think that's such a good idea."

Forget the relationship snowball, I promised myself I wouldn't do this anymore. I'm *existing* this summer, not subjecting myself to reliving the past or forming future attachments who might try to convince me to stay. I'm not sticking around for what comes next.

Reed lifts his hands in the air in defeat. "Okay, not a date then. Just to hang out."

"Listen, Reed, I don't want to be harsh—"

"I can text you!" he blurts.

I shake my head vigorously. "I don't have a phone."

"Right." He rubs his neck just like he did this morning after he admitted to knowing about my accident.

"You seem like a nice guy and all, but the last thing I need in my life right now is a walk down memory lane."

That familiar creep of panic accelerates my breathing. Maybe agreeing to work here was a gigantic mistake. *I can't do this.*

I need space. I need change. I need...

Fresh air.

I close the distance to the back door—the same one that is no longer propped open by a shoe—and slam into it before getting the hint to spin the handle. It gives way about a foot before plowing into someone else on the other side.

"Oh my gosh, I'm so sorry," I say, backing up.

The person pulls the door the rest of the way open, and it takes my eyes a second to adjust to the light. A mirage in the form of a tall figure glints in and out of focus.

"It's fi..." he starts, but his words stumble to a stop when his stunned eyes fix on me.

Miles?

CHAPTER EIGHT

SUMMER, FIVE YEARS AGO

I t's been one thousand three hundred and forty days since I've seen Bear Lake. I've kept track of every day that has passed in the back of my sketchbook. An endless row of tally marks signifies the distance between me and my summer best friend.

I've thought about Miles a million times since that first summer at the cabin, wondering how he was doing, where he went during the other three seasons of the year, and if he even remembered me. I never gave up hope that one day I'd see him again. But the more time that passed, the more unsure I became that I'd ever make it back there, or if I'd even be the same person who left.

I've been living a life so far from the summer I shared with Miles Bishop that just the thought of seeing him again has a bundle of nerves coiling in my stomach.

The five-hour drive drags on longer than I remembered it. A fleet of butterflies take off in my stomach as we round the bend at the end of the byway. The shimmering lake comes into view, and it feels like stepping out of a time machine and seeing it with pair of ten-year-old eyes for the first time.

As my dad pulls the car down the sparse driveway, Miles's trailer is the first thing I fixate on. It's parked in the same spot where the wheels have worn the grass clean down to the dirt from the weight. The startling difference is the cropped grass where a field of dandelions once grew in its place.

We take a collective deep breath with the windows rolled down.

"Well, we made it. I missed this place," my dad says.

I want to say "me too," but I've never had the heart to admit how much it meant to me after what we went through with Mom.

He rounds the front bumper as she steps out from her side of the car. He grabs on to her, hugging her shoulders as she becomes a blubbering mess.

I haven't moved from the back seat, but I can still hear her let out a sigh and stutter, "I wasn't sure I'd ever see it again."

He hugs her a little tighter.

When I work up the nerve to open the door, the surrounding view has me cataloguing all the ways it looks the same and yet feels so completely different. I hadn't expected that, and I'm not sure I can put a name to those feelings.

I cough and choke when I step into the cabin. The same stuffy grandma smell we worked so hard to get rid of that first summer returned.

"You remember the drill, people," my mom sings. "Let's open the windows."

She's beaming. In fact, I'm not sure I've ever seen her this happy. I know the cabin does something to me, but it's like it makes her come alive in a way we all need.

We unload a new summer's worth of belongings, and when I'm sure everything is settled, I leave my parents for the dock. I make it a couple of feet when I see him, standing on the edge facing the water.

My heart thunders in my chest. It takes every fiber of my being to work my way closer and closer to him.

Even from behind, he's changed. His hair is lighter than I recall. Curlier too. Of course, he's taller and broader, but that's to be expected. It's been four years. Even my four-foot eleven-inch frame has made some progress in that department.

I step on a plank, then a few more, until a loose one creaks under my weight, and he starts to turn around. As his face comes into view, a smile stretches wide across most of it. His eyebrows elevate in surprise. Mine do too.

He's... not Miles.

My smile drops, and a knot the size of a golf ball lodges in my throat.

I came back.

I finally came back, and you aren't here, my heart tells him.

What if he's gone and it was goodbye forever? I didn't prepare myself for that possibility. I shouldn't cry in front of this stranger, but I can't help it. I swallow as tears prick my vision.

"You're not..." I start to say, the wind on my face making me feel buoyant enough that it could carry me away with it.

Then a voice calls from behind me. "Teddy?"

I careen around at the sound, paying little attention to my balance, and teeter too far to the right. My body pitches off the side of the dock, fully clothed.

Despite knowing how to swim, I flounder around like a drowned cat. My mind, catching and fixating on the familiar resonance of his voice, fails to realize my feet can touch the ground. My heels brush against the mucky bottom of the lake, and when my arms are no longer treading water, I calm.

"I'm so sorry," I hear him say on a warm laugh, but I can't see him with the kelp-like strands of hair clinging over my eyes.

I probably should dip my head beneath the water and slick it back, but I don't think of that. Instead, I claw at the strands until they clump in a knotted frame and drag my eyes up the length of an outstretched hand to see his face.

Miles.

He's beaming at me as he pulls me from the water, where I want to drown in my humiliation a bit longer. When he plants me on my feet, water begins to leak down my forehead. I scrub at my eyes to be sure I'm seeing clearly and it's not all just a hazy daydream.

It's really him.

"That was not how I thought that would go," I joke, holding out my arms. Lake water drips down my white T-shirt and jean shorts, fusing them to my body like a second skin.

"Me neither," he admits, fighting to keep his gaze above my neck.

"Hi, Miles," I breathe, testing the sound of his name after all these years while my head wraps around the fourteen-year-old version of him.

He's still thin but grown into some wider shoulders that hold his chest high. His Bear Lake bucket hat has been exchanged for a Dodgers baseball cap, the tipped-up bill giving me a good look at his eyes.

That part of him is the same. I'd remember those warm speckles of hazel anywhere.

"Your hair's longer," he comments first.

I run my fingers through the wet strands, touching the ends where they drape just below my breasts. I started growing it out in middle school after Cozy and I read a *Cosmopolitan* article that said most guys like girls with long hair. But I won't tell Miles that. We told each other a lot that first summer, but we were just young kids then. There's a lot of stuff girls don't share with guys now that we're teenagers.

"Well, it's been a long time," I say, like I need to explain myself.

Deep down I was worried he might not like the about-to-start-high-school version of me—hair past my shoulder blades, post-braces, and an extra layer of freckles. He might miss that shrimpy girl with the knobby knees, a missing tooth, and locks that beveled just below her chin.

"I like it," he says with a grin.

If my heart had lungs, it would have sighed in relief. Instead, it's pounding like the start of a song just about to hit the chorus. My cheeks bloom into a faint pink as the corners of my mouth tip up in a smile.

"Thanks."

For a few beats we just stand there, staring at each other. Making up for all the lost time while also floundering for what to say next. Someone clears their throat, and I remember it's not just the two of us.

"I take it you're Teddy, and I'm guessing you live in that cabin right in the middle," the other boy interjects. "I'm Reed."

He's much sturdier than Miles, with a head of sandy brown curls and a showstopping dimple in his right cheek.

I pinch my arms against my sides, stuck on the thought of our Oreo cabins. I'm not sure I'm cut out for being sandwiched between two guys all summer. I spent my middle school years struggling to even look one in the eye, let alone two in such proximity.

"That's me."

"I'll get you a towel," he offers, pointing to my quivering shoulders. Which may or may not have anything to do with plunging into the freezing lake.

My teeth chatter. "Thank you."

"No problem."

He works his way around Miles and me before jogging toward the fully finished log cabin. Every part of it looks lived in, from the giant garden that grows past the lower deck to the speed boat tethered to their dock. They've added a sand volley-ball court on the far side of the yard and a pair of plush fabric lounge chairs with a scalloped umbrella on the upper deck.

It's finally filled with a family, I think to myself.

When I pull my attention back to Miles, it dawns on me that we're alone and his smile has faded.

"You didn't come back," he says, sounding disappointed.

I knew this part wasn't going to be easy, reliving the last four years without Bear Lake.

But then I remembered our last day in the bunkhouse. How Miles had trusted me with something he hadn't told anyone else. *That* Miles I could tell anything to. So, I motion for him to follow me to the end of the dock, and we both rest on the edge.

And I tell him everything.

CHAPTER NINE

I just slammed the door into the one guy I wasn't sure I'd ever see again, and here I am running into him for the second time in the same day.

I can still feel the aftershocks from this morning. The throbbing of my palms from where they slid down that rope swing. Those dumbfounded eyes that zeroed in on me the moment I turned around to face him. The way my words tripped over themselves in his presence. That same look of alarm stares at me now, but my eyes slip from his face and glue to his torso.

He replaced his running shorts with jeans and a T-shirt, yet the memory of sweat trickling down his bare abs is as if nothing is covering them *now*. My mouth goes dry.

"Teddy, are you okay?" Reed asks from behind, startling me.

When I rotate to acknowledge him, it gives a clear shot through the doorway.

"Miles," he hisses with disgust.

Miles acknowledges him with a nod. "Reed." Then he rubs the back of his neck, averting his eyes to the wall next to us.

An unsettling silence rests between the two of them. *I think*

I just stepped into the middle of something. Reed tightens his hand into a fist.

If I shift at all to my right, will a brawl break out? I'm not sure I want to stick around to find out.

Without a word, I do my best to squeeze around Miles's tall frame as he shields the doorway, ducking under his arm and out into the parking lot. I chance a glance back, and... Yeah. They're both ignoring each other and lasered in on me. I forgo goodbyes and book it out of there as fast as my short legs will carry me.

I don't even know why I'm running, or what I'm so afraid of. One of them chasing me? Both chasing me?

When I'm sure I haven't been followed, I slow to a walk and try to clear my head. Setting my sights on the shoreline to ground me, patches of turquoise flicker in and out of car windows. I come to a stop in front of the one car I was hoping not to see in this parking lot. There may not be a pair of binoculars pressed to the rearview mirror, but there's no denying the family hatchback with its uncanny brake lights illuminated.

Great. This is the last thing that would clear my head—my mom and her sunny disposition in the front seat of this car. There's no walking past it without her seeing me, so I knock on the passenger window. She promptly rolls it down.

"Mom, what are you doing here?"

I squat low enough to see her in the same paint-covered apron I left her in this morning. I rest both hands on the frame of the car and fix my gaze on her.

"I thought we could go get some LaBeau's together. We haven't done that in a long—"

"Mom," I interrupt, pinning her with a glare.

I can see right through her. She may have made some small compromise with bacon this morning, but there's no way she's dropping the full act for greasy fast food.

She drops her hands from ten and two, letting them fall in a heap in her lap.

"I don't like the thought of you walking home alone on that busy road, okay?" she admits.

"I did it just fine this morning." I demonstrate my safety, splaying my arms for her to inspect.

"Yeah, and I didn't like it," she argues.

"Mom, you promised you would let it go."

She exhales. "I know, and I'm trying, Teddy. I really am. But you've got to understand this isn't easy for me."

"This isn't easy for *you*?" My voice raises an octave. "Mom! I eat all my meals with you, exercise in front of you, swim in the lake while you and dad sit on the dock like I'm a five-year-old who doesn't know how to swim on her own, for crying out loud. It's all I can do to stretch my five minutes in the shower into ten just so I can breathe."

Tears well in her eyes, then her bottom lip begins to quiver. She looks away from me when she whispers, "But it's a road," and her voice cracks on the last word just like it did the day I woke up in the hospital.

"It's been seven days," my mom urged a man in a white lab coat. *"How much longer do you think we'll have to wait?"*

I rubbed my eyes with the back of my hand as they fought to adjust to the noon-day sun pouring through the bent slats of a set of blinds. A soft hum vibrated from a machine to my right, the sound of a drip from a bag strung up behind my bed. A mask covered the lower half of my face, sending a gust of oxygen through my nose every time my lungs expanded. My head felt like a morning fog had descended over every thought, making it impossible to decipher the true center.

Where am I? Seven days since what? What exactly is she waiting for?

"Severe traumatic brain injuries from blunt force trauma to

the head always include some form of unconsciousness," the man continued. "The intracranial pressure Teddy showed when she was brought in here was severe. Her body needed time to heal, and the medically induced coma was the right call. I know it's hard to believe, seeing your daughter in this condition, but she's lucky that her skull didn't fracture or that she needed surgery."

My mom covered her sob with her hand, and the man comforted her with a palm to the shoulder.

"The brain is a complex organ, Mrs. Fletcher. It takes time to heal and unfortunately, I can't give you the answer you're looking for. But I can assure you, we are doing everything possible. Based on her MRI results from this morning, the oxygen, IV fluids, and medication are doing their job. The swelling has decreased."

My mom's head nodded furiously, acknowledging his good news and letting out a shuddering breath.

I tried to sit up, but my lungs were being compressed. Almost as if a pair of pliers crimped my airway closed. I scanned my body with my palms, half expecting to find a cast somewhere amongst the skeletal structure that ached with every movement, but the only outer bandage I found was the one woven around the crown of my head.

Above and below the thick bandage I felt matted clumps of hair. One in particular was crusted on the right side. The side that hurt the most. With the realization that I was, in fact, injured, the fog became more of a haze, and I could finally string two thoughts together.

I was in a hospital room, and something happened to me.

My confused eyes met my mom's desperate ones as she pushed open the door to the room. She gasped and came running toward my bedside.

With how hastily she moved, I expected her to fling her body over mine for a full embrace, but she just laced her fingers with mine and whispered through her tears, "Oh honey, you're awake."

My mom looked broken, almost beyond repair. It wasn't even the purple rings under her eyes that suggested she hadn't slept in weeks, or the greasy knot on top of her head that alluded to the fact it'd been even longer since she'd washed it. It was the agonizing relief that sculpted every line of her face that told me something tragic happened.

"Archie, come quick!" she called out, and my dad rushed into the room.

"What is..." he started to say, but froze in the doorway, and then crumpled in a heap on the floor.

I watched them both grieve at the same time, a life they thought they were going to have to live without me. It was devastating to see.

The man in the white lab coat followed them in the room and approached my bedside.

"Hi, I'm Dr. Spalding. Can you tell me your first name?" he asked as he flashed a bright red light at my right eye.

I swallowed, and it felt like cotton balls packed my esophagus.

"Teddy," I croaked.

A smile graced his lips. "That's good."

He flashed the other eye and tipped his head to the side as he asked me his next question. "Do you know why you're in the hospital? Do you remember what happened?"

My eyes darted back and forth across the far wall of the room, trying to make sense of the missing information inside my head.

Why couldn't I remember what happened to me?

Nothing came.

The brief light ignited in my mom's eyes moments before was promptly snuffed out.

"That's okay," Dr. Spalding assured. "Give it time."

After several days of testing and meeting with specialists, we determined the TBI didn't affect my ability to walk, talk, or eat. But aside from my parents, I couldn't recall a single memory that once mapped my childhood. As we approached discharge, we were prepared for the worst-case scenario.

"What if her memory never comes back?" my dad asked the neurologist.

"With time, most patients with severe TBIs still restore full memory. If by some small chance that isn't the case for Teddy, we'll cross that bridge when we get there," Dr. Spalding said.

The gravity of what he was saying settled over the room. It settled over me.

The pressure suffocated me. It didn't matter that I had lived. What mattered was that I remember.

I combat those memories like a December cold that won't go away. I've plagued myself for months, let myself die inside trying to rebirth this person they feel like they're missing, and I refuse to do it anymore.

"Mom, I need to keep living my life. I can't spend it walking on broken glass like one wrong move will sever everything that I am. I'm walking home," I say, pushing off the car and stomping in the opposite direction.

I weave around the rows of vehicles filling the parking lot as my mom inches out of her spot and follows a safe distance behind me. My blood boils, and I start to jog as though I can outrun her car.

A battered pickup truck blocks my path, and I'm forced to circle around it. I look over my shoulder to see if I can make a break for the trees on the edge of the road when I plow into the side of a warm body.

"We've got to stop meeting like this," Miles says, his voice gruff as he disentangles us.

I check over my shoulder one more time, and the disapproval in my mom's eyes fuels this fire inside of me to do something reckless.

"I need a ride."

I meant to ask instead of demand, but under the weight of her stare, I feel pressed for time.

Miles releases me from his grip and tracks my gaze to my parents' car. "I don't think that's a good idea."

He stalks toward the driver's seat and unlocks his truck, and I follow closely behind, yanking on his arm to get his attention.

"Listen, buddy. I'm sensing you don't want to be around me, but I need this favor. So, if it's space you want, I'll give it to you. But only after a ride. Otherwise, I'm hunting you down every damn day this summer and playing a horrific version of 'Chopsticks' on the recorder," I threaten.

His eyebrows perk, a ghost of a smile playing on his lips. Then they flick over my shoulder to my glaring mother, and he swallows. He opens the driver's-side door and with a quick jerk of his head, he motions toward the passenger seat.

"Thank you!" I gasp.

I jump in and scoot across the bench. Then he slams the door closed and pulls out of the parking lot, taking a left-hand turn away from the cabin.

We ride in silence for several long minutes with me checking the rearview mirror for a vehicle that never comes into view. By the time I let myself relax and get a good look out the window, I don't recognize a single landmark around us, and I feel my shoulders instantly stiffen.

"Where are you taking me?"

"You tell me," he says.

"Oh, um..."

I didn't think this through.

I survey the unfamiliar cabin-speckled streets as if I'll find a better one for him to drop me off at than the one I live in. I don't have a clear-cut plan, but I can't expect him to meander around for half the day. He's not my chauffer, and I'm sure he has other things to do.

"You can just take me home now if you want to," I say, and if he hears the disappointment in my voice, he doesn't comment.

He nods but keeps driving in the same direction. His eyes are fixed on the road, his hand loose around the steering wheel. He seems content with our silence, but I'm struggling.

"Has anyone ever told you that you don't talk very much?"

Silence.

"You know what, this is good. It's exactly what I need. I don't like talking either."

Silence.

"Okay, fine," I burst out. "You're right, okay? I like talking. Just not about what most of this town wants to talk about."

Silence.

"Could you just please say *something*?" I beg.

He clears his throat. "I think it's best if I just take you home now."

Why does it irritate the hell out of me that he won't talk to me when I spend half my days wishing everyone else around me would do the same? But the longer the quiet lasts, the more I succumb to it. It gives me time to think.

As much I wanted to avoid my past, it showed up for the summer. I'm literally employed by one half of it, if I'm to take that drawing tucked away in my room to mean anything. I at least need to figure out *who* Miles and Reed are, even if I'm not ready to find out what they meant to me.

Ugh, I'm starting to sound like Dr. Spalding. Diagnosing my problems.

Problem number one: Reed Morgan. The neighbor I've supposedly kissed. *Now that sounds crazy.* A guy who's obsessed with—what did he say?—pickles? And who thinks I'm the most interesting girl to have ever lived. *He needs to get out more if interesting to him is a girl who has been entombed in a cabin since the last time he saw her.*

Problem number two: Miles. I don't know his last name yet because he won't talk to me. He's irritating and shows up at the worst possible times and he's... nice to look at.

Last but not least... if the fist clenching and the averted gazes weren't enough to sail a gigantic, red-flagged boat across my uncharted territory, their clipped tones proved they have some kind of beef with each other. Which only compounds my questions.

Dammit! This is why I need my phone back. Things would be so much easier if I could just look them up on my own rather than having to ask for answers from the complicated people in my life. I could care less whether Dr. Spalding thinks "rapid-moving stimuli" is detrimental to brain healing. At this point, I *am* healed. There are no cuts on my face, bruising on my skin, swelling on my head. I may not have told him about the insomnia I've been battling—it'd just be one more thing for him and my parents to worry about—but it's fine. I've been given permission to ease back into all other facets of my life. A phone should be the least of their concerns.

It will be the first thing I demand when I get home, I decide, and as far as the rest of my plan goes—well, now I need a new one. Because surviving the summer while tangoing with the past is out the window.

I can get to know them. Be their friend without learning the details from before. It'll be like we just met for the first time. I don't think Miles will have a problem with it. I just need Reed to agree. Especially now that I'll be working with him all summer.

The more I iron out the details, settle this convoluted situation, the more I relax. The voice in my head that I can't quiet at night—the one that whispers *What if you never remember* in a haunting tone—disappears. Miles keeps driving, taking two hours to circle the lake, and we fall into this serene, silent rhythm that drifts me to sleep.

I wake to my cheekbone jostling against the windowsill. There's a fine line of drool like the trail of a slug on my arm. I jolt upright, wiping it against the side of my polo and hoping Miles didn't notice. When I feel the truck come to a stop, I push open the car door. I'd rather not prolong this goodbye.

"Well, thanks for the ride. As promised, I won't ask again," I say.

I slide off the seat, stumbling to the ground, and straighten like a flagpole. I brush my hands against the front of my shorts and start to close the door but then stop it from shutting.

"Oh, and Miles? I would never have stalked you all summer and made you listen to *anything* on the recorder. Just wanted to make that clear."

I know it won't change his mind about being around me. I'm not even sure I want him to, but I'd rather him know, in a round-about way, that I appreciate his gesture.

A hint of a smile dances in his eyes as he says, "I would have never made you walk home."

It isn't until he's long out of sight that I realize, I never told him where I live.

CHAPTER TEN

SUMMER, FIVE YEARS AGO

Three weeks after that first summer ended, I was back in school in the fifth grade. Baker taught me how to play tetherball at recess, and Cozy and I learned to jump rope to the Mary Mac rhyme. If it weren't for them and the research report I got to do on frogs, I might have gone crazy thinking about Miles. Our family celebrated all the major holidays from fall to spring, and by the beginning of May, I was daydreaming constantly of long summer days on the shore of Bear Lake.

One afternoon in particular, a suitcase lay open on my floor, every bright-colored swimsuit I owned draped over the edge, when my mom knocked on my bedroom door.

"Theadora, can I come in?"

The moment she said my full name, I panicked.

Was it Dad? Was he hurt?

I cleared my throat and called out to her, and she pushed the door open.

"Can we talk for a minute?"

She gestured to the bed, and I dropped the pineapple floatie right in the middle of the room to sit by her. She looked nervous as she wrapped her arm around me. It was as if she didn't want any room between us when she told me what was coming next.

"Honey, we aren't going back to Bear Lake this summer."

Two hundred and eighty-eight tally marks doubled in the few seconds it took her to deliver that devastating sentence. My heart plummeted. I looked over at the deflated floatie and the suitcase full of summer clothes, wishing I hadn't started packing only to face the sting of putting it all back.

"I'm sick," she said.

From my earliest memories, my parents never sugarcoated anything with me. They always treated me like a miniature adult and thought I was mature enough to handle the tough stuff, including brutal honesty. But I wasn't mature or ready for anything this tough. I was a small, helpless, fragile bird who needed her mom.

"My uterine cancer returned," she continued. "It was always a possibility after I went into remission. When I started feeling some pelvic pain about a month ago, I had my doctor look into it."

My eyes went wide as I fought the shock that came with hearing news like that, and then they shrunk down to the size of slivered almonds as tears threatened to spill over.

I thought of Miles. How devastated he was when his mom left. How much I silently pleaded that day that it wouldn't happen to me. She was slipping away with that news no matter how much the strength of her arm around my shoulders anchored her to me.

"It's okay to cry. Heaven knows I have." She lifted her paint-splattered apron and blotted at her eyes.

I wasn't sure what to say or even what to ask. But there was one thing I needed to know more than anything else.

"What are we going to do?" It came out in a strangled whisper.

She let go of my shoulders and gripped my hands between hers, forcing me to face her. "We're going to fight. That's what we're going to do," she said.

A determined look shifted the soft features of her face into hard ones, and I felt relieved. There was a plan; one where she wasn't leaving me.

And fight was exactly what she did.

For the next three years off and on, she received chemotherapy treatments, shrinking the tumors until they were small enough to warrant a full hysterectomy. Her oncologist said it not only gave her the best chance of survival but was also the best scenario for stopping the spread too.

Both the treatment and the surgery demanded a lot of recovery time. My dad's architectural firm permitted him to relocate his part of the business from the downtown office on the river to our guest bedroom. He began working with virtual clients full-time like he did the summer we spent in Bear Lake.

I helped where I could. On the days my mom felt good, I paid close attention to everything she did around the house. I learned how to cook and clean and figured out how to fold laundry her way. Things were rocky, but we were a team, and I was determined to fight for our family.

When we neared that third summer, I tried not to get my hopes up. The oncologist performed scans, ran blood work, and completed various tests before the word *remission* was ever uttered to my mom. An unattainable dream came true and even then, I didn't dare pull out that pineapple floatie.

It was my dad who knocked on my door next, ready to shoulder me through more bad news.

"Hey, kiddo, what are you up to?"

"Just finishing my poster."

For seventh-grade graduation, our class made collages of all our favorite memories from the school year. We signed them like yearbooks, and it gave us something special to display in our rooms for the summer when we parted ways. My dad peered over my shoulder and chuckled at the sketch of Cozy and me tripping in our one-legged race on field day.

I smirked. "We've never been very coordinated."

"No, but what you lack in synchronization, you make up for in communication and determination," he said, pointing across the board to another drawing of the two of us crossing the finish line first.

That described Cozy's and my relationship to a tee—two competitive spirits who refused to give up when things got hard. She never left my side through everything going on with my mom, and if anything, having someone to lean on brought us even closer.

My dad cleared his throat and sat down on the edge of my bed.

"I know you felt this coming, but we aren't going to be able to go to Bear Lake again this year. Even with Mom in remission, I still think it would be best to keep her close to her team of doctors. It's safer than being so remote."

I nodded. It was all I could give him. The great thing about my dad was the way he understood me. He squeezed my shoulder and left me to finish my project while I sorted through my feelings alone.

I pulled my sketchbook from my top dresser drawer and flipped to the back, adding another mark to the depressing rows and rows. It was hard to imagine another year going by. But somehow, it did, and it was a good one.

My mom remained healthy, and I navigated the ins and outs of what it meant to fit in during my last year of middle school. I got braces, took my first drawing elective, and started playing piano for the choir.

Cozy and I became inseparable, our conversations changing

from wall ball teams and hot lunch choices to boys and note passing. We began having sleepovers every Friday night, watching *Gilmore Girls* and binge-eating popcorn and ice cream.

Baker was still a part of our social circle but less so without a tetherball court on campus. He started wearing a heavy hand of Hollister cologne and ran track for the school team, and I found I had a harder time relating to him. Relationships with the opposite gender started to slip from platonic to romantic, which made it difficult for me to even look a guy in the eye anymore.

In all my middle school years, never once did I have a boyfriend, a first kiss, or even get asked to the eighth-grade dance. I was a late bloomer in that regard, but I was fine with that. The truth was, when I thought of my first kiss, there was only one boy I could imagine myself doing that with, and it wasn't any of the guys at Treefort Middle School.

Eighth-grade graduation was the celebration of all celebrations, and I was sad when it came to an end. That was, until my parents showed up on the last day with a loaded car and a pair of grins that could touch the sun.

We were finally going back.

⁓

I feel my shoulders slump with exhaustion by the time I finish reliving the last four years of my life to Miles. It was emotionally draining, but he listened.

I end with a lame "I'm sorry I couldn't come back sooner," and it's the first time he looks at me.

"No, it's okay. I always wondered, but it makes sense now," he says. "I was just happy to see that your cabin never went up for sale."

I draw little circles in the water with my big toe to avoid looking at him.

"Really," he continues, "thank you for telling me."

A part of me wishes he were angrier. That he'd hold me accountable for breaking my promise no matter the reason. That would mean he at least cared even half as much as I do. There are things I chose to miss out on because I waited around for this moment. Seeing Reed slotted into his life, I'm not sure there is a place for me anymore.

I peer over the edge where our feet dangle in the water and catch a glimpse of a tadpole skittering by. I smile.

"It's not as easy as it once was," Miles says.

"What's that?"

"Catching tadpoles. I came out here every summer after you left. It wasn't as simple when I wasn't with you."

A lump forms in the base of my throat, making it difficult to swallow. Imagining him wading out into that water by himself physically hurts.

Just as I'm about to say, "I know what you mean," a rock flies between our shoulders and skids across the water in five long skips. We both whip around to locate the source and see Reed standing with a towel draped over his arm. He jogs the length of the dock to wrap the towel around my shoulders, an air of confidence I don't yet possess thick around him.

Miles pins him with a glare. "You could have hit us, you idiot."

"I was just making sure I didn't interrupt anything." He nudges Miles's shoulder. "I take it you two have some history."

There is no *history* like that when you're children. But then I glance over at Miles and catch him doing that thing he used to do when he was upset, twisting his hands in a Chinese death trap in his lap. His eyes flash to mine, and it's a silent plea not to tell him about our past. I don't know what it is he doesn't want

Reed to know, but I also think this is first step to getting my friendship back with him, so all I say is, "Something like that."

Reed shoves his hands in the deep dips of his workout shorts and flashes me a grin before turning back to Miles. "You ready to fish?"

"Yeah, I just need to get my pole out of the shed," he tells him as he moves to stand.

My attention ping-pongs between them, the lump in my throat disappearing down my esophagus like a boulder to my stomach. *What is this feeling? Jealousy?* I'm annoyed that they're so at ease around each other. I can't stop wondering how long they've been friends, and I realize just how little I know about their world. A small, selfish part of me wants to tell Reed to beat it and find a different dock to fish from. I don't love the idea of the two of them sharing something I'm not a part of.

As if he's telepathic, Reed says, "Teddy, you should fish with us."

I swat at the air. "Oh, that's okay, I don't have a pole."

"I have an extra one!" Miles exclaims, taking off in a jog down the dock.

Okay. This could be good, I convince myself. *The more the merrier.* So, I do what I've done for the last four years. I put on a brave face and leave the summer I shared with Miles in the past to welcome a new one. One where there is three of us, and I learn how to fish.

⌒ℛ⌒

"You want me to help you with that?" Reed offers. He encircles my waist with his burly arms to reach where my fingers are fiddling with a stringy worm.

"Uh, sure." I puff out the little air left in my lungs. I would have taken a giant breath and held it had I known I would find myself somewhat wrapped up in him.

"If you spear it in the middle instead of on one of the ends, you'll have more luck with it staying on," he instructs. He presses his lips together in a firm line as he focuses on securing the worm in place.

While he seems unfazed at our proximity, I'm glad I decided against the red swim coverup this morning. Nothing like avoiding a level of pit-stained embarrassment as my heart rate skyrockets to cardio levels. Having him this close is like the third lap around the middle school track right before you pass out.

"There!" he says, stepping back to admire his work. The worm hangs limply, impaled by the hook's tip.

So, this is the teenage version of hunting for tadpoles. It's kind of gruesome.

I watch Reed pick up his rigged-up pole and walk it confidently to the edge of the dock where he tips it back over his shoulder and casts it out into the still turquoise lake.

Well, he made that look easy.

Miles grabs a tackle box out of the shed while I follow Reed to where he sits.

Piece of cake, I think to myself, imitating Reed's swift movement of tip, extend, cast. Only, that's not what happens. Somewhere between the extend and cast part my fishing line spins around the end of my pole like a helicopter propeller, and it careens off the hook into the water with a plop. Reed howls with laughter, and I shrivel to the size of that decapitated worm that has now found a home at the bottom of the lake.

"Okay, that looked easier than it was," I say as I pull the messy end of my fishing pole toward me.

"You'll get it. It just takes practice," he says.

I grumble. "Easy for you to say. If there were Olympic medals for fishing, you'd be earning gold."

"Miles and I have been out here almost every day for four summers now," he says.

Four summers. That's how much I've missed between them.

"How did the two of you meet?" I ask.

"At the tackle shop in town. I'm sure you know Miles's dad owns it. My mom thought we needed more hobbies than just boating. Everyone else, my dad and two brothers included, thought it was stupid. I was the only one who stuck with it. When I started hanging around the shop, Shep introduced me to Miles. He said he could use a friend, that loner."

"I heard that," Miles pipes in, and we both turn to look at him. He has an old hunter-green tackle box clutched in one hand and a fishing pole with a cork handle in the other. He's traded his baseball cap for a fisherman hat, the brim hung low over his eyes like his old bucket hat used to. The sight makes my heart squeeze with nostalgia.

"I like your hat," I say, even though I want to say, *"Your hat looks good on you. It reminds me of the old one you used to wear."*

"Thanks." His mouth turns up at the corners, but his eyes dart around nervously until they land on the end of my pole. "I can help you with that."

He drops his tackle box and pulls the end closer to unwind the line. He doesn't have his arms around me like Reed did, but it doesn't matter. There's something about the way he glances at me every few seconds that I feel all the way to my toes. My heart is like a Tilt-A-Whirl in my chest, doing all sorts of confusing things I'm not used to.

Miles finishes unwinding my line, and then lifts the lid on the cup of worms. He holds it out, and I follow the steps that Reed taught me and unearth one from the dirt. Miles sits down and casts his line a similar distance to Reed's. They both smirk, waiting for me to try my own.

"We'll close our eyes if you want," Reed says.

"Okay, yeah. Please do that."

When I'm sure they aren't looking, I take a deep breath, tipping the pole back and releasing it forward. It does the wobbly thing again, but I get it far enough out there that it just whips the worm a few times on the end of the line before splashing into the water.

"See, I told you it would just take practice." Reed nudges me, and a blush creeps up my neck.

He's right. With time, it becomes more natural. Not just with fishing but being around both boys in general. We begin doing everything together. Some days we fish until we catch one large enough to eat. Then we use the timber from an over-stocked wood pile near Miles's shed and add it to our brick firepit on the patio. Miles skins our catch and we cook it over an open flame. It's not half bad when it's salted. My parents join us to make s'mores some nights, right about the time the bats swoop between the gigantic oak trees by the water. On lazy afternoons when I sketch, they swim. But Tuesdays?

Tuesdays are reserved for boating.

CHAPTER ELEVEN

"Teddy! Where have you been?"

My mom launches herself at me the moment I step through the door. There's a desperate edge to her voice, and I shrink away in irritation within the cradle of her arms.

"I'm fine."

"I'll call you right back," my dad gets out before stabbing the red circle on his phone screen and flinging it like a frisbee on top of the set of blueprints scattered on the kitchen counter. "Honey, where did Miles take you?"

I narrow my focus at them and put some distance between us.

"He didn't *take me anywhere* I didn't ask him to, if that's what you're implying. But how exactly do *you* know Miles? Because I don't have a clue how I do... did. Whatever. And he's pretending not to know me."

My dad bunches the set of plans before him into a stack and tucks away the distraction in an oversized folder while my mom clings to his side.

My dad clears his throat. "Was that the first time you've seen him?"

I growl, pulling at the strands of my hair. "Why does it even matter to you? You guys obviously haven't cared enough to tell me anything about *Miles*—or Reed for that matter—in the last nine months considering I'm just now learning they exist. Showing me some random sketch of the two of them with no explanation doesn't count!"

"Teddy, we—"

"You know what—?" I wave my hand back and forth in front of my face like a moving stop sign. "Save it! I'll figure it out myself. I need my phone back," I demand with an outstretched hand.

"But Dr. Spalding—"

"Dr. Spalding said just last week that the introduction of old activities—"

"Is something to be introduced slowly," she finishes.

If I was a dragon, the room would be black with smoke and charred from fire.

"I was there at that last appointment, remember? Or did you forget, since you spoke to each other like I wasn't on the call."

My dad steps in front of my mom, shielding her from view. "Okay. We'll agree to the phone."

He walks over to the refrigerator and fishes around on the top until his hand finds what he's looking for.

They hid it? On top of the refrigerator? Like I'm a child? It's humiliating.

I rush over and snatch it from him. Stomping off toward the stairs, he stops me.

"Teddy, your mom and I are just trying to protect you. Part of that is offering our advice when we think you need it. And right now, we think you shouldn't be spending time with Miles."

I flip around, my hair swooshing in front of my eyes, and I spit through the strands. "Oh, good. You want a say in who I spend my time with now? It's not enough that you get to control every other aspect of my life. When I'm deemed fit to have my phone back. What time I need to go bed at night. How far I can venture from the cabin alone. Well, good news for you, Miles doesn't even want to be around me. So you can save yourselves the gray hair."

I refuse to bend at the first sign of their disapproval. When it's obvious they don't have anything more to say, I trudge my way up the stairs, shouting, "And don't follow me!"

~⌇~

It's three days before I leave the confines of my bedroom. I don't have any shifts at the restaurant, I'm avoiding my parents, and I use the wee hours of the morning when I can't sleep to scour my phone for answers about my past. It took a while to charge, but when it finally lit up, I bolted upright to take in the 51 text messages, 26 voicemails, and tiny red bubble hovering at the corner of a multi-colored square with the number 283 on it.

Surprise, surprise. I missed *a lot*.

I tap on the Instagram icon, and a video starts to play. It's of a girl with wild wavy hair and a contagious smile. She's spinning, with one arm holding the phone out in front of her and the other reaching toward the sky. An enormous tower of lights flickers in the background while she lip-syncs to "Sky Full of Stars." The caption beneath the video reads *The Iron Lady is a whole vibe. Wish you were here. @teddyfletcher*

My eyes flare at the sight of my name, and I click on it. The page refreshes to a profile with one lone post. I watch in fascination as the same girl from the video and I jump off the end my dock on a hyperloop.

I can't help but compare it to everything before this summer. Just the same experiences, over and over again.

BFF <3, reads the caption.

This girl was my best friend. It should come as no surprise to me by now, but *how can I not remember I had a best friend?*

I tap all the buttons on the screen, desperate to figure out which one takes me back to her video. When I find the right one, I click on her profile name—*@callmecozy*. A grid of hundreds of pictures and videos load on her page, each one in a place of the world I've never seen before. *A traveling influencer*, I read in her bio. I'm mesmerized, scrolling post after post, when it dawns on me—*there's more.*

I close out of the app faster than I opened it to get to my text messages. The latest string is from Cozy, but I open Reed's first.

Four messages wait for me.

Fri, Sept 1 at 4:30 PM

REED: Hey! I heard from my dad you got to go home today. How are you feeling?

Mon, Sept 4 at 12:46 PM

REED: I just saw a student leave the art building on campus. The Titanic scenario might not be a thing in high school, but it's definitely one here with the way she was blushing. ;)

Fri, Sept 8 at 9:32 PM

REED: I know I'm starting to act like an obsessive boyfriend, but it's driving me crazy that I haven't heard from you. If you're mad that I couldn't stay, I'm so sorry. Believe me... if I could've, I would've.

Sun, Sept 24 at 10:12 PM

> REED: Judging by your silence, I know I need to move on. I promise after this, I won't bother you again. I just wanted you to know I miss your smile, and I'm sorry for my part in all of this.

A tear splashes on the phone screen and my nose drips so much I have to use the sleeve of my shirt to wipe it.

I pause my pursuit and reach for my sketchbook to confirm what I already know to be true. The other guy in the drawing, the one with the dimpled grin that can't hide a single thing he's thinking even if he wanted it to, is Reed Morgan. And he was my *boyfriend*.

An aching sensation blooms in my chest, and I rub at it with my fingertips, willing it to disappear.

Setting down the sketch, I go back to my phone. Close out of Reed's texts and open the ones from Cozy.

Fri, Aug 25 at 4:29 AM

> COZY: TEDDY!!!! I heard what happened from Reed! I wish I could come home!

Fri, Aug 25 at 4:31 AM

> COZY: If it weren't for this year-long contract, I'd be there!

Fri, Aug 25 at 4:40 AM

> COZY: It's killing me not to know if you're okay! You HAVE to be okay!

Sat, Aug 26 at 8:16 AM

> COZY: Reed says you still haven't woken up.
> I'm scared. I can't lose you.

I scroll past several more. Texts for *days* with the same senti-
ments until I get to the most recent one.

Mon, Jan 1 12:01 AM

> COZY: Happy New Year, BFF. It's been months
> since Reed told me you went home from the
> hospital. When he stopped responding to my
> messages and said he needed to move on. I'm
> assuming the two of you broke up, but I don't
> know that for sure, because I haven't heard
> from you. It was driving me crazy not knowing
> why, so I did what any other sane person
> would do. I googled it—traumatic brain injury—
> common side effect: amnesia. If that's what
> this is… I want you to know that I believe in
> you. One day you're going to remember me,
> and I'll be waiting by my phone when you do.
> But until then, I'm holding on to our promise for
> the both of us. I'm tagging you in every post I
> ever share because our friendship IS my
> bucket list.

By the time all 360 notifications have been read, there isn't a
single dry scrap of fabric on my body.

*How am I going to move forward? Why, after hundreds of
messages from my best friend and ex-boyfriend, can I only think
about the ones that are missing from Miles?*

I think about calling Cozy at least a dozen times. It's the
*Wondering what I would even say when I hear an unfamiliar
voice on the other end of the phone* that stops me. I also don't
have the heart to tell her that even after seeing her posts, I can't

remember her. Maybe someday I'll feel ready to do that, but today is not that day.

I look down at the face of my phone and read 10:15. *Shit*, I should have left by now.

I borrow the hatchback to save time and arrive just as a pair of flip flops emerge from underneath the ascending garage door.

"Teddy, I live next door, and I feel like I haven't seen you in weeks." He greets me with an easygoing smile and a pressed apron hanging from his outstretched hand.

I snatch up the apron, fastening it to my waist.

"It would seem we're on opposite shifts," I grunt, working hard to avoid the gaze of my *ex-boyfriend*. How I'll avoid being awkward around him from here on out, I do not know.

I glance at my watch—10:27—and then smirk. "You opened the doors three minutes early."

Reed wags his eyebrows a couple of times.

"Keeping the old man on his toes today."

I laugh and drop my attention to his sandy flip flop–covered feet. "Speaking of toes... trust me when I say, you do *not* want to wear those. I learned the hard way after our first day." I tap my pair of white sneakers together like Dorothy's ruby-red slippers.

"It's the price I have to pay, I'm afraid," he says just as Mr. Morgan comes barreling through the opening between the kitchen and the bar.

"Reed, what are you doing?" he bellows, marching closer.

"There he is now." He winks at me before whipping around on his heals. "Dad, what's up?"

"What's *up*?! Why are the garages open already? I told you not a minute before we open. And I hope you brought a different pair of shoes, otherwise you're not working today."

"Ah, shoot, I guess I'm not working today." He shrugs, sending a chimney stack of smoke from the poor man's crown.

"You better be calling Rex to cover for you then," he huffs, before flipping his frown upside down for me. "Oh, hey, Teddy."

"Hi, Mr. Morgan. Where do you need me?"

"Teddy, please. You're all grown now. Just call me Emmett. If you could fill a dozen water pitchers, that would be great. They're on the second shelf behind the bar," he reminds me, waving his hand in the general direction.

"Sure thing."

I leave the two of them to squabble, and it's not until I've started my workday that I spot Reed walking past the booths overlooking the lake to sit himself near the only window that overlooks the marina. He pretends to scroll his phone, but I catch him glancing my way the second, third, and fourth time I look up from filling water pitchers. When they line the Maplewood countertop and Mr. Morgan is out of sight, I make my way over to the camel-colored pleather booth and slide into the side opposite him.

"What are you doing?" I ask as he smirks at his phone screen.

"What does it look like I'm doing? I'm a paying customer."

I scrutinize him, but his gaze doesn't budge from his phone.

"Seeing as we've missed each other in passing for the last week and you won't agree to hang out with me outside of work, I'm going to sit in your section so we can spend some time together today."

"That's not how this works."

"Oh yeah? Enlighten me. How *does* this work?"

"You might not be working today, but I am," I remind him. "And I told you, I'm not up for the blast from the past thing."

He locks his phone screen and sets it down on the table between us. Everything about him seems more casual today, from his unkempt hair that keeps falling along his forehead to his unbuttoned polo missing an undershirt. Almost like he planned it that way.

"Well, I already checked, and this booth is in your zone. I'm a hungry guy. I can pack in a lot more than you think I can, and every hour or so when you whip out that notepad to take my order, it'll give us the perfect chance to chat." He leans back, making himself comfortable, and winks at me.

I narrow my eyes in his direction, retrieving the ballpoint pen stashed in the front pocket of my apron. "You're—"

"Trouble?" he finishes. "You'll find out just how much, soon enough." He grins before turning his attention back to his phone where his fingers tap across the mini alphabet on the screen.

Charming trouble, that's my problem.

I ready my pen on the pad of paper. "Fine. What'll it be?"

"Diet Coke for now, please, Miss Fletcher."

I scribble *DC*, tuck the pen behind my ear, and stand up from the booth just as a head of curls similar to Reed's but with a longer face comes walking out from the kitchen. He's securing his apron in place, and when he tips his head up, he nods at Reed.

"New employee?" I ask, not having seen him around before.

"Not exactly. That's my brother, Rex. He's your typical first born... follows every rule in the great big book of *Don't Let Your Parents Down*. The guy thrives off obedience."

His description strikes a nerve in me. That's the person I've been for the last nine months of my life, and I hate that version of myself. I refuse to be her anymore. If he's offering me fun over obedience, then fun it is.

"See you at noon."

He grins in triumph, tipping even further back and resting the palms of his hands behind his head. "Take your time. I have all day."

It's two o'clock before I make it back to Reed's booth. The

lunch rush hit like a tidal wave and left me jogging from table to table to keep up.

"What took you so long?" Reed teases, and I huff out a sigh as I slide into the booth with a fresh glass of Diet Coke.

"I'm exhausted; I'm not sure my feet will ever recover from this job."

He chuckles as I work my fingertips up and down my shins.

"So, what you're saying is, you take back your insult to my thongs."

"What? No." My face heats. "Don't call them that. They're flip flops."

I ignore his amused grin and stretch my legs out underneath the table. Another deep sigh escapes my lips and then turns into a desperate throat clearing as my calf brushes against his leg. I sit up a little taller. "Sorry."

Reed's face grows serious. "There isn't a world where you need to apologize to me for something like that."

I feel it again, the warmth of his leg touching mine—no accident this time. Goose bumps erupt like fireworks across my skin. I try to suck in a breath from a room that feels like the air has been vacuum-sealed out of it. We stare at each other, and this feeling of longing stirs deep inside of me. The exact sort of feeling a girl who is leaving at the end of the summer should be running from. *Why does it feel so good that I want to chase it instead?*

"Go home, Reed," Mr. Morgan barks, interrupting the spell we had over each other.

Reed and I both jump apart, but his dad continues to hover over the table with his arms folded and his lips pressed in a hard line. Reed glares at him as I slink from the booth.

"It's my day off, remember?" he argues at the same time I whisper, "I'm so sorry."

How humiliating to be caught by your boss—who also

happens to be the father of the boy you are playing footsie with —abandoning your duties while on the clock. I scamper away to check on the three tables in my zone. One of them is abandoned, the paid tab and fifty-dollar tip left beside the napkin holder.

The whisper-shouting escalates behind me, and I fight to ignore it, but the desire to hear what they're saying is too strong. I glance over my shoulder and find Mr. Morgan gesturing toward me. I jerk my head back toward the money in my hand and pretend to count.

"You're really gonna do this to yourself again?" I hear him say. "You were a *mess* last time. I thought we agreed on a plan."

My money-clutching hand drops to the tabletop, sending the bills scattering like feathers.

What plan? I want to focus on the part but the voice inside of my head reminds me, *ex-boyfriend*. He may not know whether I've read his text messages, but I know. I was his girl-friend who hurt him, and it feels too late to say I'm sorry. I should never have eavesdropped on their conversation when I knew there was chance I'd hear something I didn't like.

I swipe the money off the table, stuff it in my pocket, and scramble to the next one in my zone. I need to focus on busying myself or I'll walk out of here before finishing my tasks. I still need this job. In all the things that have changed since the start of the summer, that much hasn't.

I refill the waters at table four, drop off the check at table ten, and grab the twenty-dollar tip that was left for me at table fourteen. Three new groups are seated in my area, and it isn't until I get their food ordered at the kitchen that I glance over at Reed's table. It's empty, minus a crinkled napkin beneath his drained glass. Faint blue cursive letters scrawl the edge. I swipe the napkin as I pass by, folding it in half and tucking it in my front apron pocket. When I look up, Rex is watching me, an empty tray resting in his palm and a grin plastering his face.

"Good to see you again, Teddy. Looks like you need a five-minute bathroom break." His eyes flick to my hand clutching my apron pocket like I've trapped a mouse inside.

"Oh, uh," I start, searching around to see if anyone (Mr. Morgan) noticed.

Amusement dances in Rex's eyes. "You're not the one he's upset with, trust me."

"Has anyone ever told you you're telepathic?"

"It's a gift," he says with pleasure. "Now go on."

"Thank you."

I scurry down the dim hall adorned with pictures of sturgeon fish until I come to the door of the women's restroom. It swings inward when I lean against it and all the stalls are empty, so I stand in front of the bathroom mirror and untuck the note. A short message is scrawled across the bottom of the napkin.

Can we finally have a little fun tonight? You know where to find me.

My face flushes from how sexual that sounds, even if I know he didn't mean it that way. There are a million and one reasons why I shouldn't do this. A major one being that I don't need to anger my parents more than I already have. In every past circumstance I'd be considering the consequences, but consequences be damned. I want to hang out with Reed. He's fun and light-hearted and makes me want to do bold things.

I slip my phone out of my pocket and open our old text thread.

TEDDY: Pick me up at seven.

CHAPTER TWELVE

SUMMER, FIVE YEARS AGO

"Where's Miles?" I ask, scanning Reed's property for any sign of him.

Reed is stretched out on a lounger, a pair of boardshorts painted around his waist. We've never hung out just the two of us since I got here, and it feels weird to see him all alone. He pushes up from his spot and leans over the edge of the deck railing.

"Hey, gorgeous!" he croons.

He's called me that constantly this summer, and it makes me squirm every single time. I'm not used to being noticed by a guy my age, and I conceal the pink tint in my cheeks behind the woven sleeve of my coverup.

"He's on his way. Had to cover for his dad at the fly shop this morning," he finishes.

The fly shop. It's the thing I remember the least about this place. That and Miles's dad. I haven't seen him around much this summer, and it feels like a punch to the gut to hear that Reed knows more about Miles's life now than I do.

"Speak of the devil." Reed motions to a space behind me. I track the spot.

"Sorry I'm late." Miles jogs to catch up to me.

Before I have the chance to say anything in return, Reed's parents push open the glass doors on the lower deck, his brothers barreling out behind them.

"Dude, we should wakeboard today," Ronny says to Rex.

Rex is built a lot like Reed, but shorter for the oldest son. No matter how fitting the unfortunate nickname, Scrawny Ronny has a lot of catching up to do on all accounts. What he lacks in height and stature though, he makes up for in spunk.

"I'd like to see you try," Rex teases, shoving Ronny on the shoulders. He stumbles over his left sandal and rights his stumpy legs in a martial arts stance. Then he roundhouse kicks Rex right in the nuts. Rex drops to the ground on impact, groaning.

"Try *that*!" He chuckles, then darts to the back end of the truck.

No matter how many times they do this crap to each other (which is a lot), I fight this awkward cringe-laugh. Maybe it's the part of me that can't imagine acting that way in front of my parents. But at the same time, I find their ridiculous sibling rivalry entertaining to watch.

"Boys! Behave yourselves in front of Teddy," Mrs. Morgan barks.

They ignore her as they follow their dad, wrestling the whole way.

A few short minutes later, we coast out of the marina. Rex and Ronny take the seats at the front end of the boat and Miles, Reed, and I sandwich together on the back bench. Mr. Morgan connects his phone to the Bluetooth speakers and country music becomes the soundtrack of our summer.

Ronny milks his baby-of-the-family status for all it's worth and wakeboards first. At the earliest bump of troubled water, he faceplants and we all grimace at the sound of slapping skin on the water's surface. Reed holds the six-inch flag high in the air as the boat circles back, then nudges me in the arm.

"Teddy, you should go next."

I roll my eyes. "Sure, so you can watch me biff it like poor Ronny out there."

Reed gasps, slapping his hand against his chest. "Geez, I can't believe you would think so little of me. I happen to think you'll do great." A smile dances in his eyes.

"Right. Says the guy who made it his mission to flip me off the tube all summer," I argue.

In any other circumstance I'd be all for trying something reckless and new. I would. But even the *thought* of falling flat on my face as Miles watches... well, I'd rather suffocate in a life jacket.

"Come on, Teddy, it's fun!" Ronny says, barreling over the stern. When his foot connects with the same leather seat we're sitting on, it skids, and he shoves against Miles's back to catch himself. Miles lurches forward and knocks the wind from my lungs as he lands... Right. On. Top. Of. Me.

Forget the life jacket, I'm already dead. I'm not even on the same planet because Miles is touching me... everywhere.

Between the weight of him and the warmth of his skin, my breath ghosts out of my body. My pulse hammers through my chest and I sweat. *Is this what a panic attack feels like?*

Good. Perfect. I'm having my first panic attack with Miles on top of me. I've never been more mortified in my entire life.

But then our eyes meet. Lost in a caramel haze, only a small part of me remembers that everyone else is watching this. I should be scrambling upright, looking for a different place for my eyes to land than his. In fact, I hear Reed asking if we're okay, but his voice sounds like it's coming through a wind tunnel because every one of my senses is connected to Miles. All I can think about is the sound of his ragged breath inches from my face, the feel of his warm thighs pressing against mine.

But then he blinks and clears his throat. In one swift movement he lifts off me and says, "I want to go next."

Everyone is momentarily stunned when Miles volunteers, especially me. If there's one thing I've learned about him this summer, it's that he isn't the one who makes the decisions.

Is this him trying to get away from me?

"Go for it," Reed says, trading him spots on the bench.

I've never seen Miles wakeboard, but I know it's not his first time in the way he tightens the bindings to his feet with ease. He glances over his shoulder to make sure I'm watching, and then performs a replay with his hands.

He volunteered for me, I realize. *He wanted me to know what to do when it was my turn so that I wouldn't be embarrassed.* My heart grows a pair of wings and takes off with him into the water as the boat idles away. *I can't believe he did that.*

"So, Teddy, where are you going to high school next year?" Reed asks, scooting closer.

"Oh. Um... Jefferson High," I mumble, trying to focus on him but distracted by Miles's gaze trained on me. I roll my lips to keep from grinning and continue.

"It's in Boise. That's where I'm from. What about you?"

"Park City," he says, sweeping his hand through his hair. "We live in Utah."

I draw my eyes away from Miles, trying to give Reed my full attention.

"Cool," I say, hoping my next question comes out as nonchalant as I want it to. "Do you know where Miles is going?"

"Oh, yeah. Miles goes to Montpelier."

"Montpelier?"

"As in the city that's twenty-eight miles from here. He and Shep pack up their trailer and close the fly shop at the end of the summer. They live on his grandfather's land. He never told you where he's from?" he asks, sounding surprised.

I guess I never thought to ask. I shake my head.

Then his eyes narrow a bit as he chuckles. "Well, I wouldn't worry if I were you. I think their class size is about thirty-five kids."

My face flushes. The line of the tow rope makes a snapping sound when it's pulled taut, saving me from having to continue this conversation.

"Who's on flag duty?" Mr. Morgan hollers.

Reed shoves the flag in my hand. "You should try it."

I give Mr. Morgan a thumbs-up and then whip around to stare at the same eyes that are still looking back at me. Miles always looks at me like he's remembering something. And I'm always wishing I could hear what he's thinking when he does. I don't know if it's the breeze or the way my mouth hangs open in a trance from holding his stare so long, but it starts to feel like I'm eating cotton.

Mr. Morgan guns the gas, and Miles eases to the surface of the water, gliding back and forth between the wakes. It's the most confident I've ever seen him next to fishing and tadpole-hunting, and I can't take my eyes off him.

After landing several tricks, he lets go and dips beneath the surface, and by the time his head submerges, I'm standing up, dancing that little neon flag, my long hair fanning across my face.

Much to my surprise, a few tries and an hour later I'm doing the very same thing.

Reed—the enthusiastic, wild-mannered, shameless flirt that he is—whoops and hollers, "Teddy! You look so hot out there!" while Miles shouts, "You're doing amazing." They're both beaming at me with a sense of pride, and between the two of them, it's enough to make me feel like I'm sailing. I'm not sure I care to ever tube again.

As the end of summer draws closer, I feel a growing sense of anxiety over the thought of spending a school year without them. The pull to make sure they don't forget me has me staying up late one August evening downloading a mixtape of all the songs that remind me of our summer together.

I burn a single a copy and sprawl out on my stomach with a permanent marker in my hand. I carefully lay the disc flat on the blanket draped near the foot of my bed and lose myself to the intricate round, the disc mirroring my friendship with Miles and Reed. A friendship where I am beginning to wonder where they end, and I begin.

⁓~

"We should go out in the canoe one last time," Reed suggests over the chatter of our parents. It took all summer to coordinate, but they finally got together for a BBQ hosted on our patio to get to know each other.

We duck out in the middle of their conversation and head for the canoe. I snatch my sketchbook off a lounge chair and chase after Reed and Miles toward the dock. The boys each take an oar and row us out until our families look like miniature figurines on the shore.

It's blanketed in a dusky haze and too good not to capture, so I say, "Miles, trade me spots."

When we both stand, the boat rocks back and forth with the shift in weight, and Miles reaches out to lace his fingers with my free hand.

"Maybe you two should play chicken instead," Reed encourages.

Miles pushes on me, and I lean backward just enough to feel the tip of the boat.

"Behave," I grunt, shoving the sketchbook between my teeth so I can grip his other hand too. I ignore the flames that stoke inside of me with the sensation of his skin touching mine. They're there, but if I fall prey to them, there's no way I'm keeping my balance. I'm sure to ruin every sketch I've ever drawn from my summers here. The sketches of Miles that get me through the nine months we spend apart.

Both boys laugh as he and I shuffle in a half circle before sitting in our new spots.

"That's better," I say, tucking the paddle across the front of the boat and opening my sketchbook, eyes focused on the shoreline.

"You two may not be getting in, but I am."

Reed rips off his shirt and backflips off the back of the canoe, making a giant splash. Water droplets spray in a rain shower that drenches our clothes but miraculously avoids my book.

"REED!" Miles and I yell in unison.

He grins and swims a few laps around the canoe while I begin sketching the place where the lake meets the shore. I brush the charcoal strokes with my fingertip so they're a bit softer to match the blades of grass that sway in the breeze. The world falls away whenever I'm making art, but when I feel the boat dip forward, my hand stills.

"I don't think there's anything you aren't incredible at," Miles whispers over my shoulder.

I can think of one thing: not having the breath punched from my lungs anytime you're close to me.

Three fingertips trace down my left arm and stop at the crook of my elbow. It's nothing like the first time I felt his touch, that day on the boat, because this time it's intentional. Chills erupt on my skin with the sensation of his breath on my neck.

"Do you think you'll be back next summer?"

There's a sad longing to the sound of his voice, and I realize my response to his compliment should have been: *Leaving you. That's the thing I'm not any good at.*

I'm afraid of ruining the moment. This is the most vulnerable he's been with me since that first day I came back. Reed may be ten feet away like always, but right now, it feels like it's just him and me. Alone in this canoe.

I want to tell him *yes*, but this time, I need to be honest. I just hope my answer conveys the feelings I have in my heart.

I set down my pencil and reach my hand across my stomach to touch his fingertips. They're warm and soft. The connection feels like the kind of dream you long to hold on to and never let go.

"I hope so."

CHAPTER THIRTEEN

NOW

It's 6:58 when I hear tires skittering down the steep slope of our driveway. I'm waiting, Converse crossed at the ankle on a lawn chair, for my *fun time* with Reed. It's the one time of day I can count on my parents being out of the cabin. They take a canoe ride together down the shoreline every night before sunset. Even though I'm past the age of a curfew, I want my time with Reed as free of expectation as possible. That meant not telling them I'm going anywhere. Will they worry when they get back and find out I'm gone? Yes. But I need to do this for me.

When a familiar truck rounds the kitchen window I snatch my sweatshirt draped over the back of the chair and tuck it under the crook of my arm, moving toward him. He pops the door open and leans over the top of the frame, his broad shoulders squeezing between the gaps.

"Hi!" He grins, his white teeth popping against the deep green of his fitted long-sleeve tee.

"Hey yourself."

"You got your phone back," he comments.

My cheeks heat, and I avert my gaze to his vehicle,

nodding. I'm not ready to go there. Admit that I know we dated. So I change the subject. "You drove over? You live next door."

"What can I say, I'm a man of my word," he says, hopping out of his truck and circling the front. I feel a blush creep up the back of my neck as his eyes scroll my body.

"You look..." he starts to say.

He could be dressed in rags for all I know since I have a difficult time looking anywhere besides that hundred-carat dimple like a crater in his cheek.

"You too."

He takes confident backward steps, guiding me by an invisible string that ties our gazes together, toward the passenger door.

"Are you ready for this?" he asks with an unmistakable gleam in his eye.

"I think so?" I hold up the sweatshirt he texted me an hour earlier to bring.

He nods. "That will do."

In one swift motion, my hips are being planted in the front seat facing the view of the lake through Reed's windshield.

"Just thought the step might be a bit high for you." He shrugs when he registers my dizziness.

I somehow manage a "thank you" despite trying to calm my heart back to a steady rhythm. I rest my sweatshirt in my lap when I spot someone approaching the shed on the right side of the dock.

For as long as I can remember, the property has belonged to Shepard Bishop, the nicest man I've ever met. He was the first person who introduced himself to me the day my parents brought me back home from the hospital. I sat on the edge of the dock staring out over the vast lake feeling insignificant, lost, and confused; like someone could toss me off the edge and I'd drown because I'd forgotten how to swim, how to keep my head above water, how to even breathe.

"Teddy, you have post-traumatic amnesia," I heard Dr. Spalding repeat inside my head. *"Which is why recalling memories from before the accident is difficult for you. You might find it hard to recognize people you knew, have trouble sleeping at night, and feel irritable. Because of this, my recommendation is that we monitor your physical progress and focus on healing for now.*

"I think we should go back to Boise," my mom urged my dad.

"Actually, Mrs. Fletcher," Dr. Spalding interrupted, *"big changes are not ideal for memory reconstruction. Teddy needs as little disruptions to her past routines from before the accident as possible for best outcomes. If you can manage it on your end, we'll be able to continue our visits through telehealth appointments, and Bear Lake Memorial has a great out-patient rehab program she can start when her physical injuries have healed."*

My parents agreed.

"For the time being, I recommend limiting screen time, removing social media use, and lots of rest."

It sounded miserable. Like a death sentence to making any kind of friends.

But Shep found me on the dock that day. And like the wise man he is, told me that one day in the distant future, it would all be okay again. At the time, I struggled to believe him, but then he added, "Until then, you've got a friend in me." From then on, he'd bring me a peanut butter and honey sandwich whenever I was out there alone.

I found out Shep has type one diabetes the day my parents discovered him collapsed beside his lawn mower. He'd let his blood sugar dip too low while trimming his half acre of land. I was glad my mom found him instead of me. She already knew. Not only does Shep leave out the part about him being diabetic with most people, but he also never makes it seem like he needs help with anything either. He waters the Morgans' garden like a chameleon, picks up our mail at our driveway entrance like a saint, and never asks for a favor in return.

But it's not Shepard who's approaching the shed. This guy is much taller, in a pair of jeans and a T-shirt slung over his left shoulder. He pulls on the iron handle and the door to the shed rattles open. There's not much to see on the inside. Even from where I'm sitting, I squint to make out the handle of a lawn mower peeking past the door's opening and several weathered tools lining the shed wall. The guy reaches for an axe resting between two prongs jutting out from the back of the shed. Then he turns around and looks right at me.

Miles?

The pop of Reed's door handle snaps my attention to the driver's seat as he climbs in and fires up the engine. He's looking over his shoulder and reversing when he catches me watching something, or rather, someone, in the yard and turns to see what it is. With the few inches Reed's truck has backed up, it's become more difficult to see Miles. He's positioned on the far side of the shed and is bent over at the waist slamming an axe into a vertical stump of wood. After yesterday's run-in, I know Reed knows him, so I just say out loud what I'm thinking.

"How come Miles is at Shepard Bishop's trailer?"

Reed glares at the lake through his windshield.

"Because," he grunts. "He's his son."

That one sentence renders me speechless, and I gawk from him to Miles.

I'm sorry… son? It would seem Shepard wasn't honest with me either.

Out of all the possible scenarios, I never imagined finding my cabin nested between two pieces of my past.

Reed takes my silence as a sign to back up the driveway.

Where the top of the slope converges with the road, the trailer comes into view once more.

The sound of the tires rotating over the gravel draws Miles to a stop, but he doesn't look up from the pile of wood at his feet. Not until Reed eases the truck onto the shoulder of the road and heads toward town do I see Miles lift his haunted eyes to mine in the side mirror, watching as we drive away.

It takes five minutes to get to the marina from the cabin, and Reed parks the truck in an open spot by the road. Both the restaurant and the parking lot are overflowing.

He reaches over my lap, opening the glove box. When he pulls his hand back out, a pair of small silver keys held together by an air-filled keychain in the shape of a tube rest in the palm of his hand, and a CD sits on the center of his pointer finger. He gives it a spin, and the light from the sun refracts off the back, making tiny rainbow disco lights across the dash.

"You're a partier, aren't you?"

Smirking, he tucks it in his pocket. "I know how to have a good time." Then, dangling the silver keys in front of his grin, he says, "Come on!"

Everything Reed does is at a run. Like he's always in hurry but not because he thinks he'll be late. Rather, he might miss something good if he doesn't chase what's next. It's making me live on a steady dose of adrenaline in his presence, and it's a high I'm not sure I ever want to come down from.

In a row of white speed boats, Reed's is neon orange. He hops over the edge and then grabs my hand to help me on board. There's a seat across from the driver's side that I take. Goose bumps prickle up my arms with the wind's draft. Now I see why he asked me to bring a sweatshirt.

Reed slips the CD he was carrying into the disc reader and cranks the volume. The opening line of "Man! I Feel Like a Woman!" barrels through the speakers. We both laugh as we coast out past a series of yellow buoys, and then Reed floors the gas. My hair no longer bevels but whips behind my ears. A smile plasters my face as he jets along the shoreline. He's navigating the boat with his eyes trained on me. I grip the dash in front of my seat and force my short legs to stand. Throwing my arms in the air I screech into the wind. I'm not sure I've ever felt freer than I do right now. It's something I've been chasing for months.

Reed shouts over the sound of the boat cutting against the choppy waves. "Make her squeal, check!"

I like that he makes me feel like this.

He speeds along until he finds a deserted spot to slow the boat to a stop. It's close enough to the shoreline to see rows and rows of cabins. There's one that looks like the White House if it were planted in Bear Lake. When the boat stills, the water continues to lap against the sides. We bob along and stare at the milky clouds.

"It's really something out here," I say. My stomach floats up into the sky. I forgot how buoyant happiness can feel.

"Yeah, it is," he says.

"Any other art in the world would never measure up to this."

He rocks his head back and forth. "It's beautiful, but I disagree. I've seen art that doesn't even need color to be beautiful."

I know he's referring to my art, and I don't want to go there. I still don't even know if that's me any longer.

"Just so you know, I don't sketch anymore." There's an edge to my voice I hide behind, afraid he will press me on it. But when I look over at him, there's a playful gleam in his eye.

"Then what does Teddy Fletcher like to do for fun?"

My stomach floats back down from the clouds and twists in a knot. The truth is, I haven't done anything fun in a long time. And maybe I've forgotten how. But when Reed senses my hesitation, he grabs my hand and pulls me toward the back of the boat, stripping off his shirt.

"What are you doing?" I panic.

"What does it look like I'm doing?"

"It looks like you..." The sentence dies on my tongue as he shimmies his jeans down his legs and reveals a pair of very tight briefs. "—forgot your swimsuit," I finish, and it comes out sort of strangled.

He chuckles and a blush creeps up my neck like a thorny rose vine that just might be the end of me.

"I don't need one for what we're doing. Turn around," he instructs.

I do it on instinct, freaking out about what I'll find when I turn back. I gasp when I hear a giant splash. I spin back around to the most infectious grin I've ever seen bobbing in the water.

"Your turn," he taunts, droplets dripping from the ends of his hair. He combs them away from his forehead with his fingertips.

I don't know if I can do this. I mean, I know I said I *wanted* to do this, but maybe that was hypothetical. Maybe deep down I do need permission to do this.

My eyes flit around, searching for someone watching, but we're the only ones out here. My arms wrap my midsection to cover my clothed body.

"I'm not looking, okay?" he assures me. "I just promised you fun, and that's what I'm trying to give you."

He rotates so his back faces me while treading water. I gulp down all the air my lungs can handle as my sweatshirt lifts from my shoulders first. The more articles of clothing I remove, the more of a thrill I feel. Until there's nothing left, and I'm jumping off the back of the boat into the water.

When my head crests the surface, Reed faces me.

"And?" He grins like he's waiting for me to tell him a secret I might have to take to my grave.

"Let's do it again!"

From the marina, the inky sky makes the cabins seem brighter and other boats less visible. Reed parallel parks the boat against the dock, and then hops over the edge and ties a fancy knot, tethering us in place.

"The restaurant's closed," I notice, scanning the empty parking lot.

"Make her lose track of time, check," Reed says.

His head tilts to the side, a sea of wild curls framing his eyes as he extends his hand, helping me onto the dock. When his fingers slip into my palm, my brain registers how thankful I am that the skin there healed from the rope swing burn without anyone noticing.

"What else is on this list of yours?"

"I guess we're going to have to hang out again for you to find out."

I shake my head. "You and your secrets."

"I'd rather call them surprises." He winks at me. "I have a lot of surprises up my sleeve when it comes to you."

Reed unlocks the truck, lifting me onto the seat in a brisk fashion but less dizzying than the one in my driveway. I try to tame my smile as he races around the truck bed.

We're drifting down my driveway a few minutes later, our evening coming to an end. The truck's headlights cut a path in the dark to someone sitting at the edge of the dock. He doesn't look over his shoulder, but I know it's Miles, and when I look over at Reed, he's watching him too.

"I should go," I say, reaching for the handle, "but thank you, Reed. I had a fun time."

Reed grins. "So did I."

I'm worried things will get awkward if I make this good night last any longer than it needs to be, but as I turn away from him to push on the door handle, I stop. I can't get out of this car without asking him the one question that's been haunting me ever since I left the restaurant that first day.

"Reed?"

"Yeah?"

"When Miles came to the restaurant, it looked like..."

Reed's eyes focus on the steering wheel instead of at me. I can't finish my thought. I'm confused. Are Miles and Reed friends? Did they used to be friends? Enemies?

Before I can find the right way to phrase it, he responds. "I had fun with you tonight, Teddy. I want to keep having fun with you. So please, don't ask me about him, okay?"

The awkward goodbye I was trying to avoid erupts between us.

"Okay," I accept.

I don't want to pry, but I feel as though he already finished my sentence without saying anything at all. Something happened between them, and I have an eerie feeling it has everything to do with me.

CHAPTER FOURTEEN

SUMMER, FOUR YEARS AGO

"**D**o you need to stay the whole summer? Last year was dreadful without you," Cozy whines from where she's lounging next to me on my hot pink bedspread.

"You should come with me!" I sit up in a start, fixing the lid on the nail polish—a brilliant buttercup—that we've been passing back and forth. "Yeah! I'll ask my parents, but I don't see why they would care."

"I wish, but I can't. My mom's making me fill out an application at Old Navy in exchange for a phone *and* my license by the end of the summer."

Cozy and I finished driver's ed together in January and have been logging hours for our permits the last few months. I've learned I'd rather chauffer my dad around than my mom, who acts like a second seat belt and parking brake wrapped into one hot mess.

"Now that's a deal I'd take," I say, relaxing back on my stomach and adding topcoat to the nails on my left hand.

"Can you imagine how *nice* it's going to be to get to go off campus for lunch next year instead of sneaking out in the trunk of a junior's car?"

"Yeah, I don't want to do that again." I remember the one and only time we ever went through with it. My stomach still churns over the memory of getting caught and spending two days in detention.

"At least tell your parents you want a phone so we can text each other. And Instagram! I don't want to be posting pictures of my bestie on there when I can't even tag her in them."

"Not until my sixteenth birthday and no social media until 18," I recite with an eye roll. "Something about too many creeps on the internet." I shrug. *It's out of my control.*

She sighs. "You get to go off and hang out with two guys all summer, and I won't be able to hear a word about it until you get back."

"What if I email you?"

"Promise?"

"Promise."

That was a month ago.

⁓

"Hey stranger, I haven't seen you for a week," I call over the loud hum of a lawn mower.

Just like last summer, Miles and I are never alone. We picked up right where we left off in every regard except for that solitary moment when those three fingers on his left hand traced down my arm. That high branded itself to my memory. I searched for that feeling all freshman year and never found it anywhere else.

Miles releases the handle on the mower, letting it idle. He

jerks an earbud from his ear. "Sorry?" he hollers, pointing to the mower.

"Where have you been?" I repeat, even though I already know because of Reed. He worked the entire last week at his dad's fly shop from opening to close due to a family emergency. Of what kind, I don't know. Reed didn't elaborate.

"Oh, I had to help out my dad," he says.

I feel frustrated with how casually he says it.

"Is he home?" I ask, pointing to the trailer. I hate to go behind Miles's back, but if he won't open up to me and let me help, maybe his dad will.

He shakes his head.

So much for the lead.

"Do you want to come over later? My parents are making homemade pizzas for dinner, and we always have extra," I offer.

His lips do a small quirk to the side like they used to when we were kids, and it makes me feel better.

"Yeah, sure."

"Okay! Come by around six."

"I'll be there," he says.

I give him one last smile as he places the earbud back in and gets to work cutting even diagonal lines across the lawn.

"You need any help?" I ask my mom as I make my way out of the bathroom and into the kitchen, squeezing the moisture from the damp ends of my hair with a towel. I know it's a good day when she's wearing her paint-splattered apron tied around her waist and has flour up to her elbows.

"I'd love that," she says, giving my dad a pointed look where he's scavenging the pepperoni and sausage toppings. She holds out a ball of dough for me, then sprinkles the linoleum with a generous handful of flour and drops her own on top of it. "Just press your knuckles into it like this." She demonstrates how to knead the dough like a punching bag.

My fingers ache after thirty seconds. As if there wasn't something else to admire about the woman, the muscles in her hand are right up there at the top of the list.

"I invited Miles to dinner. Is that okay?"

I search both of their faces for approval. My dad pays little attention to anything but the can of olives he's trying to open with an electric opener. His frustration mounts with each failed attempt.

"Of course it is. We love Miles," my mom says. "Speaking of Miles, how's his dad doing? We heard he's been in the hospital."

What? His dad has been in the hospital? How am I the last person on earth to hear about this?

A rapping sound comes from the front door.

"Why don't you ask him yourself," my dad says to my mom as she hollers, "Come in."

The handle twists at the same time the door cracks.

My mom abandons her smoothed-out dough next to my glob and races to the door, wrapping Miles in a hug with her forearms. Flour flakes from her fingertips all over the tops of his tennis shoes.

I swallow at the sight of him. He's dressed up. Well, as dressed up as I think *fisherman Miles* will ever be, in a short-sleeve button-up shirt and jeans. He gives me his trademark side smile as my mom squeezes him.

"We're so glad you came!" she sings. "Aren't we, Arch?"

"What? Oh, mhm," he mutters over the sound of the can opener whirring in midair.

My mom releases Miles and gives me an expectant look. "We were just talking about your dad, weren't we, Teddy?"

His eyes snap to mine. All I can do is stare in his direction to see how he'll react. Does he want me to know?

"Is he doing better?" my mom continues.

Miles and I are standing there staring at each other like two people stuck in a crazy time warp. Miles looks away first.

"He is. Thank you for asking, Mrs. Fletcher."

He is? He is, what? Hurt? Dying? I wouldn't know because someone who I thought was my best friend doesn't tell me anything anymore. I can feel everyone's eyes volley between me and Miles.

My mom, now back at the counter, uses a rolling pin to flatten the balls into crust and lays the compressed rounds on the top of a pizza stone.

"Dinner should be ready in about fifteen minutes if you two need to catch up."

I can feel the anger bubbling up and boiling over as I stammer, "There's nothing to catch up about. I'm not feeling very hungry."

I push my way up the stairs, and I hear Miles call from below, "Teddy, wait..."

"I'm so sorry," my mom apologizes. "I don't know what's gotten into her."

"No, it's okay, Mrs. Fletcher. I got this." I can hear the hardwood groan as he climbs up after me.

I don't care that he's just a few steps behind, I shut the door when I get inside my room and pull out my sketchbook, throwing myself on top of my bed and opening to a blank page.

If he's going to tell everyone about his life but me, fine. He doesn't get to know a damn thing about mine anymore either.

Three soft tapping sounds rattle my slatted door.

"Teddy, can we talk?" he asks.

"I don't have anything nice to say."

"That's okay. You don't have to say anything at all. I'm the one who needs to do the talking," he says.

I sigh. "These are ancient doors, Miles. It's unlocked."

The door gives way with the scraping of wood. I don't look at him as he walks over to the side of the bed. I start sketching, letting my mood guide the familiar strokes of the pencil, pouring out my feelings onto the page. The bed sinks a little lower on his side when he sits down beside me.

"I'm sorry," he starts. Which is a good place to begin when I'm mad at him, but I keep my eyes trained on the thick paper, afraid if I even look his way, he won't finish what he couldn't say to my face before. "My dad... he has diabetes. I found him collapsed at the store the other day because his blood sugar dipped too low."

The tip of my pencil stops on the bridge of a nose forming in the center of the paper.

"I don't like talking about it. For a lot of reasons. Especially not with you."

I drop my pencil and sit up to look him in the eye this time.

"What do you mean, *especially not with you*. I thought we were friends, Miles."

He reaches across the bed and grips my hand. The subtle shock of how much warmer his fingers are than mine sends a jolt of heat up my arm.

"You're... important to me, Teddy. I don't want to mess that up with my family's problems."

I want to rip my hand away when he says that, but the stroke of his thumb over my pointer finger is making me too dizzy to form a rational thought. The only part of me that is still fighting and driving for answers are my emotions.

"If I'm so important to you, then why am I always the last one to know. You tell Reed. Even my parents know before me."

He drops his eyes to his lap. "Because... I didn't want you to think less of me," he lets out. "And I didn't want to scare you away."

"Think less of you because your dad has a condition out of his control? Do you hear how crazy that sounds?" Even I do, and it's coming out of my own mouth.

He sighs, letting go of my hand. "You have this amazing family, Teddy, and I... mine's dysfunctional. My mom left, my dad never puts his health first, I'm terrified he'll collapse at any moment, and I'm barely holding it together. You deserve a summer of fun when you come here, not a summer of problems." He looks up at me with the same tied-in-knots expression he had the day we sheltered from the rain in the bunkhouse as kids. Only this time it's fear in his eyes, not sadness.

It hurts seeing him like this. He means so much to me and I'm struggling more than ever to keep those feelings inside. I've gone one and a half summers now without telling him how much I thought about him all the years we spent apart. I mean, *really* telling him. He's worried he'll scare *me* away?

If I wasn't so afraid of losing him, maybe I would keep those feelings locked away. But they burst from me like a caged bird being set free.

"You're important to me too, Miles. You're my favorite person in the whole world. I'm here for you, and I'm not going anywhere."

The fear vanishes from his eyes, and a deep longing replaces it. Even before he tips forward, I feel the distance between us start to close. The bed creaks when he leans in, and my heart fumbles to meet him halfway. When I can feel his breath dancing across my lips, my eyes flutter shut. We hover there, sharing each other's air. I want to reach out and touch his shirt, feel the rhythm of his heartbeat beneath my hand to see if it's racing like mine.

"Dinner's ready!"

The sound of my mom's voice calling from downstairs jerks us apart. Miles clears his throat, and I push a strand of hair behind my ears.

"We should go down," he says, standing.

"Uh, yeah, okay." I stumble over my words as Miles exits the room in a brisk trot.

I fight to keep up with the pace of my own heart.

The one that's saying, *I almost had my first kiss.*

The one that's galloping.

Almost. Almost. Almost.

⌒⌒

Two days later, Shepard comes home. When it's half past ten and I'm sure Miles is gone to open the shop, I fill a cheap paper plate full of chopped raw vegetables—Miles told me dessert was off-limits—and take them as a "welcome home" gift to the trailer. I'm hoping the quality of the food masks how flimsy the plate feels as it collapses in my hand from the weight.

I tiptoe across the grass barefoot, the dew from the morning sprinklers chilling my feet. As I lift my fist to knock, the door swings wide open. Shep is standing, healthy as a horse, framing the doorway.

"Well, aren't you a sight for sore eyes! Come in," he says with his usual boisterous arm wave.

"Hey, Mr. Bishop. I just wanted to check up on you."

"Don't tell me *Miles* put you up to this," he grumbles.

I set the wilted plate of veggies on the counter and cringe, feeling like a homemade card would have been better. I chuckle, not sure if it's from his scolding or the embarrassment of my pathetic gift.

"No, he doesn't know I'm here."

"Well, good. Then come sit down." He gestures to a rickety table that folds out from the wall with a narrow single-person-bench on each side.

"Thank you."

I investigate the trailer since I've never been inside before. It's dated like the outside, but homey. Handcrafted quilts tuck into the edges of full-size bunk beds. There's a smaller-than-me shower and a closet (I imagine for the toilet?) on the other side. The middle section houses a single burner stove with enough room on the countertop for the overripe bundle of bananas sitting on top of it.

Shepard notices me looking around and comments, "It's not much, but it does the job."

"Well, I think it's cozy."

His smile warms. "So, what brought on this unexpected visit? And please don't tell me it's that rabbit food. I appreciate what you're doing, but I know *that* was all Miles. You don't have to convince me otherwise."

"Guilty." I shrug. "I came to see if I can help at your store. I know I don't have any retail experience or experience at all for that matter as this would be my first job, but I've learned a lot about fishing from Miles! And I'm great with people! And you don't have to pay me!"

"I don't need any favors," Shep says, and I realize why Miles has been so frustrated with him. He may be the most generous man, but he's also the most stubborn. Everyone needs help once in a while.

I lean across the table in my sudden haste to make him understand.

"You'd be doing *me* the favor. Really! Everyone's busy. My

mom's painting all the time and my dad's always puttering, and Reed's family is constantly working or going on adventures and all I do is spend time by myself on that dock." I suck in a gust of a breath.

"Woah, woah, woah." He chuckles. "Slow down."

"Sorry." I cringe.

I sound desperate. I mean, I'm over here pleading with the man over all the reasons why he should hire me. None of which have anything to do with the fact that getting this job would mean I would get to work alongside Miles every day. Nope. Nothing to do with that.

Shepard grunts a couple of times while thinking it over. I clasp my hands on top of the table. It gives me something to squeeze while I exercise that muscle I don't like to use very often... patience.

"Well, I guess I could use a little help. Can you start on Monday?" he asks.

"I can start *today* if you want!"

He chuckles again. "Monday will do. But I'll be paying you for your time. I don't expect you to work for free, and don't let anyone else in your life take advantage of you in that way either, you hear? You have a heart of gold, and that's worth everything."

His advice makes me tear up a bit, but I blink a few times before it becomes more.

"Thank you, Mr. Bishop. Thank you so much," I say, hurrying to the exit. "Oh, and can we please not tell Miles. I'd rather he think I got hired the old-fashioned way."

He slides his fingers across his lips, and then pretends to lob an imaginary key in the air.

I grin. "See you Monday!"

With Shepard feeling better and back at the store, Miles gets the weekend off. I stir in the warm cocoon of my bed as the sound of repetitive clinking wakes me. I lift onto my elbows, my room still dim and the dark shadow of the oak tree out front dancing across the wall. The clink sounds again, and I pivot toward it as a tiny seashell bounces off the glass. Using the windowsill to shield my barely there pajama top, I draw the blinds up a few inches, and like a pair of roosters, Miles and Reed stand on the edge of the patio waking me. I lift the latch on the window, sliding it open.

"What the hell are you guys doing down there," I whisper-shout.

"Waking you up! What does it look like we're doing?" Reed calls.

"You're waking more than me up. My parents are going to freak out if they hear you." I reinforce the whisper.

"Come down," Miles whispers back.

At least one of them knows how to be quiet.

I hold up a finger and draw the blinds back in place. Shooting one last, longing glance at my bed, I find the nearest pair of sweats and long-sleeve tee to change into and grab my sketchbook from the vanity drawer. Then I make the rattletrap climb down the stairs. The first step squeaks under my weight, so I hover against the edge on the next step where the sound is much softer. I hug the railing to make it down the flight of stairs after that. I'm more than halfway to the front door when I hear the coffee pot grinding beans.

"Where do you think you're going, young lady."

I whip around, and my mom, draped in a plush bathrobe, stands with a coffee mug at the ready.

"Going to see the sun rise?" It comes out more like a question than the statement I was intending to make.

She chuckles as she reads the indecision in my eyes. "You forget I was young once."

She flicks her gaze to the sheer curtains where the shadows of two boys illuminate from the patio outside. If either of them believes they'll be an undercover detective one day, they can go ahead and take an atomic bomb to that dream.

"Stay in the yard."

When the coffee maker chimes, she sets her mug on the counter and fills it to the top with piping hot coffee. I jog over to her, wrapping her in a quick hug before racing to the door.

"Thanks, Mom. You're the best!"

"Don't you forget it." She grins with pleasure. "Oh, and Teddy...? Say hi to the boys for me."

I burn with embarrassment but flit out the door before she can say any more.

I march over to where they're dinking around in the grass.

"Reed, I'm going to kill you!"

"Wow, okay. Someone's not a morning person," he says, throwing his hands in the air as if he's under arrest.

"I promise both of you, his death will be worth it," Miles says.

"Oh, so this was *your* idea?" I say to the one who I thought was the rule follower.

"Just come on," Miles says, running toward the oak tree. "We don't have much time."

I roll the sketchbook up and tuck it into the waistband of my sweatpants. The bulging roots at the base of the tree act as a steppingstone for Reed to climb first. He launches himself from a root to the first knot in the trunk, and then swings one leg over the nearest bulky branch until he's straddling it. He works himself onto his feet once more, crouching and reaching for my hand. Miles forms a makeshift step with his fingers woven together. I use it to get to the first knot and depend on Reed's strong arms to lift me the rest of the way. He hoists me onto the branch and our bodies collide against the trunk, making for an awkward moment of body contact and loss of personal space.

"Miles was right, this was worth it," he says, gripping my hips.

I punch him in the bicep, a pretty pitiful one with my tooth-pick arms, and he laughs.

"Relax, I'm kidding. Let me help you to the next branch."

He offers his laced fingers just like Miles did, and I grumble, "I should be using your head instead of your hands."

I stuff my tennis shoe in his waiting palms and use every-thing I have to make it to the next limb.

After that, the branches are a lot closer together, and I'm able to climb higher on my own. I don't have any idea how high I go. I don't inspect the drop beneath me. When the branches grow sparse, I find a set that arch out in a V-shape, allowing a seat for my legs to drape on either side.

Reed and Miles are seconds behind me, climbing so much faster than I did. They settle on tree limbs close by, and we all look out over the water.

A faint beam of light pours over the top of the plateaus, the sun hovering just beneath it. It's melting the dark blues of the night with the ambers of the rising sun. I unfurl my sketchbook and start flipping it to the nearest empty page.

In my peripheral vision, I can see Miles glancing over my shoulder. His eyes smile at the flash of a drawing I finished yesterday. The once faint shadow of his nose turned into the intricate details of his face. It's just a flash though before we're both looking at a blank page. I pretend like he didn't see it and attempt to capture the feeling of a new day with a single pencil in my hand.

I gasp as the curve of the glowing crescent peaks over the mountain tops.

"I knew it would be worth it." Reed gapes at the rising sun just like I do.

"So worth it," Miles says, but he's looking at me.

CHAPTER FIFTEEN

NOW

I figure Miles knows I'm home from the obnoxious shine of Reed's headlights, but I still clear my throat when I come to stand behind him. He moves his head to the side but doesn't make the effort to look over his shoulder at me. I'm not surprised. I'm well aware he doesn't want me around him, but I have questions, and I get straight to the point.

"I see we're neighbors," I bait him, hoping he'll fill in the blanks that Reed left empty. Deep down I know he won't. He doesn't seem to want to talk about the past any more than I do.

I sit next to him, observing the glassy lull of the water.

"Yeah," he says, keeping his gaze fixed ahead.

"Did you ever plan on telling me that or—"

"No," he cuts me off.

I have no idea what to say. He's been lying to my face and is showing no remorse for it, but I'm not done showing *him* how irritated I am.

"No? You brought me home the other day and didn't say a damn thing about it," I bark.

He sighs. "It's better that you don't remember."

"Yeah, well, now there's something we both can agree on."

Wait... what? Now I'm agreeing with him? This guy spins my head like a top. I want to ask him why he never texted me in the last nine months like Reed and Cozy did, but he'll never answer that question if he didn't even want me to know we share a property line.

"I'm just saying, it's a little hard to stay away from someone when they live next door, if that's your plan," I argue.

I can feel myself getting more and more agitated with his silence. *What is it about this guy that gets under my skin and makes me talk in circles?* Whenever I'm around him I feel like I have to fill the silence for the two of us when I know perfectly well he isn't bothered by it. It's evident in his relaxed shoulders next to my bunched-up ones.

"Fine. You know what? I don't need any answers from you. I'm fine to just sit right here and stare at this water."

A sound rumbles from deep inside his chest, and when I look over at him, I realize he's laughing. He's laughing at how much I'm rambling, just like I did in his truck the other day. I'm sure he thinks I'm unhinged. You know what, *I am* unhinged lately, and the thought is enough to make me laugh too. Even I know how ridiculous I sound when I get like this.

We're both laughing together, and it's diffusing the tense situation we were in moments ago. It's brought this sense of comfortability with it, and even though Miles isn't opening up to me, I'm beginning to gather that out of everyone in my life right now, I feel the most content opening myself up to him. If he won't answer any questions about himself, maybe he'll answer one that's more about me.

"Do you think if you stopped doing something you used to love, that you can ever get it back?"

There's a beat of silence as I wait for him to respond.

"I don't know. I stopped doing things I loved a long time ago," he whispers.

"Me too. But I don't think I can live like that anymore."

He just nods like he knows what I mean. He looks like he feels just as uncomfortable as I do talking about this.

"What's something you used to love to do?" I ask him.

He doesn't miss a beat.

"I loved to fish."

That makes sense. His dad does own a fly shop in town.

I nod. "Reminds me of your dad. Is there anything that man can't do?"

Even in the dark I can make out the grin that tugs at his lips and creeps across his face.

"Nope."

"I didn't think so."

He blows out a breath from his nose that resembles the start of a chuckle, but then he grows quiet again. So quiet it's painful. I wish I knew what he was thinking. I wonder how much I've forgotten about him.

He isn't going to be like Reed. He doesn't plan to spend time with me for me to find out.

"Teddy?"

I swivel my head at the sound of my name uttered from the cabin doorway. My dad's standing with an uncomfortable look in his eye I can't ignore. There isn't anything more to say or ask of Miles anyway. I'm better off not exploring what this gravitational pull is that I feel every time I'm around him.

"Well, good night, Miles," I say. And I walk away before he has the chance to say anything back. Even if he wasn't going to.

"Dad, what are you doing still up?"

He waits for me in the doorway in his plaid pajama pants and fuzzy loafers, his reading glasses still on the bridge of his nose. My mom's asleep on the couch behind him, her feet hanging off the end of one of the recliners. Her own pair of readers are tucked in her hair at the crown of her head and a book is draped open on her abdomen.

I fall into step behind him toward the kitchen.

"Just catching up on a little work." He hikes his open laptop to the edge of the counter and my eyes flash to the black screen —the one that should have his AutoCAD software open on it had he been telling the truth.

"You too?"

He shrugs his shoulders. "Fathers worry. It's in our DNA. Especially where boys are concerned."

"I promise you have nothing to worry about."

"Even though you're keeping things from us?" His gaze flits to the front window.

"Reed took me out on his family boat." I leave out the part about us skinny dipping. I don't think he'd appreciate hearing that.

"And Miles?" he pries.

I motion toward the dock. "You had a front-row seat to that conversation. It lasted all of ten minutes, and it was one-sided. I'll let you guess who did the talking."

He sort of chuckles then yawns. "All right, well, we should get some sleep."

I make my way toward the stairs and stop.

"Dad, why do you and Mom hate him so much? Did he do something to you?"

"He needs to tell you himself, Teddy," he says.

Figures.

"You know, it's funny... a week ago, everyone sure seemed to have all the answers about my life."

Like Margene, my dietician, with her advice to "increase omega-3 fatty acid consumption for brain cell repair." I hate salmon. And Lucas, my occupational therapist, with his "image-matching memory games for honing attention to details." The only details I notice now are the ones being hid from me.

"Now, no one wants to own up to anything," I finish.

I don't want to care, but I do. That much is obvious. I care about who Reed and Miles are. As much as I thought I could get away with leaving my past behind, I'm having to face it head-on.

I leave my dad and spend half the night staring at that damn sketch, feeling it transform me into a human mood ring. It's Reed who turns me yellow. Nervous, the color of a bright sunny day and the sweet and sour flavor of lemonade. Miles turns me green. Mixed emotions, envy, the color and uncertainty of a watermelon. You never know what you're going to get.

Observing them doesn't grow tiring, but replaying everything they've said to me since we've crossed paths does. I guess I keep thinking something they said will be the key that fixes me. The thing that unlocks this side of myself I know nothing about.

The harder I squint, the more I try to imagine them. I spend over three hours ruminating on a sketch I don't remember drawing and on memories that disappeared a long time ago until the madness gets so overwhelming, I slip into a sleep-induced oblivion where I don't have to think or remember anything at all.

At five in the morning, I creep out the front door without disturbing my parents. They relocated to their bedroom sometime after I went upstairs. Pulling the door ajar, something smooth and rectangular falls on the tops of my feet. It's too dark in the entryway to decipher the object, so I carry it tucked under the crook of my arm out the front door into the moonlight.

The chalky haze makes the gold-leaf pages of the book in my hands glisten. It's the size of a notebook with the softest leather cover. My heart begins to pick up momentum when I flip it open to a blank page and another and another until it thunders in my chest at the realization that it's a sketchbook.

The most beautiful blank canvas that feels both captivating and terrifying to hold in the palms of my hands.

I scan the front yard as if I'll spot the person who left it for me. Which is ridiculous. No one is up at this time of day but me.

The crisp air bites at my skin, and I tuck the book up underneath my shirt to keep it dry from the moisture in the air. The lake shimmers with an inch of fog along the surface. Even my bare feet blanket with dew as I make my way toward the dock.

In a soundless tiptoe, I cross the wood planks, still double-checking to see if anyone is watching. A part of me wanted to slip back inside after finding the sketchbook, use it as my excuse not to do this, but I'm here and I can't let this flicker of a flame that's been ignited inside of me die.

I grip the hem of my cotton pajama bottoms and in one tug, they drop from my waist. My tank top with my new gift tucked inside finds a home within the same heap. I cross my arms over my bare chest as my nipples pebble. I start to feel that giddy sensation I felt on Reed's boat last night and I let it wash over me. Then I shimmy my panties down my legs. Cupping my arms over my head, I dive into the water.

When I come up for air, I sweep my hair back out of my face, and I catch the backside of a familiar shirtless figure as he climbs the gravel driveway in a jog. Seconds later, he disappears behind the trees that shade the main road leading to Bloomington Lake.

I crank back the string for the eighteenth time.

Silence.

Short strands fall from my tiny ponytail with each pull, and a bead of sweat runs from the base of my hairline down the back of my T-shirt.

"What are you doing?"

I glare over my shoulder at Miles, who stands there with his hands balanced on his hips. The same guy who hasn't bothered to interact with me in over a week now, but cares about my lawn mowing struggles?

"What does it look like I'm doing?" I snap.

"It looks like you're about to throw out your back."

"Why do you care," I growl, brushing away the fresh beads of sweat that have gathered along my forehead.

I'm not mad at Miles, but he's the person interrupting me during the one time I'm trying to do something nice yet unpredictable for my parents.

"Teddy, let me see that." He sighs and grabs the rope start, brushing his fingers against the back of my hand in the process. They send a waterfall sensation straight to my stomach.

In one swift pull the motor hums to life.

"Figures. And don't you dare comment on how small I am," I lecture, pointing an accusatory finger in his face.

He holds both arms in a goal post. "Wasn't going to. But I do want to ask where your parents are. I don't want to be sexist, but your dad's typically the one out here mowing."

"They're in town getting some groceries. We haven't been getting along lately, and I just wanted to do something nice for them."

His eyes drill right through me. "You just wanted to do something they wouldn't let you do if they were here," he argues over the sound of the idle mower.

I swing my hands out wide. "Fine. Sue me. I hate being cooped up in that cabin all the time. It's either the restaurant or here, and here isn't really my favorite place to be." I give the mower a swift kick for good measure.

Miles reaches over and cuts the engine.

"If it's not here, then where is your favorite place to be?"

For someone who has done a damn good job of keeping me at arm's length, his attempt at connection just jolted my heart in my chest like the end of a four-foot-drawn tape measure.

"I think you know the answer to that." The crystal-clear water of Bloomington Lake paints across my mind.

"So, go," he pushes.

I shake my head. "Have you seen it in the middle of the day? Not like that. It will be swarming with people right now."

"Okay, well, there must be something else that you enjoy doing... you go do that, I'll finish this for you. You can have all the credit."

Why, suddenly, is he taking an interest in something I'm doing? I narrow my eyes at him. This is a new side of Miles. Helpful Miles. Not *ignoring me* Miles, or *can't stand to be in my presence* Miles.

I survey the lawn, which stands taller than I've ever seen it. I despise mowing. If I could do anything I wanted to in this moment, it would *not* be mowing. *What would it be?* As I ask myself the question a vision materializes in my mind like it's always been there, waiting for me to open myself up to it.

"Okay," I agree. "I'll take you up on it. Thank you."

He nods toward my house, and I take off in a few steps before spinning back around.

"Hey, Miles?"

He lifts his eyes to mine.

"If no one has ever told you before... you're a lot like your dad."

The corner of his mouth lifts before he refocuses on his task. Something about him inspires a creative part of me I never thought I'd feel again. I race inside to do the one thing I think I might have been missing.

CHAPTER SIXTEEN

SUMMER, FOUR YEARS AGO

I n all the times I've ever visited the fly shop, I've never seen Miles or his dad in anything other than fishing waders. I don't own a pair, so I second-guessed every decision I made when getting dressed this morning. I have a heap of clothes on my bedroom floor to show for it.

I tuck my zipper-pouched lunchbox between my knees, wiping the perspiration that formed on the palms of my hands against the front pockets of my jean shorts, and pull back my hair into a high ponytail. With it slicked away from my face, it highlights the smattering of freckles that have pigmented my cheeks with the summer sun.

Here goes nothing, I think to myself as the little bell rattles above the door in a similar fashion to my pulse. Loud and erratic.

It's just Miles today. I spot him right away, straightening a set of poles that have tipped in a tangled cluster. He pauses his pursuit long enough to glance at the door and does very little to hide his surprise when he jumps to a standing position. All the poles he worked so hard to unwind tumble to the ground again.

Maybe I should have told him I was coming.

I grit my teeth. "Sorry, I didn't mean to startle you."

His shoulders slacken and he grips the back of his neck, looking down at the mess at his feet. "Oh, that? Yeah, I meant to do that."

"Here, let me help you," I say, moving toward him.

He swipes his arm through the air like it will hide the mess under an imaginary bed. "Oh, I'll get it later."

"Or I can help you right now? Since that's why I'm here."

"You came all the way over here to help straighten a bunch of fishing poles you didn't know fell over?"

"No, not exactly that."

This isn't going like I expected.

"Your dad gave me a job, and today is my first day."

His hazel eyes widen beneath the shop's bright bulbs. "A *job?* He didn't tell me he was hiring."

I thought I could get away with not telling Miles the real reason I'm here, but I can't lie to him.

"Okay, he wasn't hiring. If you must know, I *asked* for the job."

"You *want* to work here? On your summer break?"

He sounds flabbergasted when he says it, and it's making me kind of mad.

"Is it so hard to believe that I might want to work here? It's boring without you and Reed around. I just thought this way you and I can hang out. And I do recall throwing it out into the universe that first summer." *And I can help lighten your family's burden,* I want to add, but don't.

He brightens, changing his narrative. "Thank goodness you're here then, because this a real mess."

"I can see that." I move to pick up the first pole, giggling. With it comes a web of four others, and I realize it would be better to untangle them sitting down. The wood floor of the shop has scuff marks patterning the aisles. I make a mental note to help mop it when we finish our little untangling project. "How did this happen, anyway?"

Miles grunts. "A couple of teenage guys came in here yesterday right before close and knocked them down. My dad said it was an *accident*, but the level of tangle seems too much to be labeled as one."

"We've got all day," I remind him, and I know I made the right decision in taking this job when he smiles at the comment.

I learn, from Miles this time, that he and Shepard close the shop at the end of every summer to move back to Montpelier where the roads are more plowed. Miles tells me all about the single road—Main Street—with its old western-looking stores and the high school he'll be graduating from with the tiny class size.

In return, I open up about the big city of Boise. Its capital building is in the heart of downtown. The rolling foothills we like to hike reach a plateau called Table Rock with a giant cross at the top.

We swap freshman-year stories where I tell him all about the unfortunate antics Cozy and I were at the mercy of, and he reminds me of how much of a living hell the start of high school can be for anyone in the youngest class, even him—in a class with a few dozen students.

We take a couple of breaks to help customers here and there, but the shop remains quiet until lunch time. After we straighten the poles and put them back in the rack where they belong, we eat our sack lunches behind the counter like a standing picnic. I giggle when Miles spills mustard down the front of his waders.

The afternoon brings a steady stream of customers, leaving very little time for us to talk like we did in the morning. When the day draws to a close, Miles asks if I want to stay a little later while he locks up so we can walk home together. I mop the floor with warm soapy water, making it shine, as he locks the front door and cash register. With my empty lunch pail in hand, I follow him out the back door and down the gravel side of the road back to the cabin.

The walkway between the edge of the road and the brush narrows enough that our empty hands swing inches apart. If I were to extend my pinky, it would brush against his, and it's taking every bit of restraint not to try.

"It was fun working with you today," Miles says.

"You'd still be working on those poles right now had I not stepped in."

He chuckles, looking down at his shoes. "You're probably right."

We meander like we have no place better to be than right here. It's quieter still when we reach a stop sign, and when I feel the sweep of his fingers, I hold my breath. I have no idea if he did it on purpose or by accident, but I glance over just as a car circles the bend, going well over the speed limit. Miles grabs for my hand and jerks me close. The car charges past the stop sign whipping our hair up in a vortex. An alarm goes off in my brain, and I lift my free hand to shelter my face like that would save me in the event I'm in the car's path.

"Teddy, are you okay?" he asks, looking shaken up.

I regain my footing and try to even my breathing, but when I notice Miles still has a hold of my hand, my response to his question comes out in a stutter. "Yyyeah."

"Good," he breathes.

It's the first intentional time I've held a boy's hand. *This must be what it feels like to freefall while skydiving.*

At first, he was squeezing it tight like he thought that could save me. But now, the muscles have relaxed, and he's added a stroking thumb that works a path from the crook of my thumb all the way down my pointer finger. It's a steady, hypnotizing rhythm that makes me forget where I am.

Falling, falling, falling.

When I work up the nerve to look at him, I can tell he's feeling it too in the way he holds my stare.

"Teddy..."

I swallow. "Yeah?"

"Have you ever kissed someone?"

The butterflies move from my stomach to my head.

"No. Have you?" I ask, hoping he has the same response as me. I don't know if I could bear the thought of him kissing some other girl.

He shakes his head too at the same time his eyes drop to my lips. They part, and he swallows.

I've thought about my first kiss a thousand times, wondering what it would feel like, who it would be with, if it would change me. In every single one of those times, I've wanted it to be with the boy who's standing right in front of me, looking at me the way he is right now.

The gap narrows between our bodies. His free hand lifts to my hair, sweeping it back behind my neck, and he kisses me. His full bottom lip brushes against mine, and I shudder at the soft warmth of his mouth, the gentle touch of his fingers pulling me closer to him. My heart expands in my chest, and I feel his kiss changing me. I can't believe it's taken so long for us to do this and now that we've started, I never want to stop.

But it happens in a matter of seconds, time suspending just enough for me to taste the spearmint on his breath, and then it's over even faster when someone hollers from across the street.

"There you two are!"

It's been three weeks since our kiss that Reed interrupted. Three weeks since Miles and I were alone together. All our shifts at the shop have included Shepard and all our days at the lake have been with Reed. Three weeks have passed, and we've never talked about it. If it weren't for the occasional glance Miles steals my way when neither one of them are looking, I'd have thought it never even happened at all. Worse yet, it's the last day of the summer. We leave tomorrow.

"Well, you two. What should we do on our final day in paradise?" Reed asks, standing between us with his arms slung over our shoulders. He has a pair of aviator sunglasses pushed on top of his hair and looks like he does every day: tanned and in board shorts, ready to swim.

Miles and I steal a glance at each other. The kind of weighted glance that says *We have a lot to talk about and no time to do it.*

"You and I don't leave tomorrow," Miles reminds Reed. "I think we should let Teddy decide."

What I want is a day alone with Miles. I want to feel his hand tunnel in my hair again, taste the spearmint on his lips, and feel his fingers threaded through mine. I want to tell him all the reasons why this summer has been my favorite one yet. But that would be living in a fantasy land. One where Reed Morgan wasn't our best friend.

Instead, I tell them something I don't want at all.

"I kind of want a day to just lay out in the sun. Maybe sketch. Just soak it all in."

I feel a stinging in my eyes as I say it. The truth is, I'm never ready to leave this place. No matter what I do today, it won't feel like enough time. All I can do now is try my best to bring a piece of it with me.

"We can do that," Miles agrees at the same time Reed whines, "That's what you want to do on your last day here?"

Miles glares at Reed.

"I just feel like if we go boating and fish and climb the oak tree and get raspberry shakes at LaBeau's and do all the things we've loved to do together this summer, the day will be gone. Maybe if we take it slow, it will last longer," I explain.

I want it to last forever.

Reed nods and I think even if he doesn't agree, he understands. "Okay, I can do slow. And Miles, you were born to do slow," he jokes, earning himself another glare.

"Oh, come on, I'm kidding," Reed says. "Teddy, you go get that sketchbook of yours. Miles, you bring the towels, and I'll grab the chips." He puts his hand out flat like he's ready to start a team cheer, but neither Miles nor I are feeling very cheery today.

Reed exhales. "New plan. By the time we all make it out to the dock, we're happy, okay? I can handle spending the day slow, but I can't handle mopey. Mopey is not the lasting memory you want."

Miles and I both nod, then we toss our hands on top of his.

"One, two, three, break!" We lift our arms in a collective circle in the air.

Reed jogs toward the staircase leading to the upper deck of his cabin as I turn for my room, but Miles grabs my arm first.

"Teddy, wait." He pulls me back to face him, his dark brows zipped together, and something about the way his voice lowers and his eyes scan my face makes me pause. "Can we talk about the kiss?"

Now? He wants to talk about the kiss that we should have talked about three weeks ago? It's the moment I've been waiting for, so I can hardly believe it when I shake my own head.

"I can't," I say.

An unbearable pain squeezes my throat shut.

Miles looks stunned. Then hurt.

"You can't, or you don't want to?" he presses.

"Both," I say.

"Oh."

He says it like I slapped him and drops my arm. There's so much hurt in his eyes, and I want to explain why. I *need* to explain why, but before I can, Reed's jogging back to us, his arms bursting with junk food. Even though Miles is hurt, he can't look away from me, and I'm afraid Reed will read right through us if I hold his stare any longer.

"Wow, I see we're clinging to that lack of urgency today," he says, scoping out our empty hands.

"Going," Miles grunts first. I watch as his jaw tightens, and the second stage of grief replaces the hurt.

He's angry, and that was our last chance at being alone.

I got my wish. The day is slow and quiet aside from a constant monologue from Reed. I pretend to sunbathe or draw while stealing glimpses of Miles, who swims or lies in the sun as far away from me as possible without appearing obvious. When the car is packed and my parents exchange their goodbyes with the Morgans and Shepard, Reed is the first one to pull me in for a hug.

"Have a great sophomore year, Teddy. Don't go breaking any hearts with that gorgeous smile of yours."

"Considering you and Miles are the only two guys I've ever been able to talk to, I think everyone is safe from me," I snort.

He winks at me, gripping me with both arms around my waist. "Glad we were your first."

In any normal circumstance, a comment like that from Reed

would have me ten shades of red, but Miles is waiting behind him, shifting from foot to foot, his gaze boring into mine.

"You too," I say, but I'm looking at Miles when I say it. I'm trying to convey with that one single look all that my heart longs to say about how much our kiss meant to me.

All I want to do is touch him one last time. But instead, I'm watching him walk away from me. He's already turned for his trailer without saying goodbye, taking my heart along with him. A prick of emotion stings just beneath my lash line. Reed notices and looks behind him.

"He's never been good at goodbyes," he justifies.

I want to shout *"You don't think I know that?"* as if I am right back in that place, convincing myself that the friendship I shared with Miles when we were kids was more than anyone else's. Even Reed's. I want to tell him *"I was the one who watched Miles run and hide the day his mom left him,"* and it's taking all that I have not to run to him now. But I can't do that. I'm leaving. Again. For a year. Just like last time, I can't make any promises I can't keep.

I rip my eyes from his quiet trailer and reach for Reed's hand to squeeze one final time. "Bye, Reed."

CHAPTER SEVENTEEN

NOW

A fierce cramping seizes my right hand, and I drop the piece of charcoal onto my vanity before I register just how much time has slipped by.

Hours.

Hours I've spent brushing and shading and blending and losing myself to a piece of art that bloomed straight from me. This intense need took over, and I couldn't stop until it was done.

Now, as I stare at the page, the soft lines of sloping fingers lie in the center. Long lifelines stroke across an open palm. I'm not sure whose hand it is or what it means, but this immense longing drove the idea from my mind and floated it across the page.

Had it not felt so all-consuming, I think my fear would have stopped me from finishing it. It's the first thing from my past that I haven't run from. Instead, I'm finding myself falling into it like the coziest down comforter. I'm afraid if I analyze it with a magnifying glass or dwell on how it defines who I am, that I'll do what I've been doing with everything else about my past. I'll push it away.

When a soft drum rattles my door, I panic. I don't even have time to close the cover before I'm ditching my new drawing in the drawer and launching myself onto my bed.

"Teddy, it's me. Can I come in?"

My mom peeks her head in the room, scanning her surroundings like she might find a boy stashed in the corner.

"I'm not disturbing you, am I?"

"No, just resting," I lie. I'm the opposite of that. After drawing for the last three hours, I feel keyed up.

She pushes herself the rest of the way into the room. "I just... feel like you've been avoiding me, and I wanted to say I'm sorry. I know I've said it a lot lately, so it probably doesn't mean all that much anymore. But I still am sor—" She freezes, her attention on the drawer of my vanity ajar. She takes slow, calculated steps toward it. My insides churn. It feels like an invasion of privacy, but it's too late to hide the drawing now that her fingers have closed around the edges and she's pulled the whole thing out. Her big round eyes dance.

"You're drawing again," she gusts out.

"It's nothing," I say, reaching for the notebook and slipping it from her grasp.

"It's not *nothing*, Teddy, it's incredible. The way you captured the feeling of touch," she says, all breathy. "Does this mean—"

I cut her off. "It doesn't mean anything."

It doesn't. It doesn't mean I'm remembering some part of myself or resurrecting an old talent. It means I'm acting on instinct. Figuring out what makes me happy again. Doing something fun.

"Not everything I do needs to mean something," I say, my hackles starting to raise.

"No, I know," she says, shaking herself from the fog of her

daydream but leaving the wispiness to her voice. "But how did it *feel*?"

I've *felt* my mom paint. The way it takes over her every emotion. Now I know what that feels like.

"Alive," I whisper, and her mouth swoops into the biggest smile.

"Teddy, someone's here to see you," my dad calls from downstairs.

Feeling thankful for the interruption, I dive off the bed and race down the hall to hang my head over the stairwell. When I peer over the edge, my dad has his hand clasped on Reed's shoulder, cracking a joke with him in the entryway. The banister creaks and Reed looks up.

"Hi," he says, tipping his chin back to show off his megawatt dimple.

My stomach swoops at the sight of him. He's wearing his work uniform, and his curls are still damp from the shower.

"I hope you don't mind, but I checked the schedule and we both don't work until four today. Want to get some lunch?"

My eyes flit to my dad first and then at my mom, who steps beside me. In a turn of events, they're both smiling at Reed.

"You should go," my dad encourages.

I'm a little floored. I'm not sure where their change of heart came from. Other than the knowledge that, if Reed was my boyfriend before, they must have had a relationship with him. I just can't figure out why they weren't okay with us spending time together until now.

"Yeah, you should," my mom agrees, and then whispers, "It looks like he's good for you."

It's hard not to read into all my parents' actions these days. To not believe that *he's good for you* has everything to do with that drawing she just found in my room. But ultimately I'm just thankful he saved me from having to discuss that topic any further, so he doesn't have to ask me twice.

"Okay." I jog down the stairs, grip his hand, and yank him out the front door.

"Wow, someone's in a hurry." He chuckles as I drag him along, but when I come to a complete stop in front of him, he crashes into my back and almost knocks me over.

"Shit, Teddy, I'm sorry!" He stumbles to catch me.

"I'm fine," I say. "But before we do this, I need you to promise me something."

"There she is. Overthinking Teddy."

"I'm being serious, Reed."

"Me too. You were on edge in there with them. Less thinking, more doing."

I ignore his playful banter, knowing that's just Reed.

"If we keep hanging out together, I need you to promise me you won't get your hopes up. We can just have fun."

He doesn't ask for me to elaborate. He doesn't even take the time to think about it. He just blurts, "I promise."

I don't want to think about it anymore either.

"Good, let's go then."

A quiet picnic table behind LaBeau's, with two raspberry milkshakes in hand and a cup of pickles, is where he takes me. I've got to admit, it feels a lot like a date just being alone with him, but it's less intimidating than skinny dipping, so I don't worry about it.

I take an enormous swig through the straw, letting the fruity flavor melt on my tongue. "This really is the best milkshake in the world."

Reed chuckles. "You sort of sound like your dad."

I cringe.

"Right. Forget that," he says, shaking his head and swiping

the air into a clean slate. He uses a fork to stab a pickle, dips it in his shake, then jams the end into his mouth.

When I give him a weird look, he holds one out to me.

"It's the best combination of sweet and sour. Just trust me."

It doesn't sound appetizing, but I'm having fun. Being spontaneous. I take it from him and dip it in my milkshake. Reed analyzes my expression as I bring it to my tongue and feel it explode with a salty, bitter tang.

"It's not bad," I admit.

"Ah yes, pickles and raspberry milkshakes. The perfect combination on a hot summer's day." He says it like he's quoting Cheryl from Rhode Island in *Miss Congeniality*, and I almost spray the next sip of milkshake all over the front of his shirt before choking it down.

"Make her laugh, check."

I bob my straw up and down, staring at my cup. "You still haven't told me what else is on this checklist of yours?"

He bats his eyelashes at me. "You'll have to stick around long enough to find out," he says.

I swallow. That's just it, I won't be sticking around. Therein lies the hang-up with this little thing we have going. Reed Morgan has one more month of showing me a good time, and then I'll be gone, and I've yet to tell him.

⁓⁓

I find myself avoiding Reed during our shift the same way I'm avoiding the end-of-summer conversation I need to have with my parents. I'm not sure he'd understand any more than they would. I think the only person in the whole world who might understand me right now is Miles. Which is confusing as hell. He's avoiding me. When I opened up to him the other night, I could tell he related to my feeling lost. Maybe that's the gravitational pull that keeps drawing us back together.

As if the universe conjured him up in the exact moment I needed him, I find him shirtless and fishing off the end of the dock after my shift. My spirit feels more grounded the closer I get to him. Then I smile so wide my cheeks split in two when I see the tip of a hunter-green pole dipping at the end.

"You're fishing!"

As his pole straightens, he reels in the empty line, a half-eaten worm dangling from the end. "*Was* fishing."

I grit my teeth. "Oops, sorry. I scared it away, didn't I?"

"It'll come back." He chuckles. "I guess you could say I was feeling inspired."

By me?

"Want to try?" he offers.

"I thought you'd never ask!" I squeal, and he hands the pole off to me. He reaches for a baby-food jar filled with neon-colored marshmallows and unscrews the lid. He pulls out a fuchsia one, slipping it on the end of the hook next to the mangled worm. A gamey, smokey smell wafts from the jar before he fastens the lid, and it takes me back to... something. It's gone before I can decipher the sensation.

"That smells awful," I choke.

The corner of Miles's mouth twitches. "Fish like it."

"I'm going to need all the help I can get," I warn him, staring at a host of intimidating parts and a spool of fishing line that knots just by me looking at it. Without a word, Miles tucks me in close between his arms, reaching around to grip my left hand on the rod and moving my right pointer finger in an arc, pulling back on a little metal bar. His left bicep wraps around my chest as he extends both our arms over my right shoulder. I forget every single step the moment I make it because I feel his hands everywhere.

"When I say let go, release your finger from the bail, okay?" he breathes into my hair.

A strangled "Mm-hmm" slips out as I try to focus on his instructions. *Wait, what's a bail?*

It all happens in three seconds. On one, he's flinging our arms forward in a tangled heap. Two, he's telling me to let go. On three, I do, and my heart leaps out of my chest with the hook that falls into the water, leaving a ripple effect I feel clear to my toes.

Miles's arms are tethered around me, and I stand there feeling the rise and fall of our synchronized breaths. It takes everything I have to step away from the warmth of his arms, but I do. I want to spend more time with him.

I blink up at him. "I was wondering if you would meet me at Bloomington Lake tomorrow morning. I can't promise I won't make you jump in, but I'll go for a run with you, sit on the shore in silence, whatever it is you like to do there."

Miles clears his throat. "I have to work tomorrow."

"At five a.m.?" I scoff. "Miles, I'm not sure there's a single store in the entire city of Boise—which, according to my dad, has like half a million people in it—that would open that early, let alone a sleepy little lake town. Come on, just one hour. I won't make you rope swing."

I realize how desperate I sound, but I don't know how else to penetrate this iron-clad wall he has up but to screw my own pride.

"Okay," he agrees, and it catches me off guard. He casts his line back in the water.

"Okay?" I ask again, just to be sure.

"Okay." He keeps a tight wrap on his emotions per usual.

I, on the other hand, must stand, taking rapid steps away from him before he can change his mind.

"Oh, and Miles... bring a towel, or you can bet you'll be using one with Taylor Swift's face on it."

A rumbling sound drifts from his throat again. He rests his fishing pole beside him and eases back on the palms of his hands.

"Noted."

CHAPTER EIGHTEEN

SUMMER, THREE YEARS AGO

I couldn't keep a tally of how many days I spent away from Bear Lake this time. It hurt too much. I missed Miles, and each mark was a reminder of all the things we left unsaid.

Me and my weak heart.

The truth is the moment we pulled away from the cabin I regretted not asking for a way to contact him. I was forced to resume my life in a different world than the one he lived in with me.

Sophomore year was even better than freshman. For one, I could finally talk to guys without sputtering over my words like a drunken sailor. They seemed so much more relatable than intimidating.

It took the entire first semester of writing notes, cataloguing my summer to Cozy like a bunch of diary entries, for her to forgive me. I never did send a single email, but when I got to the part about my first kiss with Miles, she could have cared less about anything else. She ran right up to me after homeroom in a squealing hug. Between that and joining the yearbook committee, the fact that we spent a summer apart no longer mattered to her. Our time together during the school year more than made up for the summer we spent contactless, and it kept me busy in all the ways I needed to be.

Max Edwards asked me to the prom in the spring. He was two grades above me and freaked the crap out of my parents, but he was just a friend. He kissed me good night at the end of the dance and had soft enough lips, but there were no fireworks.

When May came, my parents made good on their promise of gifting me a cellphone. Its capabilities felt archaic compared to the ones my friends used with internet and social media access, but I could contact Cozy this summer, so I wasn't complaining. She was in denial that I was leaving again and put together this whole summer bucket list as a way of begging me to stay.

"Just hear me out, we can spend afternoons by the Boise River where you can sketch. It's not a lake, but it's majestic nonetheless. And we can go bowling at the student union building on the weekends. I know they don't have bowling in that teeny town. Take that, Bear Lake! Oh, and we can rent one of those swan paddle boats! It will feel very lake-esque. I promise."

She may as well have been down on her knees as she proposed it. I went to my mom for advice just like I do with everything else, and she suggested Cozy and I make it a virtual summer bucket list. We could FaceTime and text each other pictures as we each experience summer memories from afar.

"Then the first thing on your list is to set the record straight with Miles. I'm not sending you there to spend all your time with someone who takes you for granted," Cozy challenged.

She seemed pleased when I cringed in fear, but I agreed. I made that mistake once, and I wasn't going to do it again.

"Sunniest... first... June... lake has seen in years," the choppy local radio host cuts through the static as the canyon gives way to Garden Valley. "Let those summer BBQs begin!"

My dad exhales, rolling down all four windows and letting the sun drench our skin. I know it's a Friday at nine, and that the shop doesn't open for another hour, but I still sit up straighter in my seat, my hands on the window ledge as we pull past All Caught Up. It's got a fresh coat of paint with this season's markdowns hand-drawn on the windows.

My mind floods with memories of Miles and me restocking the fishing lures on the middle aisle. When we reached for the same wrung, our fingers brushed together. It also reminds me of the time an ice cream truck delivered us free mint chocolate chip during our lunch break out back. He wiped a drip from the corner of my lips with his thumb and licked it clean. I wanted to be the one to do that.

While navigating memory lane, I miss the spot where we shared our first kiss and look back longingly as my dad steers the car down the driveway. The sweet floral decent of perennial blooms planted against the side of the cabin are the reminder I need that good things do come back.

Shrieking from the Morgan property drowns out the car radio. From where we're parked, I make out two guys chest-deep in the lake, each with a pair of long legs wrapped around their necks. The oak trees block my view, and on instinct, I push my way toward them for a closer look.

"I'm gonna go say hi to Reed," I call over my shoulder.

I can feel my mom's eyes on my back, but I can't even give her the time of day as another screech rings through the air.

"Okay, honey, just..."

Be careful, I know. She uses the same tone I imagine she'd use if she ever had to tell me that someone burned all the pages in my sketchbook and there's nothing left.

Something inside me screams that I should turn back. I can feel it now, but I'm a few feet closer, and can I make out Miles's dark eyes and crooked smile. I almost trip over that same damn tree root I do every year at the sight of it. The commotion of my almost-fall catches his attention, but I dodge to the left knowing from where he's standing, he won't see me behind the over-grown trunk. I don't know why I hide, but I'm glad I do.

As I squat down, I watch a beautiful brunette girl with hair halfway down her back in a pink bikini topple from Miles's shoulders into the water. It feels like time grinds to a halt as his smile doubles. When the pucker of her pouty berry-colored lips crests the water, he leans down and kisses her square on the mouth.

I don't stay for the rest.

I turn and run.

I don't care who that girl was. I don't care how long he's known her. I don't even care if they see me at this point.

I shouldn't have come back to Bear Lake.

"Teddy?" my mom says from the other side of my closed bedroom door where I've been hermitting for the past three hours.

"Yeah," I reply, wishing the whimper of my voice wasn't such a dead giveaway at the state of my mental health.

My mom pushes through the opening in her splotchy apron that protects her cut-off Levi's and tie dye tank top. Her hair is

covered with a matching bandana tied at the nape of her neck.
"I brought ice cream."

She holds a ceramic bowl out, and I straighten from my
slumped position. I take it from her outstretched hands and
notice the grandpa spoon dipped in the center. It's what we call
the largest metal serving spoon we own, and it's always been my
favorite for eating dessert.

"Thanks."

"I brought one for me too." She reveals a second bowl from
behind her back. I smile at how sweet the gesture is before cram-
ming a humungous bite of the chocolate chip cookie dough ice
cream in my mouth.

"You didn't have to do this," I say to her.

"Yeah, well, you're the Rory to my Lorelei. You want to talk
about it?"

I don't want to, but I know my mom will worry if I keep it to
myself. I stir the melting ice cream in a circle, creating the
perfect swirl shape with the tip of my spoon.

"Every year he's moved on without me. The last two were
with Reed and this year..." My voice cracks on the last word,
and even though I've already shed enough tears to overflow this
ceramic bowl, I can't stop them from coming again.

My mom sets her ice cream on the edge of my desk and
scoots next to me in bed, wrapping her arm around my
shoulders.

"Did I ever tell you about Danny Deveraux?"

I shake my head, swiping the tears with my hand as my
mom gathers my long hair into a ponytail. I scoop another bite of
ice cream to give my lips something to do other than blubber.

"Well, he was a real looker," she says, and I choke on the
bite I meant to swallow.

"What? Do people not say *looker* anymore?"

"Just say he was hot, Mom."

She nestles back in her spot with her arm around me. "Okay, fine. Danny was the hottest hotty of all the hot boys at my school."

I smirk.

"And why he liked me, the nerdy girl with paint-covered clothes, I'll never know... but he did."

"Please, Mom. You're beautiful," I say, tipping my head on her shoulder.

"Thank you, but I certainly didn't have these long strawberry blonde locks and blanket of freckles on my side." She fans her fingers over my face and brushes away my tears at the same time. "We went out for two years. He was my first kiss, my first boyfriend, my first love, really, and I thought we would end up together. I didn't see a future without him in it."

I pivot out of her arms so I can face her. "So, what happened?"

I invest myself in her story as if she's describing Miles and me. I need to know how it ends.

"We broke up, and I fell in love with someone else. Not right away, of course, but with time. You see, the heart is like a locket. There's room enough in it for more than one person in your lifetime. If you're lucky enough, they'll each teach you something that changes you. Brings you closer to the person you want to be."

"So, this is about me?" I ask, confused. "I thought we were talking about Miles?"

"Falling in love is always about you," she says. "It's about you prioritizing your happiness first."

"But he was the one who made me feel happy. What if the thought of moving on with my life doesn't make me happy at all? I'm just supposed to wait for the right person to come along and make me forget all about him?"

She shakes her head. "No, you won't ever forget. Miles

will always be a part of you. He brought you closer to who you're meant to be all on your own. Your heart still has room, and one day, when you least expect it, you'll find someone else who changes you again. In the meantime, you live. We have three months in Bear Lake, my love. Swim! Sketch! See the sunset a day or two! Staying in this room will keep you from discovering the things *you* love, and you deserve to be happy too."

What if I can't be happy without him? What if I never stop wanting what we had and wondering whether we could have had it if it weren't for someone else? There's always someone else.

"You're a wildflower in a field of daisies, Teddy Fletcher. You stand out all on your own. Go out there and let everyone see that girl!" she exclaims in an artsy rendition of what I think is trying her best to show her support. She spreads her arms out wide and then wraps them back around me. To be frank, she lost me at wildflower, but I let her press her head on my shoulder and don't tell her that.

"But if you need to wallow a little while longer, then we'll do it together. Heaven knows I have some grievances with your father. We can swap stories!" She knocks her shoulder into mine and taps our ice cream bowls together. I chuckle around another big bite.

My mom holds to her promise, cheering me up with a comical story of the time she found a piece of bacon in the pocket of his cargo shorts while doing laundry. There is something very therapeutic about ice cream and girl time amid heartache, and by the time my bowl is empty, I'm feeling better.

My mom takes the stairs two at a time to answer a knock at the front door.

"Hey, Mrs. Fletcher, is Teddy home?"

I don't have to lean over the railing and see him to know Reed is the one waiting there. I run my fingertips under my eyes in a post-tear mascara check before his face splits in a cheeky grin the second he sees me.

"Teddy Fletcher, you come all this way, and you don't bother to say hello? I'm hurt!" He's resting his forearm against the door frame, his hand over his heart.

It looked like you and Miles were pretty busy to me, I think to myself.

My eyes dart to my mom before I say my white lie out loud. "Just helping unpack."

"A few of us are going out on the boat." He dangles the keys from the tip of his pointer finger. "They're letting me drive it this summer. Isn't that amazing?! Want to come? That is, if it's okay with you, Mrs. Fletcher."

This feels like a twisted game of Would You Rather. Teddy, would you rather go boating with the guy you like and his new girlfriend, who there's a good chance he'll make out with right in front of you, or sit at home and drown in your own tears?

"Um..." I look to my mom who lifts her chin high in the air. It's always been her symbol whenever she wants to convey silent affirmations like *I am brave, I am smart, I can do hard things*.

"Okay," I concede. "I just need to change."

"No problem. We'll wait for you at the dock."

When he rushes back down the lawn and my mom closes the door, I feel another tear slip from the corner of my eye. I'm not sure I want to do any part of this summer.

My mom climbs back up the stairs and takes my hand in hers. "A wildflower among daisies, remember that."

A wildflower who decides to wear the black bikini Cozy convinced me to buy on clearance last fall. I was freaked out by it at the time, just like I'm intimidated at the thought of spending an entire afternoon with the boy I like who likes someone else. It seems fitting. I change into it, along with a new coverup.

Confidence. That's what I'm bringing on this boating trip.

I'm halfway across the lawn when I spot them all waiting for me on Reed's dock. Miles is holding her hand and joking with the group, and that familiar pang in my chest threatens to let loose another dam of waterworks. But I tip my chin a little higher.

I'm a wildflower, I'm a wildflower, I'm a wildflower, I chant as I close the gap.

I try not to look at Miles, and I avoid looking at *her* at all costs. I wade into the water until I'm thigh deep, and Reed notices me first. He reaches for my hand and pulls me onto the dock facing Rex and Ronny. Somehow over the last nine months, Rex has surpassed Reed in height, and he's wearing a pair of thick, black-rimmed glasses. Another guy with tattoos, wider shoulders, and a narrow waist touches his arm. Ronny is still... well, scrawny.

"Hey, guys," I say, forcing a smile.

"Hey! Teddy! This is my boyfriend, Alex," Rex says, tucking his arm around the tattooed lineman.

We exchange a hello.

"And this is Ruby." Reed extends his arm to the blonde girl who was sitting atop his shoulders this morning. Her name matches her red lipstick that frames her smile.

"Hi," I say.

"And, of course, you know Miles."

I finally do what I've been avoiding since the moment I ran back to the cabin this morning... I look at him. My whole nervous system screams at me to hug him, but that would be awkward since his arm is attached to someone else.

"Hi, Miles," I manage without my voice cracking.

A whisper of a side smile ghosts his lips at the sound of his name before he reciprocates a hello. He's quick to look away from me and at the girl clinging to his arm.

Unlike Ruby with a full face of makeup, this girl doesn't even have to try to look pretty. There isn't a single angle to her face that doesn't remind me of a Disney princess—from the way her long brunette hair frames her sloping chin to her mascaraless eyelashes fanning her big round eyes. The swell of her lips looks like she just ate a handful of raspberries, and unlike me who burns just by stepping out of a shadow, every part of her shimmers in bronze. She leaves her right hand laced with Miles's and extends her non-dominant hand to shake mine.

"Hi, I'm Lexi. I'm Miles's girlfriend."

Girlfriend.

Miles has a girlfriend.

A beautiful girlfriend.

I flick my eyes back to Miles, and he's watching me.

WILDFLOWER.

WILDFLOWER.

WILDFLOWER.

I choke on the words as I mutter them over and over, but I clear my throat at the same time to cover the sound.

"It's nice to meet you."

"Now that we've gotten the introductions out of the way," Reed interrupts, "let's do this thing!"

Miles follows Lexi to the front of the boat where they cuddle up on one side, Ruby on the other. Rex and Alex share the captain chair facing Reed. That leaves Ronny and me at the back of the boat... on a bench that screams *We're single.*

Rex unwinds the rope tethering us to the dock while Reed kicks the engine to life. We idle out past a sole red buoy, and all I can stare at is the dock that Miles and I shared getting smaller and smaller in our wake.

Boats and jet skis pack the lake, leaving us to go quite a ways from the cabin to find a spot vacant enough to wakeboard. I volunteer as the flag girl, which seems like a good idea up until the point where Reed suggests Miles wakeboard with Lexi balancing on his shoulders. I have a front row shot that requires me to watch him hold on to her ankles while she giggles and runs her fingers through his hair. When Miles wobbles too far to one side, she tips off his shoulders, and they both sink beneath the water.

Reed circles the boat back to them. Miles is no longer laughing along. He's looking right at me like I have something he needs.

Reed's brothers are horsing around with Ruby at the front of the boat and for a moment, it feels like it's just the two of us. Looking at him I see my best friend—the boy whose every monumental summer intertwines with mine. But it's not true. He has a whole different life here that I know nothing about. At that thought, I can feel my eyes mist over again, and I pinch them together to control it.

"That was awesome!" Reed hollers.

I plant my eyes anywhere other than the place in the water where Lexi circles her legs around Miles's hips. They take turns climbing onto the back of the boat, and Ruby hands them a towel from the bench next to me to dry off with.

"Hey, Miles, you take the boat, I'm going next," Reed says.

"Dude, I should be the one taking the boat," Rex complains.

Reed shakes his head as he clips his lift jacket buckles together. "You won't go fast enough. You can be the flag person." Then he falls like a tree, arms outstretched into the water with the wakeboard.

Rex grumbles, grabbing the flag from my hand and positioning himself on the bench beside us.

"Come on, let's go sit in the front. I want to get to know the girl who broke Miles's heart," Lexi says, grabbing hold of my hand.

I didn't know a person could swallow their own tongue, but

that's what this horrible knot that just asphyxiated my lungs must be. She grabs my hand and clutches the towel around her middle. Miles and I exchange a concerned glance as she yanks me next to her.

"I can't believe you're from Boise! I've always wanted to go there. Tell me everything you love about it."

She knows Miles and I have history and that I'm from Boise... what else does this girl know about me?

"Uh, there's not much to tell," I say in my desperate quest for distraction from this conversation.

She leans closer, resting a hand on my knee. "There's got to be a lot of hot guys at your school, right?"

My eyes flash to Miles, where he's boring a hole in the side of my head waiting for my answer. I swallow once. Blink twice. Then I turn back to Lexi.

"Yeah, you're right. There is." The vindictive side of me hopes my answer travels through the wind that's whipping in his direction.

"I knew it!" she squeals. "Living in such a small town doesn't provide a lot of options in that department. Luckily, the hottest guy in the whole school was single and somehow had an interest in me." She giggles again and looks over at Miles, who stops my heart with the cock of his sideways smile I missed so much. The one he used to reserve for me.

Dammit, Lexi.

The wave of jealousy is enough to make me want to barrel over the side of this boat mid-movement. It might be a gentler death sentence than the one I'm living right now.

"Yeah, you're lucky," I say, not caring if it travels downwind.

I ask a stupid question next; one I don't care to know the answer to. "I take it you go to school with Miles?"

"Yeah, we've lived in the same town for years. My dad's a farmer, and my parents homeschooled my little brother and me so we could help during the on-season. It wasn't until they were successful enough to hire a helping hand that they agreed to let me finish out my high school years at public school. Miles and I had homeroom together. We've lived our whole lives in the same tiny town, and we didn't meet until now. Isn't that crazy?"

"So crazy," I deadpan.

"I come up on the weekends, but my parents agreed to let Ruby and me stay at the Morgans' cabin for boating Tuesday. I'm so jealous you get to spend all summer on the water. It's so beautiful here!" She sweeps her eyes across the skyline in front of us.

Lexi? Jealous of me? I'd trade her spots. That grand city of Boise she was talking about earlier... take me back there. Maybe Cozy and I were meant to do our bucket lists together this summer.

After Reed finishes his turn wakeboarding, his brothers do a round, and I volunteer to hold the flag again. No one ever brings up tubing, which I'm thankful for. I'm better off not having to relive any more of the past when I was the only girl in their lives.

CHAPTER NINETEEN

NOW

I feel like a ship anchor at the bottom of the ocean as my morning alarm sounds from my phone on the bedside table. Insomnia hit again. I dozed off around two a.m., and now the three hours of sleep beat at my temples like a percussion instrument. I need a dose of caffeine in the form of a polar plunge.

I slip off my striped sleep set and replace it with a ribbed one-piece swimsuit, cut-off denim shorts, and running shoes. I reach in my closet and grab the popstar icon–covered beach towel. Then I slide down the banister and slip into the bathroom to brush my teeth.

The engine sputters when I turn the key, and I cringe. My parents' REM cycles must hit dead status around 4:40.

Ten minutes later, I'm pulling into a parking lot after traversing down the dirt road through Bloomington Canyon. An old Ranger pickup with an exaggerated bumper is the lone car there. I pull up next to it, peek out the window, and see Miles leaning against the driver's side door. A pair of swim trunks plaster his legs and a towel drapes between his folded arms. His face splits into a rare grin at the sight of me until I step out of the front seat in my swimsuit and his smile humbles.

"You waited for me."

"I thought we could walk together," he says, pushing off the side of the car.

"We're not running?"

"Not today."

I wave one foot around. "And to think, I wore these beauties for you."

"I mean, if you really want to—"

"Nope! You already agreed we weren't."

We both chuckle.

Where the end of the parking lot and the start of the trailhead converge, there's a large rustic sign that pays homage to the vegetation and wildlife that can be spotted on the trail. It feels like a scavenger hunt when I see a patch of purple wildflowers a few feet ahead depicted on the sign. We climb the initial slope until it tapers off into stretches of rolling land. It's quiet and peaceful, and I'm enjoying just taking it all in.

"I know why I come here, but what brought you to this place the first time you found it?" I ask.

"You first," he says.

As we crest the top of the first hill, I take in the scenic expanse of pond lining one side with wildflowers on the other. The path is wide enough we can walk side by side with room to spare, and even though we're not touching, there is something about the brisk morning air that feels like an electric current keeping our steps in sync.

"I come here to get away," I say.

"Away from?"

"My parents. Bear Lake. The past. All of it."

"And does it help?" he asks.

"Sometimes. Sometimes it's not far enough."

Our steps slow as the questions get deeper. Miles trains his attention on the pond when he asks, "Would you go any farther?"

I nod. "I am. I'm leaving at the end of the summer."

He pins me with a look of surprise. "Oh."

When he doesn't follow it up with another question, I give him an answer anyway.

"It feels like something I need to do."

I can see him chewing on the inside of his cheek like this conversation is making him uncomfortable, so I turn it back to him.

"You go. What brought you to Bloomington Lake?"

I expect him to deflect the personal question, but then he says, "My dad."

"Really?"

I didn't know Shepard ever came up here.

"He has diabetes," Miles says, and peers over at me to gauge my reaction.

I appreciate the gesture. That he doesn't assume I already know when I confirm that I do.

Our steps are slow and methodical, and I try not to look at his face in hopes it gives him space to continue opening up to me.

"He's had it for as long as I can remember, but my mom knew a time when he didn't. The two of them loved to travel together. They grew up in Montpelier and were high school sweethearts. Both were tired of small-town life and dreamed of seeing the whole country, living life on the road."

It's hard to imagine Shep going anywhere farther than a thirty-mile radius. When he's not at the trailer or helping a neighbor, he's working at his shop.

"They used the money they saved from odd jobs during high school," he continues, "and the summer after they graduated, they spent all they had on the trailer. My grandfather owned undeveloped land on Bear Lake. He told them they could park it there for the summer while they worked more odd jobs to save more money. She got a job waitressing at an old pizza place that has since closed, and my dad worked at a little tackle shop that connected to a gas station. That same summer he started showing signs of frequent dehydration. When my mom found him collapsed one morning, they took him to be seen by a physician, and he was diagnosed with type one diabetes. Between insulin and shots, it's an expensive disease. They were living in a small town on borrowed land with nothing but high school diplomas to their names, and they got stuck there."

I fixate on the word *stuck*. In the stubborn yet peaceful way he carries himself, I would have never pictured Shep as stuck anywhere, especially not in Bear Lake. It's the only place I've seen him. When you know someone as one thing, it's hard to picture them any other way. For me, Shep has been a small-town man with a kind heart. In the version of him that I don't know, he could be someone longing for more. He could be someone like me.

"When enough years went by scraping the bottom of the barrel, seeing nothing but this side of the lake, my mom grew tired of the life we lived. She left when I was ten. When I got older I started running to clear my head, and my dad showed me this place. He felt like the trails were safer than the streets in town I resorted to."

My heart sinks for the both of them. "I'm so sorry, Miles."

I expect him to retreat inside himself, but instead his chest puffs up in frustrated gasps.

"You know what the worst part is?" He scuffs the ground with his shoe, sending a puff of dust in the air. "I don't blame her for leaving. It broke my heart, but I get it now, feeling trapped by his diabetes."

Trapped. The next word I fixate on. A word that I've come to know well.

"I was gone for a year, and the second I was able, I came back for him. But in all honesty, I wanted him to be okay enough that I wouldn't have to. I just couldn't do that to him."

He catches my eye, and I want him to know that feeling that way doesn't make him a bad person. He can want to leave and still be noble.

"You're a good son, Miles."

He shakes his head. "I still think about it... leaving this place."

It's obvious Miles is giving so much of himself to his dad. He deserves for someone to do the same for him.

"Why don't you?"

"I can't. I see how frail he's become in the last year. Sometimes he even puts himself at risk with a low insulin supply, just to cut corners. I can't leave him again."

I grip his forearm so he will stop walking and look at me. "Miles, if you ever wanted to leave... here, I mean, I would go with you."

My eyes flare. *Woah, where did that come from? We barely know each other, and I'm inviting him to leave with me?*

His eyes knit together in confusion too. Like he's considering it, even if he thinks he shouldn't. Somehow in the short amount of time we've spent together it's feeling harder to imagine leaving here at the end of the summer.

"I can't," he says.

And a part of me feels saddened by that. *Did I just want this for him, or do I want him to come with me?* I can't want someone from my past to come with me. That goes against the entire purpose of leaving. But Miles doesn't remind me about my past every second. In fact, he doesn't remind me about it at all. I'm not sure I even want to know the Miles I used to know when I'm starting to like present Miles so much.

"Okay, well maybe you don't have to go very far to get that feeling, ya know? What if you could go somewhere new for the day. Somewhere you've never been before," I suggest.

"You speak about it like it's some exotic place. We're in Bear Lake, Idaho. The most exotic thing within twenty miles of here is the new gas station in Paris that has a rainforest-themed bathroom."

I giggle. "That actually sounds awesome. But if I think of such a place..." I start as Miles gestures for me to traverse a log that stretches across a section of the lake leading to the rope swing. It's a wooden tight rope as I plant one foot in front of the other, but the idea of going somewhere new with Miles has me feeling like I could skip across the damn thing. I spin around to face him.

"Would you go with me?"

Miles cocks an eyebrow. "You know, you really should keep your focus forward. One wrong move and you'll be plunging into this thing fully clothed."

"Answer me, and I'll turn around," I taunt, extending my arms wide like a gymnast on a beam.

"I've never have been able to say no to you," he says.

I blanch and almost miss a step, but still I say, ever so quietly, "I'll take that as a yes."

Satisfied, I whirl back around, lose my balance, and plummet with my Taylor Swift towel into Bloomington Lake.

～～

"You're pretty glad you asked me to bring that towel right now, aren't you?"

A smug look paints Miles's face. My own towel lies in a

sopping wet heap in the grass while he pulls his taut around my shoulders.

"Very funny," I stammer. The towel isn't big enough though to get my shivering under control.

His eyes pinch. "Okay, maybe I should have brought a blanket." He analyzes my lips—most certainly blue—and the uncontrollable chatter of my teeth. His arms wrap his shins, hands fidgeting.

"I don't know how to ask this without sounding forward..." he says carefully. "But can I hold you? I don't like seeing you cold."

My skin is a live wire in anticipation. "Okay."

He moves closer to me. I pull a quaking stream of air through my nose to calm my erratic heart. It's an impossible situation with his body pressing against me. He pulls me so close that my legs drape over his lap. His arms stroke up and down my sides. Heat begins to build with the friction between my skin and the towel, the flush rising straight to my cheeks. But it feels so good I don't dare ask him to stop.

I hadn't realized just how much I was trying to keep it together, but I lose all sensibility the moment I nestle into his warmth. A soft moan escapes my lips.

"This feels nice."

I don't have time to get embarrassed. His arms wrap tighter, tucking my head beneath his chin as he groans along with my sound. "Yeah, it does."

Even with the blanket between us, it feels good to be hugged. But Miles isn't just hugging me; he's holding me like I might disappear. We keep finding ourselves in these situations where we want to cling to each other, like there's an invisible magnet drawing us together beyond our control. Not until the quivering in my body subsides does he let go. I feel the loss as his arms fall away from me. I want to hold on to him like *he* might be the one to disappear.

Miles clears his throat and shifts back so there is enough space to look at each other. His irises are a shade darker, and his lips rest in a flat line. I can't live with serious Miles without my blood turning to lava.

"Kiss, marry, kill," I blurt. "Emma Watson, Blake Lively, Emma Stone."

"Huh?" Miles says, and I know I've successfully caught him off guard.

"You know, the game."

"I can't say I've ever played this game, no."

"You choose which person you'd kiss, marry, and kill." I repeat his options.

"Wait, I have to *kill* one of them? What is this game?!"

I roll my eyes. "Come on, you've never played it before?"

"I have not played it before."

"Just answer the question," I say.

"Okay, but I'd like to have it on record that I don't want to do any of those things with any of those women."

"Ugh, it's just a game, Miles. Which person would you rather have one fleeting moment with, spend the rest of your life with, or never have to see again."

"All right," he says, leaning back on his palms in the grass and crossing his feet at the ankles. He looks up at the sky, his face pinching in agony as if the idea of answering this dumb question will determine his own death penalty.

"I guess if I had to pick, I'd kiss Emma Stone, marry Emma Watson, and kill Blake Lively."

I gasp audibly. "You would KILL Blake Lively?!"

"Okay, see, this is why I didn't want to answer, because no, of course I wouldn't KILL Blake Lively. What kind of a criminal do you think I am?"

I burst into a fit of giggles.

"Can I explain myself at least?" he asks.

"Please do," I choke out over my laughter.

His grin falters as he locks eyes with me. "While Emma Stone is beautiful, her red hair is not the one I want to sink my hands into when I'm kissing someone. Emma Watson is talented and smart, but her art form is different than the one that gets me. And like someone else I know, the world could lose Blake Lively, but she'd be remembered long after she's gone."

I swallow as I dissect the way he's looking at me. The way he took something that was meant to be silly and made it hard for me to breathe. He might as well have said, "Kiss Teddy, marry Teddy, kill Teddy."

"Miles..."

There is this burning desire within my chest—like a bird whose wings are trapped behind my ribcage, desperate to break free. It's begging me to ask Miles about his memories. About the past. About... us? But as if he knows what I'm going to say, he sobers and stands, sweeping away the opportunity.

"We should get back. We both have work today," he says, eyeing the ascent of the sun for a moment before turning back to the trail.

"We never did the rope swing," I remind him.

"I think you got cold enough for the both of us," he teases. "Besides, we need a reason to come back tomorrow."

He smiles at me over his shoulder, the one where one corner of his mouth tips up toward his eyes. And I forget all about why I ever cared about the past.

All I really need is the future.

CHAPTER TWENTY

SUMMER, THREE YEARS AGO

W hen I get back to the cabin I have three missed calls, two voicemails, and seven unread text messages, all from Cozy. Ninety-nine percent of them say something to the effect of "Please tell me you're making out with Miles right now!!!"

I flop onto my bed like a starfish and dial her back.

"So? How was it? Did he use tongue?"

"Cozy," I cut in.

"Did he lay you on your back? Straddle your lap? Kiss you senseless?" she continues.

I yell this time. "COZY!"

She silences.

"He has a girlfriend."

I hear her scream on the other end. "WHAT?!"

"Yeah..." I groan, hiding my face under the crook of my arm.

"Do we hate her? Because if you want me to, I'll hate her."

"No, we don't hate her. We *can't* hate her. She's too nice to be hated."

"Damn. I knew this whole bucket list from afar thing was a

bad idea. Call Birdie up there! I need to have a word with her," Cozy demands.

"About that… can we just maybe curb the bucket list concept on my end this summer. I'm not leaving this room ever again," I moan, rolling over on my stomach and suffocating my face into my blanket.

"You got it, babe. Consider it canceled. I just wish I was there to watch *10 Things I Hate About You* and binge ice cream."

I picture a wild mess of curls bouncing to the tempo of her outstretched accusatory finger as Cozy eviscerated her first scumbag of a boyfriend when she'd caught him cheating on her in the back seat of his car. Not a single person who witnessed that moment had any idea what a mess she was later when the heartbreak settled in. For Miles's sake, I'm kind of glad she's not here. Even if what Miles is doing with Lexi is fair, I know Cozy would react the same for me.

"My mom's got you covered on the ice cream part, but let's watch it together on FaceTime tonight, okay? I could use a distraction."

She groans. "I hate to do this to you, but do you remember Tetherball Baker?"

She doesn't pause for me to answer.

"His friend Peter invited me to join them bowling tonight, and it was on the bucket list, so I said yes. You don't hate me, do you?"

I chuckle, and then sigh. "No, I could never hate you. You go and do something fun. One of us should be. Just remember… if there's no picture, it didn't happen!"

"Do you even know your best friend? This *influencer* wouldn't miss the chance to post about it."

I laugh because if I don't, I'll cry, and I don't want her canceling her plans for me. I'm just regretting not staying is all.

"Hang in there," she says.

"I will. And Cozy, for what it's worth... I don't hate Miles either. He deserves to be happy."

"More like he doesn't deserve *you*," she argues. "But there's always Reed!"

I shake my head. "Bye, Cozy."

I watched Julia Stiles poetically confess all the ways she hates Heath Ledger in front of an entire classroom of peers last night and cried myself to sleep.

I hate the way I don't hate you, Miles. Not even a little bit. Not even when you shock me with a girlfriend and rip my heart out. Not even at all.

But a tiny smile graced my lips when my phone chimed me awake with a message from Cozy. It wasn't just the picture she promised but a whole reel slowed down to match the upbeat of "We Will Rock You." Bowling pins tumbled down in front her in a strike as a guy collapsed her knees under the weight of his arms. He hauled her in the air, spinning her in a circle and holding up the number one.

She got *me*—a pathetic, heartbroken girl—to feel lighter. She may have been joking about being an influencer, but I think it's her calling in life. It fueled the courage I needed to do what's next.

With every footstep that leads me closer to the trailer, I plead it won't be Miles who answers my knock. To my pleasant surprise, the door swings open, and it's just who I'm hoping to see.

"Teddy! It's so good to see you." Shep leans in to hug me, swallowing me up in his arms.

"You too."

He keeps a firm grip on my forearms and pulls back to look at me. "You haven't grown an inch."

"That's the thing about middle school puberty... when it's over, it's over." I shrug.

He chuckles, pressing his palms into the door casing. "Are you looking for Miles?"

I shake my head. "You, actually. I was wondering if my summer job is still available? I think I need to keep myself busy."

I know that means I'll have to work with Miles sometimes, which sounds like another form of torture right now, but sitting at home doing nothing sounds worse.

"Of course! I'm about to head there now if you'd like to start today. You can catch a ride with us," he offers.

Us?

A throat clears behind me, and I turn around to find Miles naked from the waist up in a pair of running shorts, sweat dripping down his chest. I swallow. It's not like I haven't seen him like that before, but it throws me off-kilter when there's no warning.

"Teddy, what are you doing here?" It sounds accusatory as he pulls a pair of headphones back to rest on his shoulders.

I can't stop staring at his shirtless torso. "You took up running."

He drops his focus to figure out what I'm looking at, and then makes matters worse by sweeping a hand down the defined planes of his midriff. "Oh... yeah. I decided to run track at school last year."

He bends over at the waist to untie his shoe and slips it off.

You started a lot of new things it would seem, I think to myself.

"Cool."

"What do you say we give Miles five minutes to shower and wait for him in the truck?" Shep asks.

I knew I'd have to face Miles at the shop, but being smashed inside his dad's truck next to him was not what I had in mind.

When my eyes settle on Miles, I regret ever coming over here.

Why did I think working with him all summer would be a good idea?

But now I'm at a crossroads. His dad is waiting for me to answer, and I'm backed into a corner. Literally. On the steps between them. I offer him an out hoping he'll take it.

"Only if it's okay with you."

Miles brushes past me. "By all means."

I deflate.

He didn't take the out.

"Are you *sure* this is okay?" I ask Shep.

"Oh, yeah," he chirps. "The more the merrier."

I can't tell if he's oblivious to that little exchange we just had or if he's egging this on. He reaches for a pair of keys dangling from a hook on the back of the door and holds them out. "Why don't you wait for us in the truck. We'll be right there."

"Sure," I say, grabbing them in the most unsure fashion.

We ride in silence. Miles drives, and I'm pressed in the middle like mayonnaise in a peanut butter and jelly sandwich. We find tasks on opposite sides of the store to keep ourselves busy all day—I eat lunch out back with Shep like Miles and I used to do, while he stays inside and talks on the phone to Lexi.

This becomes my daily routine for the next two months. Eat, sleep, be ignored by Miles, repeat.

It's a joyful summer.

It's Reed's idea to have a bonfire the last night of summer break. With the way my chair is positioned, I snatched a front-row seat to the Miles and Lexi show through the flickering flames of the campfire. *Lucky me.*

Her fingers lace up and down his, and I fight to stare anywhere but their touching hands. She invited her friend Ruby again, who sits between Ronny and Rex in fold-out camp chairs, and I'm in the middle of Alex and Reed.

I scroll my text chain with Cozy, smiling at every bucket list photo she sent this summer: A hike to Table Rock, riding the Bogus Basin coaster, floating the Boise River on a paddle board, and winning a french fry–eating contest at Five Guys with Peter (who became her new boyfriend, by the way).

"We should play spin the bottle," Ronny suggests, pulling me from my phone scroll and wagging his eyebrows up and down in Ruby's direction.

"Yeah, no." She winces like she wouldn't be caught dead sitting next to him on any other occasion than this one.

"Fine. Truth or dare, then," Ronny taunts.

"I'm down," Alex says.

A collective sound of agreement waves through everyone as I groan.

Reed prods my leg with his foot. "You okay?"

"Oh, yeah. I'm good," I lie, peeking over at the happy couple who are giggling about some inside joke no one else gets.

Reed nods at me and lets it go.

"Okay, who wants to start?" Ronny asks. "How about you, Rex."

A grin blooms on Rex's face as he turns from Ronny to Ruby. "Truth or dare."

"What are you smiling about?" Ruby folds her arms over her chest. "Dare."

Rex scans the yard. The edge of the water is nonexistent from where we sit. "I dare you to jump in the lake."

She plants her hands on the cupholders of her chair to stand.

"Naked," Rex adds.

Everyone gasps.

I look over at Ronny, whose eyes look like they're about to explode, and I stifle a giggle. Maybe this game won't be so bad after all. Entertaining at least.

"Fine," she says, pushing out of her camp chair and plunging through the darkness toward the dock. My mouth gapes open right about the time I see her top come off. We lose sight of her the moment she is more than five feet away, but a splash sounds a minute later, and everyone cheers.

I can't believe she just did that, I scream inside my head. Well, come to think of it, it's Ruby. I can. But *I'm* not doing that.

"I'll get her a towel," Ronny says, jumping from the edge of his seat.

"Well, that might be a while," Alex jokes, and I almost laugh along with him until he turns to me. "Your turn. Truth or dare, Teddy?"

I fidget in my seat, wishing he would have chosen anyone else. *I won't be caught dead choosing dare if everyone's idea is to skinny dip in front of these people.*

"Truth."

"How many guys have you kissed?"

I can't answer that in front of everyone! What if they ask *who* I've kissed next? I'm itching to bolt out of my seat, but as I glance around the circle, everyone is grinning at me. Everyone except Miles.

"Well, go on," Alex encourages.

I have no escape. No backup plan. No white lie to get me out of this. I just have the truth. A truth that may or may not hurt someone I don't want to hurt no matter how much he's hurt me.

"Two."

I can't look at Miles. I don't want to know what my answer means to him. Alex nods in appreciation, like he expected my answer to be zero, which irritates the hell out of me, so I fire it back at him. "Truth or dare, *Alex*."

He folds his arms and crosses his ankles. "Truth."

"How many guys have YOU kissed?"

Seems like a good question. An eye for an eye.

"Fifteen." His lips lift in a cocky grin, and he tips his chair back on its back feet.

FIFTEEN? Judging by the calm written on Rex's face, he already knew that.

"Guess I get to go again." Alex's smug eyes sweep the circle as he looks for another puppet to play show and tell with. "Reed. Truth or dare, bro?"

"Dare."

A smirk slithers across Alex's face as he turns back to me. "I dare you to ask Teddy on a date."

My eyes go wide, and then I glare at him. "I leave tomorrow."

"The start of next summer then," he presses.

I've hung out with Alex a few times and thought he was an okay enough guy, but right now, I don't appreciate him. What does he think he's doing? What did I ever do to him? Reed is just my friend. I've already made enough of a mess with Miles, I don't need to play out that same mistake with Reed.

But he reaches for my arm with no hesitation. "Teddy, will you go on a date with me next summer?"

"You can't be serious?" I blurt.

"Who says it has to be serious?"

I don't mean to, but that's when I look over at Miles. To... what? Seek his permission? His approval? I don't owe him anything. But his chair is empty.

Reed pouts his bottom lip.

"Fine," I cave.

"Man, make the guy feel like he's your last choice," Alex comments.

I could punch him in the face right now. He's trying to start something, but I can't even argue with his comment when he's sort of right. It's not that I don't find Reed attractive, I do. I just haven't considered him in that way. I'm the "settle down with one person" type. Reed plays the field with his heavy flirting. We would never work. Not to mention the fact that I'm hung up on his best friend.

I swivel my head around the circle of chairs until I land on his. It's still empty. It *stays* empty.

Another summer where Miles and I don't say goodbye.

CHAPTER TWENTY-ONE

"How are your shifts at the Morgans' restaurant going?" my mom asks as she deposits a pancake with peanut butter in front of me. She's eased back on her kale smoothies and avocado toast, but I can forget about maple syrup. She's not bending to that yet.

"It's great. I like getting to look out at the lake as I work, and the people vacationing are always in a good mood."

"It's Bear Lake. What's not to love," my dad adds.

"Good point," I say, but inside my gut is churning. There's a handful of things I can think of that I don't love about Bear Lake anymore, and while they don't need to hear that, they do need to know I'm leaving. I'm not sure I'll ever be *ready* to break the news to them. It's more of a *now or never* situation, and I guess *now* it is.

"Since we're all here, I wanted to tell you guys something," I say.

My mom pauses mid–pancake scoop, and her attention flits to my dad. They communicate the same questioning glance—*Do you know what she's going to say?*—before trapping me with the same confused stare.

"We're listening," my mom says.

"I'm moving away at the end of the summer," I announce.

The spatula crashes to the wood floor, sending a pancake splatting against a kitchen cupboard.

"What! Where?" my mom gasps.

"Maine," I say, sounding far less confident than I did a month ago when I made this decision. *As far away as possible*, I remember thinking, because it was the furthest thing stateside. But it was a verdict I made before I knew there was more to my life here. Before I met the two people who have me questioning every choice I make.

"Maine?" my mom wheezes, ignoring the pancake batter clumped to her feet. "That's clear across the country! How are you *possibly* going to get there?"

I wring my hands in front of my lap, trying to calm my racing heart.

"I've been saving my wages and tip money from the restaurant to buy something used from an old car lot in Montpelier. I'll need a lift getting to town of course, but then from there—"

"I guess I should have seen this coming," my dad interrupts, scratching his head. He looks sad, but my mom is scowling. I don't know what I expected from them when I knew they weren't going to take this well. Just this once I hoped they would trust me enough to believe I was making the right decision for myself, even if it was one that was hard for them to understand. But a scowl? There's no trust in a scowl.

"What is it?" I push.

Maybe if I know her why, I'll be able to understand *her* perspective.

"It's just... your dad and I always thought you'd put that money toward school... maybe get an art degree..."

"Or, y'know, something in architecture so you could work with your old man," my dad interjects, winking at me.

My mom shoots him a glare. "To become an *artist*. Like you always planned."

Her shoulders square in a fighting stance, and I realize she doesn't care about understanding at all. She's still trying to impose her own dreams on me.

"Why, because you got one?" I hiss.

A look of pain radiates from her eyes.

Increased irritation is a common side effect for someone with my kind of TBI history, but it doesn't make it any less frustrating to experience firsthand. I don't *want* to feel mad at them. How am I supposed to be who I want to be and who they need me to be at the same time?

"No, because you *are* one," she fires back. "That sketch you did the other day... it's still inside of you, and you're wasting your talent if you don't pursue it."

"Just because I have a book of sketches in my room from my childhood and drew ONE new thing does not mean that's what I want to do for the rest of my life!" I holler. "It's not what defines me. I can be whatever I want!"

"You're right, Teddy. You can. You should go off and be that person. You won't see me stopping you." She sighs, and for the first time ever, she leaves the room before me.

"Dad, I'm sorry, I'm just tired of pretending that I'm okay being someone I'm not anymore."

He reaches his palm out as if he planned to clasp my shoulder, maybe give it a squeeze of support, but then drops it back to his side. "It's okay to be someone else, Teddy Bear. But what you're not is someone who hurts your mom like that. I'm saddened to think that you believe you've changed so much that you're willing to be that person now." He pushes away from the counter and trails behind her.

His soft-spoken words sting more than any yell ever could. I *hate* this feeling. I don't want to feel it anymore. My hands shake, tears on the verge of spilling over, as I pull out my phone from my back pocket and send a text to the one person who promised to help me forget.

> TEDDY: Meet me at Maverick's at six. I'll be the one with the microphone.

Outfitted like a '50s western saloon, Maverick's is the sole spot for family-friendly country line dancing and karaoke in Garden City. With half swinging oak doors in every room but the bathrooms, a mechanical bull in the corner, and a disco ball above the stage, it's the type of place you wear a pair of cowboy boots and cue up Nitty Gritty Dirt Band on the jukebox. Which is precisely what I've done while waiting for Reed to arrive. With a microphone in my hand and at least four dozen people in the audience, I take a deep breath.

"Fishin' in the Dark" filters through the speakers, and a terrible static follows it. The nervous shake of my hand rubs the microphone against my pocket, and I jerk it away from my body like it's caught fire. When a handful of people in the audience laugh, I look up to find everyone hunkered over stilted tables on stools, watching my every move. I swallow again as the first verse begins without me, wondering why I thought this was such a good idea. I should have just waited for Reed.

Then someone whoops from the back. Thousands of tiny, brilliant lights bounce off the disco ball and scatter across the room. I try to block the light with my forearm, but I can't see who it is. The cheer sounds again, louder this time, and I giggle.

Stop taking yourself so seriously, Teddy. You came to have fun.

I shake off the jitters, my bob swinging from side to side in front of my face and my hips bouncing to the rhythm of the music. When I feel the energy travel all the way to the toe tap of my suede cowgirl boots, I lift the microphone to my mouth and begin to sing.

My voice shakes at first, but then more and more people join in, singing along and cheering. A grin splits across my face, and it fuels my hips to sway a little more, laugh at myself, have a good time.

My head clears. It feels like I'm floating as I dance down the stage steps, interacting with the audience. *It's working!* I forget all about my conversation with my parents or the fact that I was ever nervous to do this in the first place. But most of all, I forget there was someone encouraging me to sing from the back of the room. Someone no longer disguised by bright lights as I descend the bottom of the stage steps.

Miles pushes his way through the crowd of people until he finds a stool to sit on. His eyes track my hips, and he tilts his head—a subtle nod that bolsters me through every new note I sing. He's glowing as I hit the chorus and I grin, singing right to him.

He looks good. A pair of jeans hug his thighs, and a white T-shirt fits snug against the width of his shoulders. *What is he doing here*, I wonder as he starts mouthing along to the words, and for a moment, the song becomes a duet. Even though the rest of the room can only hear me, the lyrics volley between his lips and mine, and everyone else falls away.

I don't just forget about earlier; I transcend to this space where my soul feels connected to someone else. It feels so good to be seen for *me*. When the song starts to fade, I bend myself in half in a great big bow. I'm breathless from dancing and attempt to restore my lungs, but the inhale turns into more of a gasp. It feels like the wind has been knocked out of me as I right myself. I almost stagger backward, and my heart skitters to a stop. Reed is frozen a few feet behind the barstool Miles sits on. His venomous glare murdering him from behind.

I pant a couple of times into the microphone before remembering where I am and drop it from my lips. The crowd continues to cheer as I look around for a place to set the microphone down. I sort of stumble over to the nearest table and deposit it on top of it.

When I look back up again, there's a hint of concern that has zipped Miles's furrowed brows together. I'm sure he's expecting me to come say hello. I *want* to, but I think I owe Reed an apology. An explanation after inviting him here and then forcing him to witness an intimate moment between Miles and me like that. He had to have seen it with the look of devastation that's on his face. I mouth *I'm sorry* to Miles as I brush right past him to where Reed stands waiting for me.

"You were great up there," Reed says.

I want to look back over my shoulder and make sure Miles is okay too. *I don't know what to do.*

"Thanks. I'm... sorry I didn't wait for you. It's just that, they had my song on the jukebox, and I really needed to let loose."

His lips lift in a smile. "I see that. Just like the old Teddy."

My heart crashes from my chest to my stomach at his words. As if there's an old Teddy that needs to be reincarnated. As if I'm not standing here in front of him as the truest version of me. I was *living* on that stage. It's the first time Reed has indicated he wants me to be someone else.

As I sort through my feelings, Miles forces his way past us to the exit. Between me not acknowledging him for Reed's sake and the fact that Reed didn't appreciate my performance in the way I hoped he would, I start to feel upset.

I press a finger into his chest. "You promised me you wouldn't get your hopes up. Is that all you want from me?"

Reed stumbles back a step. "What?"

"Is that all you want from me?" I repeat. "To be the old Teddy?" I fold my arms across my chest.

"What? No, of course not. I want you to be *you*. You *were* you up there, that's all I'm saying," he clarifies, and then reaches for my hands.

When his warm fingertips snake through mine I feel safe. And I hate that this is the moment reserved as the first time he's really held my hand. They drown mine in the best way, and I want to be focusing on that feeling instead of this big gaping hole between us. I'm not sure I'll ever measure up to the Teddy that Reed remembers.

"I just need you to know that I've tried," I say. "I've tried so hard to remember that girl you used to know, but she's not coming back." I start to cry.

"Hey, hey, hey, I'm sorry," Reed says, bending over so he's eye level with me and brushing the tears that fall down my cheeks. "I'm sorry if I made you feel bad. Can we go outside and talk?"

A group of teenage girls belt their rendition of "Goodbye Earl" from the stage, and it's impossible to compete with their volume. I nod into his hands that are cradling the sides of my face, and he leads me to the green Exit sign. We walk in silence across the gravel parking lot to his truck where he pops the tailgate down and hoists me on top of it.

"That surprises me every time," I laugh through my cry.

"You're barely five feet, Teddy, I don't expect you to pole vault."

The topic change diffuses the tension between us, but I falter in the silence. The night sky matches the mood, shifting into a somber, dusky blue. There's a group of teenagers piling out of a truck bed near us, but they're all loud laughter and witty banter, so they don't even notice us. There's a girl with them, and her attention lobs back and forth between the two guys she's walking with. She grins in a light and easy way that makes me jealous.

Maybe that's where I've gone wrong. I can feel myself slipping from the friend zone with both Miles and Reed, and it's a dangerous position to put myself in. It's making all three of us insecure.

"I didn't know he was coming," I admit.

Reed groans like he's in pain while he stares straight ahead, but he nods.

"I know you asked me not to, but I think I need you to tell me about him. At least the part that makes you despise him so much," I say.

There's a long, weighted pause where Reed studies the etchings on his cowboy boots before he asks, "Why hasn't he told you himself?"

His question confuses me. I don't have an answer for him. The past is one big secret with Miles, but every moment we share in the present is so nice that I don't even care. I don't pry. He doesn't open up in the same way Reed does, and admitting that to Reed will look like I compare them. Which I don't. I hope someday Miles will open up to me, but Reed has already proved he can.

"I don't know why, but I *need* this to move forward."

Reed sighs then says, "We used to be best friends."

I straighten. I didn't expect for him to give in.

"Used to?" I ask.

He nods. "As a kid, Miles had everything I didn't. A simple life, a close relationship with his father that I envied, and he lived right next door to the girl with the constellation of freckles I was sure mapped my future."

Reed ghosts his lips in a heartbreaking half-smile.

"It helped that we got along so well. My brothers and I were"—he puffs out a laugh—"always in competition with each other. But with Miles..." His voice drops to a whisper like he's about to tell me a secret. "He never tried to be better at something than I was."

I fight a smirk. Even the Reed I've gotten to know would appreciate being the center of attention.

"At first, I thought the foundation of our friendship was fishing, but I soon realized the greatest thing we had in common was you." He shrugs, and then looks down at his boots again, crossing them at the ankle.

He's quiet for more than ten seconds, and I do what I'm best at—I spiral in the silence.

Am I supposed to say something? What comment could I possibly follow with that doesn't just sound like a sympathetic friend. I mean, I AM a sympathetic friend. I can't imagine my world orbiting the same person someone else lov—

The thought dies in my head with the identical sensation I experienced while fishing with Miles the other day. That gamey smell drafted from the fish bait, and it was like it unlocked a door just out of reach in my brain. I close my eyes and extend that impression just a bit further, fighting to reach the memory. Trying to...

"We bonded over the fact that we missed you when you weren't around," he continues, and that figurative door bolts shut again. I try not to look frustrated, but I don't have to try very hard when he meets my eyes and there's a level of grief living behind them. I instantly regret allowing my inner torment to get the best of me.

"When you started coming back every summer, it always took a little adjusting at first, like things do when two becomes three. For the first couple of summers, we were all so in sync that we never spent a moment apart. It was easy as kids. But then we became teenagers and boundaries started getting messier. The moments where three became two were harder to ignore."

I nod. I'm right there with him. I'm feeling that *now*. There's me and him, and there's me and Miles. It's beyond complicated.

"Deep down, I think I always knew Miles looked at you the same way I did, but I never wanted to admit that to myself. Doing so would mean you might choose him over me. I knew if that ever happened, I would be losing both of you, and the thought of sacrificing my two best friends was too much."

No kidding, I want to say, because it's feeling like he's about to make me do the same.

"I'm sure Miles felt the same way, but I have no way of knowing for sure. We never talked about our feelings for you. They were just there... changing us."

Tears prick my eyes with every word Reed utters. I hold them back though, afraid if I fall apart, I'll never hear how this ends. Reed's sole focus will become consoling me, and I need for him to finish.

"You guys can still be friends. We all can be," I justify.

"We can't just be your friend, Teddy. Don't you see that? It's impossible. People change, and I don't know who to blame anymore." There's a note of frustration to his voice that I wish I could soothe.

"Yeah, people do change, but it doesn't mean you have to let them go because of it," I argue. "You can grow with them through it."

Reed shakes his head. "It's always going to be there between us, and we can't survive it... watching who you choose. We tried it once before, and it's what got us here, in the mess we're in."

I'm even more confused than before Reed started talking. I

IF I NEVER REMEMBER   193

jump off the bed of his truck, which feels more like a fall, but I need to face him.

"You're still not telling me what happened. I need to know *the moment* your friendship fell apart."

"I can't do that. I'm sorry. That part is either for Miles to tell you or for you to remember."

CHAPTER TWENTY-TWO

SUMMER, TWO YEARS AGO

I f I felt like a third wheel all summer, my junior year was even worse. Peter and Cozy were attached at the lips, giving me no choice but to try things out with Tetherball Baker. I wasn't sure I was even attracted to him. Especially when his middle school cologne–wearing levels paled in comparison to high school. I found myself in a coughing fit every time I was in his presence. And I mean, we didn't exactly date, it was more of a forced proximity thing. Not just on my part, but his too. But we had a lot in common when it came to delighting in teasing Cozy and Peter about their PDA. He was good for me in the sense that I needed a distraction and a friend.

My parents passed down the family station wagon as a school commuting vehicle. That thing can pack people *in*, and we had fun taking big groups of kids out to various fast-food chains in town on our lunch breaks.

I lost a lot of my desire to sketch after last summer. Maybe it was that I lost my inspiration—spending my days sketching someone else's boyfriend seemed a little desperate. Either way, not sketching during the school year was a choice I don't regret.

I tried a watercolor class instead and found a love of bringing charcoal drawings to life with the rainbow. My mom was thrilled to see me taking up her medium.

Cozy wasn't all that sad to say goodbye to me this summer. She had Peter. I'm happy for her, but had she not been with him, this might have been the first summer I asked my parents to stay behind. Instead, I found myself working eight days straight on my first week back at the fly shop with Shep while Miles was in Montpelier working with Lexi on her family farm.

The first day I asked for a day off was today. It's boating Tuesday, and I'm rummaging through my closet for a swimsuit.

"No, no, no," I moan out loud, kicking over the laundry basket filled with wet swimsuits. They don't make it any farther than a sopping heap on the floor. A tiny black bikini mocks me from the lone hanger.

I scan the room wondering if it would be possible to fashion a last-minute one-piece out of the quilt at the end of my bed. That's how bad things are. When I have no other option, I rip the bikini from where it hangs and shimmy the black bottoms up my legs. The top gathers in a knot in the middle of my chest, my hair falling in waves to cover it. My dad would kill me if he knew I ever even bought something like this. So, to avoid dying today, I cover it up with a pair of denim shorts and a T-shirt, then leave my room without another thought.

"Yeah, I'll have those plans drawn up for you by Thursday. Structurally, I don't see why we can't add that couple of feet to the entryway your wife was requesting."

I listen to my dad conversing with someone over the phone from the stairs, the soles of his shoes clunking against the wood floor in a pacing pattern. I descend the bottom flight in a tiptoe, manifesting the belief that he'll be absorbed enough in his client call that I can slip out the front door without a word.

"Hang on," I hear him say into the speaker, and all hope slithers out that exit without me.

"Woah, woah, woah. Where are you going so fast?" he asks, tucking his hand over the phone receiver.

"It's a Tuesday," I say, as if that's supposed to answer his question. His blank stare makes me realize that while I've had a routine here every summer, between keeping his business afloat and looking out for my mom, he lives his life day by day. He has ever since her cancer diagnosis. While she's still in remission, he hasn't left the life where she isn't. Guilt consumes me, and I consider canceling.

"I should stay... help with something around the cabin."

"Nah, you go. Have fun," he says.

I nod, but as I turn from his bedroom door to continue down the stairs, he stops me.

"But those shorts stay on, you hear?"

My face heats. "Dad, are you... trying to have the sex talk with me right now?"

He coughs, growing flustered. "All I'm saying is boys have a one-track mind. I know. I've been one." He smirks.

"Okay, I did not need to know that, but thank you. Shorts on. Got it," I holler over my shoulder as I barrel down the rest of the steps.

There's a towel draped over the barstool by the door and a bottle of sunscreen on the counter that have my mom written all over them. I grab them both, sliding on a pair of sandals and slipping out the front door.

When I cross the lawn, I see Reed sprawled out in his lawn chair on his second-story deck, scrolling his phone.

"Hey, stranger, what are you doing today?" I holler up to him.

He moves the device so it's no longer blocking his view of my face.

"Waiting for you!" he calls. "Stay there!"

He descends the steps from the upper deck down to the grass. "My dad got tied up with a work call this morning, so we can't leave on the boat for a while. Want to swim?"

I swallow, my promise to my dad disintegrating with my answer. "Sure."

Reed grabs an American flag towel hanging from a drying line across a set of trees and leads me knee-deep through the water to get to his floating dock. We climb on top and lay our towels across the deck. He grips the back of his tank top and hauls it over his head, the muscles in his arms bunching with the tug.

The knot in my stomach grows, and I can't stop staring. If Reed is the quarterback of the made-up Bear Lake football team, I'm the nobody who he'd never even recognize in the bleachers. Yet I'm very aware that we're here. Alone together. There's no one else around to diffuse the situation when I act awkward or make a complete fool of myself.

Reed on the other hand is unfazed by my presence. It's clear he does this all the time, interacting with girls his age. He motions at the clothes still clinging to my body like a chastity belt.

"Well... I imagine you wore a swimsuit if you planned on going boating."

Yeah, I did, but not the Speedo one-piece you're used to seeing me in, I want to argue with him.

"Turn around," I say instead. I'm not feeling brave enough for him to see me in it just yet.

I see him swallow. Hard.

"You DID wear a swimsuit, didn't you?" he asks.

"Yes," I say, and his shoulders wilt a good foot with his sigh.

I didn't peg Reed to be the afraid-of-skinny-dipping type, but then again, I still don't know him well. When I work up the nerve to strip off my clothes, I'm not even looking to see if Reed notices. I'm fixed on the front windows of my cabin to make sure my dad isn't watching out of them. I shed them a lot faster than I put them on and dive feetfirst off the dock into the water. When I come up for air, Reed is still standing there watching me, a smirk playing on his lips.

"You look good in black," he says before cannonballing off the edge.

He swims closer to me as we both tread water.

"Want to play a game?"

"Something tells me I'll regret saying yes given the way you're looking at me right now," I say.

There's a wicked grin on his face.

"Say yes anyway."

I hesitate. He's pushing me far out of my comfort zone.

"Okay, yes."

We swim back to the edge of the dock so we can grip the side with one hand.

"Two truths and a lie. I'll go first," he says.

I knew I was going to regret this.

"Rom-coms are my favorite movie genre. I sleep with the hall light on. I can count the number of girls I've kissed on one hand."

I study his answers. There's *no way* all three of those aren't a lie. I have no idea which one to pick.

As if he can sense my growing distress, he says, "I'll make it easier on you. My favorite movie is *The Holiday*."

What?

"As in, Cameron Diaz and Kate Winslet?"

"Yes," he says with a grin.

"I *love* that movie, but I'm kind of shocked that wasn't your lie. Most guys our age like *Silence of the Lambs*, not watching Cameron Diaz cry over Jude Law."

"What can I say, I'm a weeper," he says, quoting the movie.

I giggle. "You are not!"

"Are too. Now are you going to guess or what? You have a fifty-fifty shot at this point."

His lips lift in another shameless smirk and draw my attention to how full they are. There's no way he has only kissed a handful of girls by now.

"You don't sleep with the hall light on. The darker the better," I guess.

"Wrong. Total wimp."

I burst out laughing, thinking he can't be serious, until he doesn't laugh with me. Reed's a teenage boy afraid of the dark, and that means he's only kissed a few girls.

Next to the water, his eyes glow a deeper shade of blue. "I also lied about how many," he confesses. "It's not a handful." He eyes me sheepishly through his lashes. "It's not anyone actually."

I'm thankful he is difficult to embarrass because I gape at him with an unhinged jaw, close enough to resemble a nutcracker. "You've *never* kissed someone?"

"Is there something wrong with that?" he asks simply.

"Well, no, but—"

"But what? Because I'm a teenage guy, it means I just give it away to the first girl I come across?"

The hole I've managed to dig for myself has become a trench at this point. More like a burial plot where my casket belongs.

"I'm just—"

"Speechless?" he finishes. "Good to know I have that effect on you."

He winks at me, and I freak out internally. I have no idea what to do with myself in this situation. I'm embarrassed and nervous. Terrified he can read every single one of those emotions with my face on fire, so I dunk my whole head straight under water to put it out.

When I come up for air, he's still unfazed. He wraps his biceps along the top of the dock, resting his chin on his forearms. "All right, your turn."

I think about it for a second before deciding to say the first thing that comes to mind.

"I've been the same height since the sixth grade. I'd rather eat a pickle than a cookie any day. And I can't keep my eyes open past ten."

He chuckles, shaking his head. "Please tell me the ten o'clock bedtime is a lie, because if you say it's the pickle one..."

I cringe. "It's the pickle one."

"Dammit, Teddy. I'm appalled that you would diss on pickles when they're my favorite food group."

"Pickles? Seriously?"

He nods. "On burgers, with peanut butter, dipped in a milkshake, on the end of a stick, you name it, it's my favorite thing."

Now I'm the one laughing. "I would have never guessed that. But seriously, dipped in a milkshake? That's just ruining a perfectly good milkshake," I say.

"When we go on that date you promised me, you're trying it," he wagers, holding out his pinky.

"Oh. I didn't know we were still doing that."

"Why wouldn't we? You have something against me, Fletcher?" He squints and then splashes water at my face. I whip my head to the side just before it sprays my cheek.

"You're going to pay for that," I call, but he's already paddling backward out of reach. When I give up, he swims back to me and extends his pinky in the air.

"So, do we have a deal or not?"

Hanging out with Reed and trying milkshake-dipped

pickles sounds like the most fun I've had all year, so I say, "Deal," and wrap my pinky finger around his. Then he leans forward and kisses it, and it's a good thing we're in icy lake water. My body flushes the hottest shade of pink.

"Now let's play the game you want to play. The one where we jump like elementary-school-aged children on that trampoline you've been eyeing all summer."

I don't even try to hide my excitement. "Yes!"

We spend the next thirty minutes teasing each other and jumping. Reed does a flip off the side, and then we both jump off together holding hands. I like being around him. He's fun and playful and has a way of making me forget everything else.

It takes a surprising amount of leg muscle climbing the steep ladder to get back on again so by round ten, we're both taking ragged breaths. We flop on our backs in the center of the fabric and stare up at the bright blue sky.

"What are you parents like?" Reed asks. "I've only ever spent that BBQ and a couple of bonfires with them. They seem pretty great."

"Yeah, they are," I agree. "Maybe a little overbearing at times, but it's just because they care about me. My mom battled cancer a few years ago, but you'd never know that aside from the scars on her forearms from all the IVs."

Reed's palms rest on his bare chest, and droplets of water glimmer from the tips of his curls as he looks at me. "I'm sorry, Teddy. That had to have been hard to watch."

"Yeah, it was. It's why we didn't come back here after my first summer. She's in remission now though, and her doctor thinks she has good odds of keeping it that way. She's happy here too."

"That's good." He smiles. "And your dad?"

"He never leaves her side," I say, turning to take in the

cloudless sky above me. I think of my dad and how, just the other night, he covered my mom's shoulders with her grand-mother's afghan when she fell asleep in front of the fire. Thinking about that sweet gesture, I gaze at the abyss above me. "I want a love like theirs one day."

"Sounds nice." He sighs.

"What about your parents? They seem happy together." All I have to pull from are our weekly boating trips. Never once have I seen them raise their voices at each other.

"They are, and they aren't. I think my dad has a lot of want. He's a dreamer, and my mom is content with her lot in life."

"I can see why." I shift my head, getting a good view of the Morgan property. The garden, the wildflowers, the trees... it only looks *lusher* from out on the water. "Do you ever think they'll sell this place?"

"No, that's the one thing I admire about my dad. He brings his dreams to us. He won't ever leave her for them. Not like..."

When he trails off, his face looks like he's said too much, and I can't help but wonder if he was talking about Miles.

"What do you do for fun when you're not here for the summer," Reed asks, changing the subject.

"The same things I do here, honestly. I'm not any different there. I used to draw, but just took up watercolor last fall."

"Used to?"

"Still do. Just haven't felt very inspired lately," I admit.

"Miles said you're amazing. You should show me your art sometime... you know... if you want to," he says.

"Okay." I nod, taking in his smile and melting at the sight of that carved dimple that I'm now noticing properly for the first time... when it's right in front of me... beckoning me to move closer.

"Speaking of Miles... did anything ever happen between you two?" he asks.

"What?" I falter from staring at his dimple.

"Do you like him. Miles, I mean. You know, as more than a friend."

"Miles has a girlfriend," I remind him, as if he doesn't already know that.

"Reed, Teddy, it's time!" Mrs. Morgan shouts from the upper deck of their patio, and relief washes over me.

I don't want to lie to Reed, but I know how close the two of them are and I would have, just so my feelings didn't get back to Miles.

"We should head back," I say, standing first.

"Last one there eats a pickle!" he yells, and sails off the side of the trampoline.

When his hair flicks away from his face, spraying water from a streak of curls, he backstrokes to the shore, immobilizing me with his grin. I shake my head, get a running start, and pray it will be enough to close some of the distance between us. Otherwise, I'm having a pickle for lunch.

Reed shows up at my door with a single wildflower clutched between his hands the night of our dare date. Instead of holding it out to me, he fashions it in the half-up clip of my hair.

"Beautiful," he says.

I don't know if he meant me or the flower, but I pretend it was the flower so I don't blush in front of him.

"I see you're driving more than just boats this summer," I comment as Reed walks with me toward a brand-new oversized truck.

"My parents tend to buy my affection to make up for their busy schedules," he says.

Where most teenagers would be thrilled at the gift of a shiny new car, Reed looks embarrassed, and I regret pointing it out. I don't know what it's like to have absent parents because of work, but I know I'm more thankful to have overbearing ones than parents too busy to give me the time of day.

"I'm sorry, Reed."

"Nope." He stops me. "We're supposed to be having fun!" He jerks the car door open and whisks me in with one steady motion onto the front seat.

"Wow, like rollercoaster ride kind of fun?" I giggle, feeling my heart beat faster.

"Exactly!" He beams before shutting the door.

As his F-150 whirs to life, so does the soundtrack of my fourteen-year-old summer. I'd recognize the CD I made for Reed and Miles anywhere and for a moment, it stings a little bit to realize that Miles must not have wanted it. But I bury those feelings under the ones that tell me Reed did. We exchange a knowing smile and jam out to Garth Brooks on our way to LaBeau's, our arms out the windows.

As promised, he orders two raspberry milkshakes and two pickles. He pauses as I dunk the pickle into the shake and lift it to my lips, crunching down around the end as milkshake dribbles down my chin. He chuckles and catches the drip with a napkin before it falls onto my denim shorts.

His dimple pierces his cheek. "It's good, right?"

His eyes are on me as if he doesn't want to be anywhere but right here.

"You always surprise me," I say, taking another bite of my pickle.

"Because I like weird food?" he jokes.

"Because you love life."

"I do when I'm with you," he says.

His comment throws me off, and I drop my gaze to my lap just as another drop of milkshake lands on my shorts.

"I'm a mess." I chuckle.

"I'm just glad I met someone as messy as me," he says.

This feels so easy.

So easy, in fact, that nothing about it prepares me for the situation I find myself in not twenty-four hours later.

CHAPTER TWENTY-THREE

NOW

The entire next week Mr. Morgan keeps me busy with closing shifts. Miles's truck is gone by the time I finish breakfast with my parents most mornings. I can't tell if he's avoiding me or just working. With one cabin separating them, Miles and Reed have managed to dodge each other all summer.

I don't see Reed either. Our shifts at the restaurant overlap just enough for us to wave in passing. After the day he skipped out on work and angered his father, I have no doubt that it's on purpose. Mr. Morgan doesn't want me getting any closer to Reed than I already have, and I get it. He doesn't want me to hold him back, just like I don't want anyone to hold me back from what comes next either.

At the end of a long-awaited opening shift, I come home to Shep and Miles fishing together off the end of the dock. They have a cardboard box–sized cooler parked next to them with the lid open, and Shep reaches to pull out a Ziploc bag, handing it to Miles. On the other side rests a tackle box twice the size of the one Miles pulled those slimy marshmallows from the last time we fished together.

When I get close to the dock, I think about turning back

around and giving them space, but I've waited an entire week for this opportunity, and it's too long to let another day go by.

"Hey, Miles, can I talk to you for a minute?" I ask.

"I'm a little busy," he grumbles, not even taking the time to turn around and look me in the face. But Shep does.

"Now there's a face I haven't seen in a while!" he exclaims, resting his pole next to him and standing to hug me. My smile broadens at the sight of him, and I stand on my tiptoes to hug him back. His cheeks look pinker today, and he has on a pair of fishing bibs with one of the straps undone.

"I was just thinking the same thing," I add.

"Yeah, well, it's because this pain in the ass thinks he needs to do everything for me," he gripes.

I chuckle before sobering when Miles still doesn't turn around.

"It must be nice having him home again though," I say.

"He's around a little too much if you ask me. Keep him a little busier, would you?"

"As a matter of fact, I plan to," I say with little thought as to bringing this up in front of his dad. "He'll be out of your hair all of Friday evening, so you just tinker away to your heart's content while he's gone."

Shep sighs, then shoots me a contented smile. "I thought this day would never come."

"I missed you too, Dad," Miles deadpans.

"Oh, you know I love ya. I just don't need a second mother. I've already had one of those, and she'd watch over my shoulder while I washed my underwear. You're one step away from doing the same damn thing."

"I hear you loud and clear," he grumps.

"You seem way better at this than me." I point to the fishing pole that Shep has propped between his legs. He fiddles with the reel, and then he walks over to fish something out from his gigantic Mary Poppins tackle box.

"Aw hell, I've got a few years on ya," he says, thumbing through the top layer before extending it up on its hinges to get to the next one.

Now is not the time to get into a karaoke night apology I see, so I start backing up a few steps toward the cabin.

I call out a final "See you on Friday, Miles. Four o'clock. My patio," to the back of his head, then leave the two of them to do what they do best. Fish in solitude.

On Friday afternoon, I wait for Miles an impatient fifteen minutes past the time I told him to meet me before I give up and march over to his trailer. Long, driven strides lead me to a latched screen door with the sound of a baseball game playing from a fuzzy screen inside. Three firm raps alert my arrival before I shout through the opening, "Miles, are you in there?"

The creak of a wooden bench echoes through the space and two shuffling feet brings a smiling Shepard to the door to greet me.

"Well, hey there! Doesn't sound like you came by to see me."

"Hey, Shep. Is Miles here?" I bob my head around to snoop behind him. I make out a pair of size thirteen tennis shoes. They're dusty like the Bloomington trail where we've met several mornings now, except for the last ten since he started avoiding me. I crane my neck and peer around Shep to try to get a good look at his son. He chuckles and leans against the door frame.

"Hang on, let me get him," he says, amused with himself as he pushes open the screen door to let me in. "Miles, your girl-friend is here."

"I'm not his..." I start to say as I take one step up, but then I get a clear view of Miles and my thought dies away. He's stretched out on a barely full-sized bed (hence the shoes hanging over the end), and he's scrolling on his phone acting like I'm not three feet away from him.

"Tell her I'm busy," Miles says, avoiding looking up.

"Miles, we had plans tonight. Or did you forget?"

"Nope, didn't forget. Just didn't agree to it, and I'm not going," he mumbles, continuing his perusal with his finger.

"Quit your moping, boy, and talk to this pretty girl who is waiting for you," his dad buts in.

I came to offer him an apology, but I don't want to stick around and waste my time if he won't even look at me.

"I'll wait by your truck for the next five minutes," I threaten, "and then I'm going without you."

That gets his attention. He catches my eyes when he glances past the edge of his phone, but I don't wait to see if he'll say anything. I turn right around and march back down the steps, calling over my shoulder, "Have a good night, Shep."

"I like her," I hear him say just before I'm out of earshot.

I shove my hands into the front pockets of the terry cloth swim coverup I'm wearing and stare out at the lake. The sudden glide of majestic white wings catches my eye as a pelican floats through the air out past the dock and dives toward the water's surface. Its domed beak hangs open as it scoops a mouthful of something and lifts back into the air. I'm caught up in imagining what its meal looks like when I hear Miles open the driver's-side door. He's looking at me through the window like he's the one who's been waiting for me, and says, "You coming?"

I huff and jerk on the handle, climbing into the passenger seat while fighting the urge to roll my eyes. Miles pulls the car in a U-turn and climbs the driveway to the main road. I reach over and fasten my seat belt as he puts the car in park at the top of the driveway.

"So, where are we going?"

The plan didn't just come to me like a lightning strike. It took a bit of research and creativity after googling recreational activities within a fifty-mile radius during my lunch break. Among the top five were the watercraft rental at the marina (too close to work) and the Pickleville Playhouse (already been). I plug the destination into my phone and wedge it in the dash's cupholder for him to follow.

"Looks like you've got one hour and twenty minutes to tell me where your head's at," Miles says.

He pulls out onto the street, and I realize this is where my apology comes in.

"I'm sorry," I say.

He clutches the steering wheel with his fists like he's ringing out a wet rag.

"I promised Reed I'd meet him at Maverick's for karaoke. I didn't expect to see you and..." My words fail me again.

"You didn't expect to sing with me," he finishes.

"No."

The pained look in his expression makes me suck in a gust of air.

"Did it mean anything to you?" he whispers.

We're alone together in this car and yet, I struggle to say the words out loud, as if anyone other than Miles can hear them. I nod up and down instead.

I thought admitting that would make me feel better, but the sadness that hovers like a rain cloud over Miles makes me feel worse.

"It made me feel alive," I whisper. "That's what I would have said had I taken my chance and spoken to you after the song. I would have told you that there isn't anyone in the world who makes me *feel* more than you do."

In a bold gesture, Miles reaches across the seat and laces his fingers with mine. Just like his shadow, his hand dwarfs them.

His fingers are warm, and they remain still for a while as we both stare out opposite windows. A part of me wishes he would say something, but I know that's not Miles. We drive in comfortable silence, my eyes taking in the rivers and cliffs and bridges while my heart traces the pattern of his hand against mine.

After a while he stops being tentative and begins stroking his thumb back and forth over the top of my hand. It's a repetitive pattern that leeches all of my focus until we reach our destination. We pull into a tiny town with mismatched buildings and a giant banner that greets us with the city's name.

Lava Hot Springs.

"How have I lived all my life in Montpelier and never known this was an hour away?" he asks, admiring the quaint historic buildings and a charming bed and breakfast with a hot spring on the left.

"Because you've never set yourself free enough to see it. Let's go check it out," I say.

For the first time in days, Miles's smile comes back to me.

It's quiet for a Friday night, a handful of people scattered around the river-like hot tub. Nestled low in a valley of foothills the sun has already disappeared behind, steam evaporates just above the surface of the water. We dip our toes in first, then ankles, getting used to the spicy temperature.

When we're calf-deep, Mile says, "I take it this won't be like plunging into Bloomington Lake? I thought you might dive in headfirst."

I laugh. "I know you think I'm crazy, but I'm not *that* crazy! I'm pretty sure the temperature of this water could fry a few brain cells if I dunked my head under it."

Miles squats down, dipping his bare chest beneath the water. "I don't think you're crazy," he says, and I hold my breath, waiting for his next words. "I just think you're searching for something that's better left unfound."

I rip off the rest of the Band-Aid and dip myself in too. It's sobering in the opposite way of Bloomington Lake. We're all alone in a quiet little corner, and something about it has my walls tumbling down around me.

"It was you, wasn't it?"

I track my fingertips as they trace long strokes on the surface of the water out to my sides. Even if I can't see them beneath the thick cloud of steam, it's better to focus on their invisible movement than in front of me. I can't look him in the face. My walls might be down, but they aren't crumbled to pieces.

"What was me?" he whispers, and I lift my gaze just enough to catch his swallow. A harsh bob of his Adam's apple.

"The one who left the sketchbook by my front door. For someone who believes my past is better left unfound, you sure have a way of encouraging *that* part of it." I study him like a forensic scientist.

"That's different," he says, looking away.

"Different how?" I press.

He settles onto a step behind him so his torso is exposed.

"I remember the first time my dad took me fishing. I was maybe five, clueless about how the whole thing actually worked, but enamored at the idea of walking away from the experience of having caught a fish from a giant body of water. No one had to tell me I'd like it or that it would make me smile. I tried it, and I just knew. When you're a kid, you're the most *you* you'll ever be. Not tainted by the expectations of others, no fear of failure, not worried about whether or not it will be a valuable skill that will serve you throughout your life. If you like to fish, you do it because it makes you happy. Because it makes you feel like yourself. You deserve that kind of happy in your life, Teddy. You deserve to feel like *you*."

Tears spring to my eyes. "How did you know drawing would make me feel that way?"

"Because you did it when you were ten, and it lit up your whole face."

"Miles..." I croak, reaching for him.

He leans away from my touch.

"Please don't push me away again," I plead.

His eyes settle on me with a look that's stripped bare. I watch his own brick wall—the one that's kept us apart for so long—detonate in one swift motion. He cups his hands over my hips and draws me onto his lap. His eyes flit between mine, and he lifts a dripping hand from the water, tucking a strand of hair behind my ear.

"That's my problem, Teddy. I can't stay away from you."

His eyes draw a path down the bridge of my nose to my lips.

"I can't either," I breathe, and his lips capture the gasp that follows it.

My legs circle his waist, and his hands tunnel into my hair. To my heart, it feels like finding the place I've longed for. To belong. He steals each breath I draw in, slanting his mouth over mine. When we part, his thumb brushes over my bottom lip.

"I've waited years to do that," he says, pressing his forehead into mine.

"Yeah," I say, because after he pulled away, I realized how long it's *felt* that way for me too.

He holds me against him while taking in the view. "Thank you for bringing me here. No one has ever done something like this for me before."

I rest my head against his chest, feeling the vibrations of his pulse. Between the heat of the hot pool and the comfort of his arms, I'm wrapped in the coziest blanket.

"I think I'd go anywhere with you," I say.

On the drive home, I sit in the middle seat close to Miles. I rest my head on his shoulder, our hands entangled in my lap. It's hard not to think about what happened between us or what will happen when we wake up tomorrow and realize we're both on different paths. I don't want to wonder what it means for me, for him, even for Reed. I'm afraid if I overanalyze any of it, I'll ruin what we have. I want to just be. Him and me. Nothing but a calm in my heart, and the stars in the sky above us.

With his gaze fixed on the road, I feather my fingers across my lips, the taste of his kiss still lingering there. It feels too good to be true being this close to him.

The drive to Lava was too long, but the drive home is too short. I feel the ending of our evening in the pit of my stomach before we've even parked between our cabins. Miles circles the front of the truck, opens my door, and laces our fingers together.

"Thank you for the sketchbook."

I take the slowest steps possible to my front door.

"You don't have to thank me, Teddy. I'd give you the moon in the sky if I thought that's what would make you smile like that again."

As we stop beneath the porch light, Miles turns to face me, threading his fingers between both of my hands.

"I'm not ready to say good night yet," I admit.

A smile traces his lips. He glances over his shoulder and draws me beneath the covered bay window and out of the porch light. He crowds me up against the side of the cabin.

"Me neither," he says before leaning in and kissing me.

Our kiss in the hot tub was one of hunger. Years, maybe, of wanting and waiting boiled down to one moment. A moment that obliterated the wall between us.

This kiss... our second kiss... is one we savor. It builds and builds into something more. A new wall. One that stands to never keep us apart again.

My mom waits for me at the kitchen counter, an enamel mug warming her hands. She's sipping on her favorite sleepy time tea.

"Did you have a good time tonight?" she asks.

Her question feels loaded, and I'm worried she'll ruin my perfect evening if I tell her too much, so I settle on, "I did."

When she doesn't respond, I take it as my sign to head to bed.

"I just don't want to see you get hurt," she confesses to the darkness.

I turn around to face her. "You know the other day when you found that sketch," I say. "It was him who inspired me to do it. And when I told you it made me feel alive? He makes me feel that way too."

"He'll keep you here," she blurts out. "Is moving away what you still want?"

I can read between the lines. She's asking if I want him. If I'd give up leaving here, give up Reed, even her, for him. I don't know how to answer that when I don't know yet. All I know is that I don't want to ruin the happiest night I've had in a long time by putting a label on anything.

"Yes, it's what I still want," I say.

"Then you have to be honest with each other, Teddy. You with him, and especially, him with you."

All I can do is nod, and for the first time since the accident, I fall asleep the moment my head hits the pillow. I sleep in past nine, my body soaking up every minute like a sponge. It's too late for Bloomington Lake but not too late for a swim before work.

I slip on my black Speedo one-piece, not bothering with a coverup. I'm surprised when I find the house quiet and the kitchen empty. When I peek through the curtains over the sink, the car is gone too. There's an even giddier pep to my step knowing I'm home alone, and I bound across the dock, diving off the end in a great big splash.

"Don't tell me I'm too late," I hear someone holler from the shore.

"Too late for what?" I ask Reed.

"Skinny dipping!" he yells back.

"Yep, you're too late," I say, planting my feet, my upper body catching the breeze above the water.

"Dammit." He grins at my swimsuit before pulling his shirt over his head and jogging into the water. He dives under, disappearing in the dark shadows beneath.

The five seconds he's under there I take three backward butterfly pulls with my arms and allow myself to freak out. I kissed Miles last night and don't want to hurt Reed. I'm out far enough now that I'm treading water and can't see below the surface. I scream when I feel a pair of hands squeeze my thighs. Reed's head emerges right in front of me, and he wipes his hair out of his eyes and grins a mile wide.

"You jerk," I shout, splashing a gush of water in his face.

"Make her flirt with me, check," he says.

"Forget flirting, there's payback where you're concerned."

"I'm ready, bring it on!" he says, splashing back.

I tangle my arm around his neck and shove against his shoulders, trying to force him under as he grabs me around the waist and lifts me. Then he throws me in the air, and I catch one of his arms before dunking under.

When we sober, we're both gasping and staring each other in the eye with chemistry swirling between us.

I can't kiss both of them, I panic. In five swift strokes I put as much distance between us as I can.

"My dad's throwing this summer soiree at the restaurant next Saturday night. I normally avoid those kinds of gatherings, but I thought since we both worked there this summer, maybe you'd want to go with me?" he asks.

Like a date? I swallow.

"I don't know, I'm sure your dad is going to ask me to work it."

"I already talked to him about it and told him not to. You'd be doing me a big favor."

I groan under my breath, my resolve crumbling with his very blue puppy dog eyes staring back at me.

"Okay. Do I need a dress?"

CHAPTER TWENTY-FOUR

SUMMER, TWO YEARS AGO

"Hey, Dad, I'm back. I asked Lex's parents to just drop me off at the shop and..."

I feel the breeze of the half door swing open and the clunk of a duffle bag drop near my feet as he roots to the spot.

"Teddy," he says, making startled eye contact with me. "I didn't know you'd be..." His voice dies with his sentence.

"At the shop?" I finish. "I kind of gathered that."

"It's just, my dad hadn't mentioned—"

"That I've been working with him the last week? I can see you're real thrilled about it."

I push past his shoulder, partway through the half swinging door. There's a lull in customers, and now seems like the perfect time to mop the scuff on the floor I've been meaning to buff out.

My eyes drop to the place where his palm grips my forearm. The warmth of his hand seeps through the linen of my button-down shirt, and I close my eyes like I could sunbathe in it. It's wild how months apart only make my heart grow fonder with him.

"No, I am," he argues. "It's good to see you." His hand falls away, signaling the end of his moment of vulnerability, and he wraps his arms across his chest to confirm it.

"You too, Miles." I turn back toward the dusty old broom closet where I have to step over at least a dozen different spider and mouse traps to get to the bucket and scrub brush I'm looking for.

"How'd farm life treat you?" I ask, making small talk from the crack in the door. I can see him sweep his hand through his hair out of the corner of my eye. It's longer than it's ever been as it threatens to hang down in his eyes.

"Oh, it was... good. No, actually... it was awful." He chuckles to himself. "I am not cut out to shovel manure for a living, that's for damn sure."

I turn up my nose. "That's why you smell so bad."

He draws his shirt to his nose. "I do not!" he calls after me as I drop to my knees and begin working the scrub brush in firm circles with a smirk on my face. I slow the strokes and stare at a different spot on the floor, working up the courage to ask him the question I don't care to know the answer to.

"How's Lexi?"

He pauses to look down at me.

"She's Lexi. I don't think there's a single thing in her life she's not bubbly about."

That holds true to even the version I know of her.

"Have you and Reed been hanging out?" he asks.

I pick up the speed of the brush strokes. "Yeah, we've gone boating a couple of times, swam once, had milkshakes at LaBeau's..."

"Wow, so you guys went on that date after all."

When I stop scrubbing to look up at him, he's scrutinizing me like he's holding a magnifying glass.

"He said that's where he'd take you."

"You talked about it?" I ask.

"Come on, Teddy. We're best friends. It's no secret he likes you."

"What? No, he doesn't," I argue.

"Yeah, okay," he scoffs.

"And you're okay with that?"

He shrugs. "It will be nice for Lex to have another girl around to hang out with."

He's not just acting like he doesn't care; he's encouraging it. And it makes me sad.

"Yeah," I manage, giving up on the black spot that has made a permanent change in the pigmentation of the floor.

"I'm going to check in with my dad, and then I'll take over the till, okay?"

"Sure," I say, changing my mind about the spot on the floor. I scrub it until I can no longer see straight. It seems to have transformed into something more that I'm not ready to give up on just yet.

A week later, we were lying on Reed's trampoline, looking up at the stars after a night swim, when he suggested a double-date with Miles and Lexi. We've hung out several times alone now, but nothing has happened between the two of us. Except for how he clings to my side right now, proving his fear of the dark.

I'm not even sure I want anything to happen between us, but I keep saying yes to spending time with him. I love being around him. He's become the best friend I never knew I needed.

We do stupid stuff together like prank his mom by forking her garden, wrap his truck in lights to celebrate Christmas in July, and dress up in Hawaiian shirts and perform the Macarena to get a laugh out of Ronny.

Reed does sweet things too, like gushing over the smell of my hair and leaving a bouquet of wildflowers taped to my front door every morning before I leave for work. We've been dancing in this space between friends and something more.

Your heart still has room, and one day, when you least expect it, you'll find someone else who changes you again, I hear my mom say inside my head.

I definitely didn't expect this, my heart making room for Reed. The confusing part is that Miles has been a good friend too. He doesn't ignore me at the fly shop like he did last summer. Instead, we talk while restocking shelves about trivial things like the weather and the crazy amount of mosquitoes we've had this year. But also, about important things too, like plans for our senior year and updates on our parents' health.

We talk about everything except Lexi and Reed.

Mere minutes before Reed is scheduled to pick me up for our double-date, I'm buried in clothes searching for what to wear, when Cozy FaceTimes me. I flip the camera as I answer.

"Wow, are you not dressed?" she asks to my bare legs as I survey the huge heap of clothes on the floor.

I groan. "Does it look like I'm dressed?"

"Woah! It does not. Watch the camera angle or you'll be giving me more of a show than you intended."

"Shit. Sorry," I say, flipping it back so it's on my face.

"What are you guys doing again?"

When I look in the camera, Cozy's face is resting in the palm of her hand, her feet swinging in the air behind her head as she lounges on her four-poster bed.

"Karaoke and a movie, I think?"

"Hold up! That would make the *best* Instagram reel. I never thought I'd say this, but I think I've run out of content here. Maybe it's time for me to take this show on the road."

"Cozy, you can't become a traveling influencer at seventeen."

"The brands I'm working with would say differently," she argues. "Why do you have to be such a realist all the time?"

"A realist," I mumble under my breath. "That's exactly what I am. A realist who knows there isn't a piece of clothing in the world that's going to make me feel confident about this double-date."

"What was that?" she asks, straightening to a listening position.

"Nothing."

It's way too difficult to keep the camera angle aimed at my face, so I flip it back to my feet.

"Wait. Show me that black dress again," she bosses, pointing her finger at the pile on my right.

"This?" I pinch the hem of a strapless dress.

"No, the halter one. Keep digging." Cozy chuckles.

I fling clothes around the room until I uncover the one she's referring to.

"Yeah, that! And some cowboy boots! This place has a western vibe, doesn't it?"

"I guess," I say. "I've driven by it, but never been in there."

"Well, he won't know what hit him!"

"Cozy. We're just friends, remember?"

"Yeah, just friends... with a guy you've been spending all your time with this summer. Don't even make me mention that this is also a double-date with Mr. First Kiss. I am so upset I'm missing this," Cozy pouts, grabbing her phone with both hands and rolling onto her back so I'm looking down at her.

"Ha-ha. Very funny. Are you and Peter doing something tonight?"

"Are we ever!" She wags her eyebrows, and I scold her with her first and last name.

"What? From your stories about this Reed guy, I'm shocked he hasn't tried to put the moves on you yet."

I fall back on my bed, mirroring her. "Did I tell you he hasn't kissed anyone?"

"WHAT?!" She screams so loud I fling my phone on the mole hill of clothes. A muffled *"Is there something wrong with this guy? No upper lip?"* sounds from the pile.

I chuckle as I race over to pick the phone back up. "He has an upper lip."

"Oh, so you *have* noticed his lips! Are they soft? Pouty?"

I panic when I hear my mom's voice raise an octave as she answers the door. "Cozy, I've gotta go," I say.

"Does he lick them when he talks to you?"

I laugh. "Goodbye, Cozy."

"Call me later!" she shouts before I end the call.

The last time I took Cozy's advice and bought the black bikini, I landed myself in a situation with Reed I wasn't ready for. The black halter dress seems like a potential for round two, so I toss it back in the pile and slip on a pair of jeans and a black strapless top. I do take her advice on the cowboy boots though.

Reed whistles from the front door as I descend the stairs, and it makes me blush even more than when he comments on how good my hair smells.

"Wow, you look—"

"*Way* too young to be going to a karaoke bar," my dad interrupts.

"I promise this place is not like that, Mr. Fletcher. It's family friendly. More of a restaurant with dancing, really. You guys are welcome to come if you want! It's just a bunch of silly singing followed by a movie on the lawn out there."

"No, we trust Teddy," my mom reminds my dad, placing her palm flat against his chest and staring him down. "Have fun, you two!"

"Thanks, Mom. Love you, Dad," I say, taking turns kissing them both on the cheek before guiding Reed out the door.

When we make it to the truck, Reed hoists me by the waist into the passenger seat, and I'm greeted with a double "Hi" from the back seat. When I look over my shoulder, Miles and Lexi are sitting next to each other, his hand perched on her thigh.

"Oh, hey guys," I say, somewhat surprised. I didn't realize they'd be riding with us too, but it makes sense, I guess.

"Teddy, you look incredible!" Lexi gushes, grabbing me by the arm.

Miles stares at me through the rearview mirror, but I flit my gaze away faster than I have time to assess his reaction to that comment and peer at Lexi's outfit over my left shoulder. We're both in denim which makes me glad I opted for the wardrobe change at the last second. One thing I *don't* want is to stand out.

"Thanks. You too."

If the parking lot is any indication of the popularity of this place, karaoke is about to be a party. When we push inside the doors, we are shoulder to shoulder with people. I feel Reed's breath against my ear as he hollers over a group of girls in cowboy hats singing on stage to "Cowboy Take Me Away" by The Chicks.

"Can I get you something to drink?"

The feeling sends a shiver down my spine, and I want to lean in a little closer and see what it would feel like if his lips were *touching* my skin, but I refrain. Miles is right next to me guiding Lexi through the crowd by her lower back. In his own subtle way, he's watching every move I make just like I'm doing to him. It's difficult to let myself be touched by Reed with Miles looking at me like that.

I put a little space between us.

"No, thank you. Let's sing!"

I pull Reed by the hand to the sign-up table. A gentleman a

decade older than us with a regal beard and a suede cowboy hat takes our song request on a clipboard. Then Reed ushers us to an open table the moment a group abandons it for their turn on stage. He pulls out my chair and scoots me in as I sit down across from Lexi.

"So, Teddy, what are your plans after senior year?" she shouts over the belting quartet.

To be honest, I haven't given it much thought. All I've ever loved is sketching. That's what I *want* to be doing after my senior year. It's *when and where* I don't have the answer to yet.

"I'm not sure. Maybe art?"

"Oh, that's right. Miles said you do these incredible sketches."

I flash a glance at Miles who is wearing a genuine look of pride—the one he used to wear as my best friend who championed everything I did.

"I do love it," I say.

"That's great!"

"What about you?" I ask her.

"I'm just hoping to settle down with someone who has an interest in helping me take over the family farm one day," she says as she eyes Miles up and down.

He looks anywhere but at her. If the conversation I had with Miles at the beginning of the summer is any indication of his feelings on the topic, I know he's not who she's looking for. He doesn't want that life for himself. But what he does want? I don't have a clue anymore.

"And what about you, Reed? A child of two attorneys... is law school in your future?"

Reed laughs out loud. "Hell no. I can't think of anything worse. If there's no adrenaline rush, it's not for me. I've been thinking a lot about smokejumping."

"You have?" I gasp, grabbing his bicep. "You've never told me that! That's amazing!"

"Yeah." He shrugs. "It does something good for the world while also allowing me to jump out of airplanes for my job. It seems right up my alley."

My lips turn down at the corners, and I whip my head toward the stage to hide my frown. I think I might be envious of Reed. I've always known he's a confident, decisive person, but he's also a dreamer, which is something I don't think I've ever let myself do. Dreams are risky and daring. The concept of failure scares me too much. What if I don't live up to the idea of Birdie and Archie Fletcher's perfect only child. I don't know if I can take that chance. But I have no doubt Reed will make an incredible smokejumper someday, and I'm happy for him.

Out of the corner of my eye, Miles's shoulders shrink back in his seat. He looks as uneasy as I feel. I wish we were alone so I could ask what he plans to do with his life. Maybe I'm not the only one in this room afraid of dreaming. But the bearded cowboy shouts, "Double Trouble" and Reed says, "It's our turn!"

***

"I can't believe they let us sing two songs," Lexi says as we pull up to the side of Reed's cabin.

"*That's* what you thought was surprising? Who knew Miles could sing!" Reed exclaims.

We all look at Miles and laugh, but it really was impressive. He was the one who kept us all on pitch. Too bad we didn't stay for a solo performance.

Instead, Reed guides us over to the outdoor theatre he set up on the lawn, complete with a projector propped up on the back of the brick firepit, a sheet hung from two limbs of the oak tree, and two blankets spread out by the dock. I settle on the one that looks like a plaid bedspread, pulling off my cowboy boots, stretching out my legs, and resting on my palms.

When I look over at the other blanket, Miles and Lexi are a set of shadows. A light filters between us, cascading the opening credits to *King Kong* on the sheet, and they disappear completely. Reed joins me on the blanket as the movie begins to play.

"This is not the rom-com I imagined watching with you," he leans over and whispers in my ear.

He must not have picked it. He did say they were his favorite, but to be honest, I don't really care what's playing. It's impossible to pay attention to anything with how close Reed's hand is to mine. If I shifted a few inches to my left, I could touch him. Feel the giddy sensation that I know will sweep my stomach at the stroke of his fingers on my palm.

And maybe I'm imagining it every time he repositions his body to get comfortable, but his hand seems to drift closer, the gap between our bodies shrinking. I pretend to stare at the homemade screen in front of me. But by the time his pinky grazes the outer of edge of mine, I'm squirming and flush all over.

I hold my breath, and he shifts again. Two fingers overlap mine now, and every nerve ending in my body sparks to life. They graze a path back and forth and if I don't concentrate on stiffening the muscles in my left hand, they're going to tremor at his touch.

Too late.

"Are you cold?" he asks.

He moves so that he's sitting behind me, his legs straddling my back as I tip against him. A small sigh escapes my lips.

"Is this okay?" he asks.

I nod, thankful I don't have to look him in the eye. I know I'm blushing. A part of me wants to feel his big arms wrap around my waist too and hold me close to him, but then I remember we're watching this movie with company, and this already feels intimate.

I miss King Kong saving the girl on the Empire State Building. I miss the groan of the dock next to us as it rocks on the surface of the lake. Instead, I count the thumps of Reed's heartbeat through his shirt against my back, wondering why I never paid attention to them before.

Every morning until the night of the Morgan soiree is the same thing. I wake up at four, hop in Miles's truck, and ride to Bloomington Lake. We take the trail holding hands, watch the sun come up from the water's edge, and steal a kiss before parting ways. Everything about my stolen time with him feels easy. It's hard to believe I wasn't always doing it with my life.

We talk about places we want to go someday. Miles says he wants to see the Grand Canyon, and I share my dreams of hang gliding off the coast of California. When it comes to the past though, we never talk about it. I'm beginning to think that whatever happened between Miles and Reed isn't for me to know anymore. And if there ever was an us before that, it can't be as good as the us now.

While it doesn't scare me not talking about the past, the thought of not telling Miles about the soiree does. I lean against his chest, his arms wrapped around me and his face out of view.

"So, there's this thing at work tonight," I start. "I mean, I'm not working, but Reed's parents are putting on an event. I think there's food and dancing or something like that."

"Oh yeah? Are you gonna go?"

I hesitate. "I was thinking about it."

"I'll go with you if you want me to," he offers.

This is so much harder than I thought it would be.

"Reed invited me."

I turn in his arms to gauge his reaction.

"Oh... okay."

"Okay as in you're cool with it?"

"Yeah, I mean, I have no claim over you. You get to do whatever you want, Teddy." He sighs.

"I know, but is it what you *want* me to do?"

I want him to say no. We haven't defined anything, but I want him to admit that this is more.

"How could you ask me that."

"Because you don't seem to be fighting for me!"

"When it comes to you and Reed Morgan, I won't fight you on it. You need to do what's best for you. Don't worry about me," he says, drawing his arms away from where they were wrapped around my neck a second ago.

It stings to hear him say that. But he's never fought for me, has he? It's always one step forward, ten steps back with him. I should have expected this.

"No, you're right," I say. "It is up to me. I just wanted to let you know I'm going." I scoot away from him and stand up.

"We should get back," he says, deflecting like usual.

Maybe my mom was right all along. Whatever this thing is that's happening between us, I should pull back before I get hurt.

"Well, don't you clean up nice!" my dad says. He's in his khaki pants and Hawaiian shirt, and he gives me a twirl as I reach the bottom of our stairs. I'm in a full-length black dress that splits up the leg and wraps a single shoulder.

"Thanks, Dad."

I kiss him on the cheek, and he tucks his arm back around my mom, who is wearing something tea length and suitable for a Cinco de Mayo party. It has every bright color in it, as if she painted it herself. It's so her.

"You look amazing too, Mom," I say, hugging her.

"Thanks, sweetheart. I imagine you don't want to ride with us old folks anyway, but I think there's someone waiting for you on the patio."

She winks at me, and my gaze drifts to the front door where Reed paces behind the glass cut-out window. His slicked-back curls look darker with hair product in them, and I can't deny that he's good-looking, no matter if his hair is windswept just after a boat ride or in a perfect part like a restaurant owner's son would be.

"I'll meet you guys there," I say, squeezing their hands before closing the gap between me and the front door. When I pull it back, Reed startles, pivoting to face me. I swear I see a glint shine off his dimple like you would a cartoon character.

"Too dressed up?" I ask, twirling in front of him.

He shakes his head, not a curl falling out of place. "Perfect."

I smile. "You, too."

"This old thing?" He pulls on the collar of his pinstripe short-sleeve dress shirt.

I drop my gaze to my feet before I blush any deeper.

"Do your parents want a ride?"

I look back over my shoulder and catch them watching us from the opening to the laundry room. When they see me, my dad spins my mom toward the back door, and they hustle away.

"I think they're good."

"Well, okay then." He offers me his arm, and I take it.

I steal a final glance at the trailer. The truck is still parked outside, and a part of me hopes Miles isn't watching this all play out from one of the windows. With the start of the ignition, "Why Can't I?" by Liz Phair drifts through the speakers.

"Is this that CD you played the first night we went boating?" I ask.

I didn't know it was possible—or for what reason—but Reed's smile broadens.

"It is."

"I like this song," I say, turning up the volume just as she gets to the chorus. With her words, I think of... Miles. And a lump surfaces in my throat.

The parking lot is packed with illegally parked cars. It will be a miracle if anyone can get out of here without rear-ending someone. My parents, in their haste, beat us here, and I catch them entering one of the garage bays and greeting a woman in a satin tea-length bodycon dress. Mr. Morgan wraps his arm around the woman's shoulder as he reaches out to shake my dad's hand, and I realize it must be Reed's mother. I haven't met her... well, I guess more like *seen her* all summer.

Reed takes my hand as we weave through the parking lot and before I know it, I'm being wrapped in the same woman's arms.

"Teddy, I'm so glad you're okay," Mrs. Morgan bellows, making a bit of scene.

"Um, yeah... I mean, thank you," I fumble.

"Mom, please," Reed cuts in.

"Sorry, I'm just happy to see you two together. I'm glad you could both make it."

"Dad." Reed addresses him by ruffling the collar of his dress shirt.

He hurries to straighten it. "No pranks tonight, understand?" he grunts.

"Yes, sir." Reed salutes him and pulls me into the crowd.

His parents went all out. I scan the room, my eyes following the strands of string lights draped across the rafters in the peaked ceiling. Cream-colored candles float in centerpieces on each table. Soft music plays as people mingle and at first, I feel like a third wheel following Reed from table to table. He "introduces" me to people who I've already met at some point in my life, and my cheeks heat. I've loved working at the restaurant all summer, but I've never once felt this uncomfortable here. Now, with Reed parading me around like this, I feel so out of place.

"Dance with me," he says, pulling me to a small area where the tables have been cleared. A few couples are twirling across the open space and gazing into each other's eyes in a way that is far from the friendship I'm trying to keep with Reed.

I pull back on his hand. "I don't know."

"Oh, come on. It'll be fun," he says. "Better than interacting with these people."

I look around the room filled with strangers. If I have to be surrounded by people I don't remember, I'd rather not be talking to them about it.

"Okay," I agree, letting him pull me a little closer. His gentle hand rests on my narrow waist and mine on his broad shoulder. He sways us in slow circles to the music.

"Make her dance, check," he whispers in my ear.

I tilt my head back to see his smile. "You've checked off a lot of things on this list of yours this summer."

With two weeks left, I imagine saying goodbye as the last thing he'll check off.

"I'm just getting started," he says.

I was afraid of that.

CHAPTER TWENTY-SIX

SUMMER, TWO YEARS AGO

The glimmer of the August moon shimmering against the strokes of the lake one evening has me glued to the end of the dock in a peaceful state of solitude. It's rare to find myself alone these days, so I dip my bare toes in the water, sketching the lines that ripple like snakes and then fade into glass.

A familiar crash of a screen door startles me and the light on Miles's trailer shines a spotlight on him and Lexi. They're standing inches apart, his hands clasped around hers, and I turn away before I see anything even more intimate.

I've gotten in a good place with Miles as friends, but it still stings to see him kiss her. I try to push the thought of them several feet behind me out of my mind and go back to shading in the crest of the moon against the page when I hear his voice escalate.

"Why are you doing this?"

"Miles, please understand," she begs through her tears. "It's better this way."

I can't help it. The emotion in her voice has me peeking over my shoulder. Miles drop his grasp and takes a giant step back.

"Fine. Go!" he shouts, kicking the trailer door with his boot.

She clasps a hand over her mouth to cover her sobs and runs to her car. She's gone before Miles ever looks up.

He drops to a squat and scrubs his hands down his face. His heart is breaking, and my first instinct is to go comfort him. But he doesn't know I'm out here watching his very private breakup with Lexi.

Weighing my options, I pretend I wasn't here at all. It's not hard to blend into the darkness. When I look back at my sketch, it doesn't seem dark enough to mirror the weight in the air, the deafening silence all around. I shade darker strokes on everything... the water, the sky, the spot on the dock where I sit invisible.

"How long have you been out here?" his angry voice booms from behind me.

The jerk of my shoulders sends a giant black gash across the page as I lift my hand to cover my heart. "Miles, you scared me!"

"How long, Teddy?" he presses.

"Long enough to know that you could use a friend right now."

I gesture for him to sit beside me.

He sighs. "I was thinking I'd go fishing. You want to come with me?"

I stretch out my hand and watch it disappear a few feet in front of me.

"Like... night fishing?"

He laughs softly, holding out his hand to me as an invitation. "Yeah... you want to go fishing in the dark?"

I look up at him, and the light bounces off the water and hits the caramel speckles in his irises.

Do you want to hunt for tadpoles with me, Miles? flashes in my memory. I smile up at him and grip his hand as he pulls me to stand.

"Yeah, I do," I say.

I slip inside to tuck away my sketchbook, throw on a sweatshirt, and tell my parents where I'm going while Miles gets the gear from his shed. They aren't happy about it at first, but when I promise to wear a life jacket and not go too far from shore, they give in. Miles has a canoe filled with two fishing poles, a Styrofoam cup, and an extra life jacket by the time I return.

"How'd you know I'd ask for this?" I hold up the life jacket.

"I didn't, but I know your parents."

"Good thing too. It's the only reason they agreed to let me tag along." I laugh.

I slip my arms through the holes and snap the buckles down the front. Sliding onto the wooden bench, Miles strides a handful of steps into the water before he hops over the rear side. I grip the edges of the boat as it jostles with his weight, and he picks up the oar, rowing three long pulls that wades us out just deep enough for our hooks to drop a few feet into the water.

"It's kind of convenient you have a father who owns a fishing shop," I say as Miles pulls back the Styrofoam lid revealing a cup of worms.

"Yeah, it has its perks."

He finds a thick one to string on the end of my hook. Once it's attached, he hands me the fishing pole. I hold it over the dark black water and release the bail, watching it drop below the surface and drift out of sight. Miles does the same on the opposite side of the boat as I witness his lips tip in a frown.

"Do you want to talk about it?" I ask.

Man, I hope that was the right thing to say.

He stares at the water for a long time before he says, "Everyone leaves. I should know that by now. First my mom, then you, now Lexi. Everyone leaves eventually."

I feel the sting of his words in a place in my heart I haven't felt for so long. The place that always had me learning from

Miles... *I hope I don't lose my mom too. I hope I don't lose Miles too.*

"Miles, I wish I had never left," I admit. A tear cascades down my cheek, hot and heavy and burning a path in its wake.

Miles looks up at me and rushes to wipe it away with the pad of his thumb. "Wait. Teddy, I know, I'm sorry. I didn't mean that. I know you didn't have a choice. But Lexi does, and she's choosing to break up with me because she thinks it's easier this way. To do it now before we make even more memories our senior year and have a harder time letting go. She knows we want different things," he says, sounding frustrated. He's no longer denying playing a role in their goodbye.

"What *do* you want, Miles?"

He shakes his head. "I'm afraid of what I want."

"You don't have to be afraid with me," I say.

He takes a deep breath and blinks at me. "I want for one day to feel like I'm not tethered to anything. That's the part that scares me. All along I've been terrified of being left behind, when all I've ever wanted is to be taken along."

"And Lexi still wants to live on her parents' farm," I say, like I'm putting together pieces of a puzzle.

He nods. "Is it so bad that I wanted the companionship part, but not her dream part?"

"No. No one wants to be alone. But her dream isn't yours, and she did the right thing for herself letting you go if you couldn't give her that. You'll find your way. I know you will."

He offers me a sad smile. "Can I ask you something?"

"Anything."

"Did it mean something to you?"

He searches my face like he's looking for a sign that I understand him. That he won't have to fill in the part of that question he left blank.

Everything about him has always meant something to me, so it isn't until his eyes fall to my lips that I know.

"It meant everything," I whisper.

He nods as if he thought that's what I would say, and then looks away. I can't blame him. He's fresh off a break up, and I'm... well, I don't know what I am. Someone who is more confused than ever, but not about our first kiss.

The point is, neither of us is in a place for that conversation to go any further than a clarification that should have happened years ago. Maybe there will never be a right time for us. If not, I hope we'll always have Bear Lake.

I feel a gentle *tug, tug, tug* on the end of my pole and sit a little straighter. "Miles, I think I got something!"

It tugs again, and this time, he sees it too.

"Well, reel it in," he reprimands with a laugh, and I begin spinning the handle as fast as I can.

I've caught many fish before. Sometimes it's a struggle, but this one takes me two seconds to reel all the way in. A tiny little minnow, not much bigger than a tadpole, thrashes at the surface. I giggle at its size as Miles grabs my line and plucks the poor thing off the end. He transfers it to my palm, and it dances around as we grin at each other. I ease my hand back toward the water, and we both lean over the edge and watch it swim away. He grins at me and starts singing the chorus of "Fishin' in the Dark." A song that makes us both feel better in a way nothing else could.

Despite the high-pitched squeak of the front door's hinges, my parents don't even flinch when I come in from fishing. They're a heap of tangled arms and legs sprawled across the couch, the credits to a movie still climbing up the screen. I smile at the sight, reaching for the knitted afghan on the recliner across from them. It's enough to drape over their laps, but the accidental brush against my mom's arm tells me they're warm enough.

I tiptoe up the stairs to my room, leaving the light off. I draw the curtains to the top of the window frame so the light of the moon spills over the windowsill and onto my pillow before grabbing my sketchbook and flipping to the last page.

Most of my drawings begin with an idea, but without giving this one any thought, my pencil moves in a shape the size of my closed fist. A soft line runs down the center, creating two chambers. Memories from summers we spent together come pouring back, flowing through every line, every mark, every shade, every movement. It's as if my mind shuts off, my brain turning on autopilot.

I focus on what I love most, and when my pencil stills and I'm brought back to reality, a very confused heart stares back at me. A tear trickles down my cheek and splashes in the center, smudging the outline of their faces.

My mom said there'd be room to fill the empty spaces, but what I wish I'd asked her that day on my bed is if a heart can love two people at once.

CHAPTER TWENTY-SEVEN

NOW

W e sway for a full two songs until Reed freezes.
        "What are you doing here?" he asks over my
shoulder.

When I turn around, Miles is standing beside Shepard, observing the room.

"Your parents invited us," Miles says, looking from Reed to me and the place where Reed's hand rests on my waist.

Reed's eyes flash to his parents who are making the rounds with their guests.

"Enjoy your night," he says, not letting go of my hand and pulling me out toward the lit-up wraparound patio.

I look back over my shoulder to find Miles watching me, that unreadable expression I haven't seen in weeks painted across his face.

Reed walks us to the edge of the balcony overlooking the water and leans against it.

"I don't know why my parents invited him."

"Maybe to be nice?" I say, trying not to sound as irritated as I feel on the inside.

"What would be nice is if there was one place in this town I could go and not find him there. But it's Bear Lake. Everyone is everywhere all the time."

"Why does it have to ruin your night?" I ask, trying to get him to look at me. "Look, he's not even out here. He's hanging out with his dad."

Reed looks inside to see Shep and Miles engaged in a conversation with a couple of older gentlemen. His body relaxes.

As we both tip against the wrought-iron railing, I feel the energy shift between us. Maybe it's the way he notices the chill in the air sparking goose bumps against my skin that encourages him to lean closer to me. To share his warmth.

"There's something on my list I haven't done with you yet," he whispers, and I learn I was wrong before. He's not about to say goodbye.

When I spin back around, he's staring at me, lost in my eyes.

"What's that?" I swallow as a bundle of nerves weaves a knot in the base of my throat.

Then he leans in and kisses me. Soft and sweet like he has all the time in the world to drink it in. He pulls away just enough to whisper, "Kiss her, check." Then he's dipping in for another kiss.

It's not the sound of a barstool tumbling over on a hardwood floor that has us jerking apart. It's me.

A flash of red lips, the grey of an overcast sky, the feel of grass beneath my fingertips, and the devastated face of Miles Bishop as he catches my first kiss with Reed. A memory, so crystal clear it's like it was downloaded into my mind. As if it's always been there—part of me that nothing could have erased forever.

I see Miles reaching to pick up the barstool one second and gone the next.

I panic, a feeling of devastation clutching at my heart when I can't find him, and Reed notices.

"Teddy, what's wrong?"

"I'm sorry, I have to go," I say. Gripping the hem of my dress, I cut through the crowd of people, looking for Miles. I knock into several shoulders, apologizing in my wake. The last people I see are Reed's parents, who take one glance at me and look back to where their son is crumpled over the railing, watching me run out of his life for a second time.

When I make it to the parking lot, I spin in circles in search of his truck, but it's already gone. I yank off my heels and start to run. I run as hard and as fast as I can toward our cabin, my lungs feeling like they're going to implode with each stride I take. Hot tears streak my cheeks as memories of Miles and me as kids rush back like an old family movie.

He's holding my hand at his dad's shop. We're sharing our first kiss along the side of the road. I'm walking away from him, and then he's kissing her. Reed's there for me when I'm left devastated and needing a friend. He's making me laugh and doing nothing wrong but falling in love with someone who doesn't love him back. I'm drowning in memories a handful of yards down the main street on the edge of the road when the hatchback pulls up beside me.

My mom leans out the window and calls, "Get in."

I need to keep running, but I don't know if I'm still running away from the memories now or toward them.

Ones with my parents come rushing back too. My mom sick; my dad scared. *And Cozy.*

I've never needed my best friend more than I do right now.

"*I promise I didn't want to do anything or be anything that would disappoint you,*" I hear the voice in my head telling my parents, "*and yet that's all I've been doing.*"

I wish I could say it out loud.

I can't imagine they'll support me in this... running toward Miles. But they're here now, and they're offering their help, and my lungs are screaming to say yes. I pull back on the handle and collapse in a heap in the back seat. My dad starts to pull away as I quake against the headrest.

"Stop the car, Arch," my mom demands. She wrestles her dress over the center console. When she settles in beside me, he keeps driving, and she holds me in her arms, rocking me back and forth like an infant.

"You're a wildflower," she whispers, and the fourteen-year-old version of myself brokenhearted and weeping in her arms flashes through my mind. She comforts me like I'm the only thing that matters to her, and I realize how wrong I've been in pushing her away. I need my mom.

She offers to help me inside when we get back to the cabin, but she knows I won't say yes. She gives me an understanding nod, watching as I pick myself up and rush to the edge of the dock where my first love hurts because of me.

I need to tell him.

When I trip and fall on my knees on the first plank, he stands and sprints for me, lifting me in his arms.

"Teddy, are you okay?" he gasps, and I cling to his shirt.

"I remember," I cry.

His arms stiffen around me. "You remember what?"

I lift my eyes so that when I tell him, he won't just hear it, he'll see it too. It's written all over my face.

"You remember what, Teddy?" he repeats, cradling my face in his hands and brushing the tears away with his fingertips.

"You," I breathe. "I remember you."

And then I kiss him. I kiss him in the way my heart has wanted to for the last five years of my life. I kiss him for that ten-year-old version of me who loved the way his bucket hat flopped over his eyes. I kiss him for the fourteen-year-old girl who was just trying to figure out what it meant when she missed him for four summers as more than a friend. I kiss him for the girl who didn't want that first kiss to ever end and the one who lost her first love because she was stupid and selfish and couldn't tell him how she felt. But most of all, I kiss him for the me now. The one who isn't scared to live in the moment. Because he taught me that. He made me feel like I didn't have to remember. I don't even have to run to what's next. I can just live.

So, we live. Together. In this moment, like it will last a lifetime.

CHAPTER TWENTY-EIGHT

SUMMER, ONE YEAR AGO

I grip my hair in a fisted heap. "Go any faster and my parents will find a way to fuse their headlights to our bumper."

Cozy abandons the steering wheel, drawing a pair of over-sized Ray-Bans down the bridge of her nose and wagging her eyebrows at me. "We wouldn't want that, now would we?"

Her graduation present lurches forward at the same time her fingers wiggle out the sunroof.

Honk.

My phone dings in the palm of my hand, and I swipe to view the message.

I didn't agree to a Nascar audition! A canary yellow Mini Cooper is a billboard on this road. Don't make me regret your month-long invitation to Cozy.

I chew on the ends of my worn nails before flipping the notifications to silent.

"How are you feeling about the breakup?" I ask, changing the subject.

Cozy shakes her head. "Nope. Prom sucks. Peter sucks. I don't want to talk about him when we can be talking about your awaiting love interests."

I groan and tuck my feet against the dash. "Don't remind me."

"No, it's good! You've lived *the summer of boy meets girl* and *the summer of boy kisses girl*, and then it was *the summer of boy breaks girl's heart,* and finally, *the summer of girl dates boy's best friend.* I want to know what this one's gonna be!"

"How about *the summer of girl graduating and living it up with her best friend.*"

"Hell yes!" Cozy screams, throwing both hands in the air.

Honk.

Great. My parents are sending Cozy packing the moment this vehicle stops.

One, two, three, I count, calming my jittery heart. When I've made it to a hundred, I count the number of times Cozy says the word cute (fifteen) while winding around the lake through Garden City.

Not two minutes in the cabin driveway, my past summers find me. Reed runs for me first, sweeping me into an air-spinning hug. My face plants against the dip of his tank top, and his bronzed skin makes mine look like a fluorescent lightbulb that's been rolled in a layer of speckled sand.

"You're really here," he says. "I don't have to text you to ask about your day anymore."

"Or about my art class," I add as he sets me on my feet.

He raises his arms above his head. "I don't want to know."

I giggle. "I told you... high school art is nothing like in *Titanic.*"

My knees bow at the sight of that damn dimple in his cheek.

"Well, now I know what all the fuss is about," Cozy interrupts. She scrolls Reed's body and then leans in to hug him.

"Hi," Miles says with a grin that could split the sky in half. He's different. More content than I've seen him in a long time, I think. He squeezes me around the shoulders.

"Hi back," I say.

A hand peels me away from him, and he staggers backward with the tackle of Cozy's bear hug.

"Wow, you are friendly," he says.

"I like them already!" Cozy squeals before pushing off Miles and running toward the water. She throws her arms wide with a spin, her chin tilted to the sky. "And now I get why you never wanted to leave. This place is amazing!"

"Yeah," all three of us say in one unified sigh.

She pulls her iPhone from her pocket and records a panoramic video starting with the lake and ending with the three of us.

"So, what's first? Do we climb the oak tree? Fish off the dock? Karaoke at Maverick's?"

"Are you sure she's never been here before?" Reed jokes.

"She's my best friend. I tell her a lot, okay?"

"Don't worry, pretty boy. All good things," Cozy says. She stuffs her phone back in her pocket and skips over to us, tapping Reed on the shoulder at the same time Miles says, "I have an idea."

Somewhere along the spectrum of Antarctica and the polar ice caps of Greenland registers the temperature of the Minnetonka Caves. The warmest thing Cozy and I packed for a summer beach town are a pair of crewneck sweatshirts that do very little to alleviate the chatter of our teeth. Miles leads us through a dome-shaped opening much smaller than the initial one we went through. The walls feel closer somehow. Cozy follows behind him, frowning at the lack of cell service bars on her phone screen. A tour guide leads us through the cave, rattling on an impressive number of facts about stalagmites and stalactites.

With their backs to us, I feel Reed's lips against my ear first, then his breath hot on my skin as he says, "For warmth's sake." He nets his fingers with mine, and a tingling blooms in the palm of my hand. "I missed you," he adds.

I smile up at him. "I missed you too."

With not a lot of room to move or air to breathe, I'm pressed against his side, surrounded by the scent of him—something woodsy with a hint of cinnamon.

"I was thinking this could be our summer," he whispers. When he sweeps his thumb back and forth over my knuckle, I shiver. "Will you be my girlfriend?"

It doesn't make sense, two opposing feelings, but I freeze as my heart speeds up. *I like him.* I like the way he makes me feel and the humor that we share. I like the dimple of his smile and the thoughtfulness of his actions. I like that I can be myself around him.

But at the same time, he flirts with everyone and airs on the side of arrogant sometimes. *What if he hurts me?* I don't know why I feel the need to weigh a pro and con list with him when all he's ever given me is every reason to trust that he's the right person for me.

My attention flashes to Miles, who stares in wonder at a bunch of rocks like he's seeing them for the first time. Then I think, *Maybe what scares me is that I'll be the one to hurt him.* But Miles and I have been "just friends" for more than two summers now, and whether he's with Lexi or not, it feels time that I let him go.

Without more thought, I agree.

Reed's eyes drop to my lips like he wants to kiss me, but then thinks better of it. It would be our first kiss in a cave full of people.

I motion to Miles running his fingertips along the jagged edges of a stalactite as the tour guide explains their texture, then to Cozy, who scrolls her phone next to him.

"Do you think we can keep it between us for now? Just until I get the chance to tell them."

Reed lets go of my hand before anyone else can see, and relief washes over me.

"I can do that."

The tour lasts thirty minutes, and as we exit the limestone cave through the same formation we came in, Cozy says, "Thank goodness we're done with that!"

"I'm sorry if it was boring," Miles says. "I've always wanted to go."

"I think that would have been cooler when we were like, ten." Reed laughs.

It's obvious that I'm the only one who sees the change in Miles. He's stepping outside his comfort zone and doing things for himself. I hate that he's apologizing for something that made him so happy.

"My first activity as a tourism influencer, and all I have to show for it are some rocks in my hair," Cozy complains.

"I thought you said your contract didn't start until you leave here?" I question.

"It doesn't. But I agreed to showcase a portfolio of my work with the eDreams team before becoming the voice of their 20 European Countries in 20 Months campaign. I just wanted to have the best content I could. It's a dream opportunity for me."

"Well, I liked it," I say to Miles, and he beams at me. Then I turn to Cozy. "You still have several weeks left to capture whatever you need, but I'm sure Bear Lake will pale in comparison to where you're headed next."

"Where *we're* headed next," she emphasizes. "I'm not giving up on convincing you to come with me." Then she spins to face

Reed. "*Please* tell me you're the one planning what we're doing next and that it's video-worthy."

⁓

A campout. That's what Reed planned. My parents agreed, so long as we sleep in separate tents. It was Cozy's bright idea to challenge the guys to a tent set-up race—winner gets the insulated sleeping bags. She's propped her phone in the nearest tree branch to record the whole thing. Considering I'm an infant when it comes to the cold, I scream at Cozy to hurry up as she struggles to wedge a broken pole through the tent tabs.

"Just hold the broken part flat. Stop bending it," I instruct warily.

"I'm trying! This isn't a fair race when we've been given shotty parts," she complains.

I steal a glance at the guys. Seventy-five percent of their tent stands to our one. Cozy should have never made this bet with a bunch of Boy Scouts.

"There!" she shouts.

The pole is far enough through the loop that it pokes out the other side, and I'm able to pull it through the rest of the way. I thread it through two more loops on my side before staking it in the ground.

"Done!" Reed yells, high-fiving Miles, and Cozy collapses to the ground on her back in defeat. I wipe the perspiration that accumulated on my forehead from all the straining and stress. Shielding the sun from her eyes, we all gather over Cozy's body.

"Reed, I'll pay you five bucks to use the sleeping bags," she gasps.

An hour later, we say good night to the guys and crawl in

our tent. Minutes after her video uploads, Cozy is snoring in the downy comfort of her mummy bag.

Not me. There's a circle of uncovered netting at the top of our tent just large enough to see a smattering of stars. They flicker and twinkle in time with the crackle of the dwindling campfire outside. I don't know how long I lie there before I give up on sleep altogether. I wrap the striped blanket I stole off the end of my bed around my shoulders for warmth and unzip the tent. The fire is nothing more than ashes now, but the moon is bright enough to light a path toward the end of the dock where I go to sit.

"Can't sleep?" a voice asks from behind me.

I look up to see Miles in a pair of gym shorts and a T-shirt looming over me.

I shake my head.

"Me neither," he says, sitting down beside me.

A water skipper skims the surface in front of us, performing an ice-skating dance that would be comical if it were any other creature.

"So, Cozy's pretty entertaining," Miles says.

"Yeah, she is." I laugh just thinking about her dramatic sigh as she slipped into her paid-for sleeping bag. "But she's a great friend."

"I can tell."

I should tell him about Reed, but this is the first moment we've had alone since the end of last summer. What I want to talk about instead has nothing to do with Reed and me.

"I know we texted each other a few times but I never did ask you... how was your senior year?"

"Oh, it... wasn't my favorite," he admits. "But the ending was good."

"When you threw your cap in the air?"

He looks at me. "How did you know?"

"Because you're my best friend. And we're similar in a lot of ways. Also, because it was my favorite part too."

The corners of Miles's mouth lift. Then he grips the edge of the dock with his palms and looks out over the water.

"She married Duncan."

"Duncan?" I gasp. "As in, cowboy karaoke announcer Duncan?"

"That's the one. They eloped at the town courthouse the day after graduation."

"Well, that was... fast."

He shakes his head. "Not for Lexi. She was clear about what she wanted from the beginning, and she found it."

"Wasn't he like ten years older than us?"

He chuckles. "Fifteen."

"Are you okay?"

He turns his head to face me and smiles.

I knew there was something different about him this summer, something lighter, and I'm seeing it now.

"I am," he says.

"Does that mean you know what you want now?" I ask, feeling hopeful that Miles will finally get to do something for himself.

He nods, gazing into my eyes. When he swallows, I swallow. He leans against the palm of his right hand, the one on the dock between our thighs. We're closer than we've been in a very long time, and he's not looking away. Instead, he's got this look in his eye that's open and vulnerable and honest. I'm unable to breathe with his lips inches from mine, unable to think, unsure of how to stop.

"Miles wait..."

Dropping my face so our foreheads touch, I place my hand over the top of his pounding heart. I pull back far enough to see confusion swim in his eyes, and it kills me knowing I'm about to crush him.

"Reed asked me to be his girlfriend."

I get it out before I have the chance to take it back, because I can't take it back. I already committed to giving this summer a shot with Reed.

"When?" He gapes at me, righting himself and making the space grow larger between our bodies.

"The Minnetonka Caves."

"Oh."

Miles squints at his reflection in the water as if he's reading an ancient text written across his features that he can't decipher.

"Miles."

"I'm too late."

He sweeps a hand through his hair as he stands, and he studies the ground near his feet while I stand too.

"No, you know what..." He grips on to my shaking hands, clasping them close to his chest.

"Teddy, I love you. I've loved you from the moment you came toppling down this dock with a pail in your hand and a missing tooth in your smile. I've loved you when I've been at my worst, when I lost my mom, and every moment at my best. I let my pride get in the way when you left that summer after we kissed. I wanted you to say it meant as much to you as it did to me, but I get why you didn't. You couldn't promise you wouldn't leave me behind because it wasn't your choice at the time. I know you didn't want to leave back then. And I was wrong to date Lexi. She was around when you couldn't be, which wasn't a fair comparison. But now, with this summer being different, no school to have to go back to... I just thought it was finally our time. But I waited too long. I waited too long to tell you I love you. I always have, and I always will."

Miles doesn't even give me the chance to respond. My

fingertips slip through his, and he spins on his heels and walks away. He leaves me alone on our dock with no more chances for tomorrow.

CHAPTER TWENTY-NINE

NOW

W e crash into each other. Miles sweeps my feet off the ground and carries me toward the bunkhouse. My legs encircle his waist and I grip the nape of his neck. He fumbles with the handle, so I drag open the glass door with my foot. He deposits my feet on the linoleum floor and pushes me up against the wall next to the bunkbed. There's plenty of space to move around but not an inch separates our bodies. My lips part and his tongue sweeps through my mouth, pulling a whimper from the base of my throat. He drags his hands down my arms and threads our fingers together.

"Teddy," he groans. "I've wanted this for so long." His lips fuse to my neck, leaving a trail of warm kisses to my shoulder.

My breathing stops as his lips rest just above my exposed collarbone. When he presses against me, I can feel all of him.

"Me too," I say.

He plants another feather-light kiss against my chest, and all I want is for him to go lower, to feel him closer. I reach behind me. My fingers close around the zipper of my dress when he stops me.

"Wait. We don't have to do this," he says. "I didn't mean—"

"I know what you meant. I want to," I say.

"But I wasn't expecting... I mean, I don't have..."

I drop my hands to my sides. "Oh."

He cradles my face. "But I can go get one, if you're sure."

I nod. "I've never been more sure about anything."

He weaves his fingers into the curls of my hair, leaving me with a breathless kiss, before he pulls away.

"I'll be right back then," he says.

I watch him disappear through the sliding door and breathe a sigh of relief as my head fights to catch up to my heart. I slide my back down the drywall, and chiffon fabric pools at my feet.

The longer he takes the higher the brick tower of nerves build, too tall to fit in the small space of my chest.

I've never done this before. *What if he has, and I don't measure up?*

I close my eyes and listen for a sound to distract me. It's the brush of the oak tree leaves I hear first. After the accident, I used to lie on my bed and listen to them rustle, longing for the day when I could climb them instead of just pretending.

Those same limbs now wave in the wind. The light on the porch reflects off them and casts dancing shadows on the wall by the bed. That same yearning comes back, but it's for a different reason this time. Not for what I can't have, but what I can.

A tall figure jogs across the lawn, and I jump to my feet.

"Sorry that took me so long," Miles says, fumbling his way through the sliding door.

My eyes flit to the foil wrapper tucked in his palm, and my hands start to shake at the sight of it. I *want* to do this, but I'm also terrified of being this vulnerable with another person.

Miles reaches for the comforter on the bottom bunk, jerking it from where it's tucked in. "Are you cold?"

He wraps me up in it and runs his big hands up and down the backs of my arms.

"I think just nervous," I stutter, dropping my gaze to the floor.

He presses a kiss to my forehead and holds me until my body calms down.

"I'm nervous, too," he says.

I jolt my head up to look into his eyes. "You are?"

He palms my face, and a look of disbelief knits his eyebrows together. "Of course I am."

My shoulders sag. "Then we can be nervous together?"

He pulls back further and tips his head at an angle. His eyes bounce over every plane of my face. "I meant what I said; we don't have to do this tonight. Just getting to hold you like this will always be enough for me."

He tucks me under his chin, and I melt against him. That gesture alone makes me feel safer than anything I've ever experienced. I could drown in the shelter of his arms.

Standing on my tiptoes, I breathe into the collar of his shirt. It's open just enough that the top of his chest peeks through, and I place a kiss there. Feeling braver, I nudge my nose against his bare skin, drawing the neckline of his dress shirt a little lower, planting another kiss below his sternum.

"You smell good." I sigh. *Like spearmint gum.*

He drops the blanket from around me and runs his hands up the back of my dress until they tunnel in my hair.

"You feel good," he whispers in my ear. His hand fists in the tangle as he kisses me again, taking his time.

I'm trembling when I feel him grip the zipper on the back of my dress, but he captures my stare. I nod in approval as he draws it from my upper back, down my spine, to the edge of my panties. I feel him skate his fingertips back up the sides of my arms and stop as his right hand slinks beneath the strap of shimmering fabric, dropping it down my side.

The dress falls in a heap at my feet.

A puff of an exhale escapes his lips as he gazes down at my bare chest. "You are so beautiful."

His eyes lift to meet mine again. "You always have been. The brightest light in my orbit, Teddy. The only thing that I see."

I blush and bite my lip to keep from grinning. I reach for the buttons on his shirt next, undoing them one at a time. Slipping my hands beneath the fabric and running my fingers over the hard ridges of his chest, he shudders.

There were so many times I wanted to this, to touch him when his shirt wasn't on. Now, I get to, and it all feels like a dream I don't want to ever wake up from.

I rest my hands over his heart, feeling its steady beat, and a part of me wants them to stay like that. They belong there. But an even bigger part of me wants his shirt to meet my dress on the floor.

I take my time working it over his shoulders, feeling the places where his hard lines meet his soft ones. He unfastens the button on his pants, then slides down the zipper, the sound filling the tight space. When we're both left in nothing but our underwear, he guides me by the small of my back to the edge of the bunkbed and lays me on top of it with enough room so he can fit beside me.

"Tell me this is real," he says. "Tell me I'm gonna wake up tomorrow, and you're still gonna be here." His desperate eyes search my face.

"I'm here," I say, covering his heart with the palm of my hand again so he'll feel it, *believe* it. "I'll always be here."

I feel his touch lower from the place where it seared my neck, down my chest, until he's cupping one of my breasts in the palm of his hand. His mouth replaces it, and I forget to breathe. He works my underwear down my legs, pulling them free, before I reach for his. I get them halfway down his thighs before he works them the rest of the way. As we explore each other with nothing left separating us, a mountain of sensations crest and fall over and over again.

I don't hear the condom wrapper tearing or see when he slides it on. I just feel him push inside of me. It burns at first, and he stops when I stiffen.

"Are you okay? I don't know what I'm doing."

His voice is quivering.

"You don't?"

"Of course not. It's always been you for me," he says.

Searching beyond the chocolate brown of his eyes, I find the reason it's always been *him* for *me*. It's taken loving more than one person in my life for me to know that when you give your heart to someone and put their needs above your own, it comes at a risk of losing a part of yourself. The part that serves to protect who you are at your core.

But with Miles, I don't lose myself in him at all, I find *me*. I find my reason to live. I find where I belong.

I pull him in to kiss me, and he groans when he pushes inside of me a second time. This time it doesn't hurt as much. We fumble through awkward positioning and clumsy movements, but we never stop. Neither one of us slows down for a single second. We dive headfirst into the most intimate moment you can share with another person, and I discover I was wrong before. No amount of thrill-seeking can ever compare to this.

Loving him sets me free.

A beam of golden light shining through the glass doors wakes me. Sprawled out on my stomach with my arms stretched like a starfish, I lift my head.

I scrub my eyes as the bunkhouse walls drift into focus, along with the memories of last night... the gentle hands that caressed every part of me, the strangled sound of Miles's voice as he told me how beautiful I was.

I remembered him.

I melt back into the sheets in a happy yawn until my hand feels nothing but the empty pillow next to me, and I shoot up. Without the sheets pressed to my ear, a muffled call echoes from outside.

"Teddy? Teddy?"

My parents!

I wrench my dress from the floor, shimmying it up my waist and over my shoulder. In one swift movement, I zip up the back and barrel out of the sliding glass door. I shield my eyes with my arm, scanning the yard.

Miles's truck is gone.

"Teddy? Teddy?" my parents call again.

I leap over my abandoned shoes in the grass and bound up the cabin steps.

"I'm here," I call.

My parents halt their rush toward the back door. There's a blanket tucked under my mom's arm and a pair of keys dangling from my dad's hand.

"There you are! When we got the call and couldn't find you, we thought you'd already be at the hospital."

I rush toward them. "What hospital? What are you talking about?"

Fear drips through my veins like an IV with each blink of my parents' stunned eyes.

"You haven't heard?" my dad asks.

"Haven't heard what?"

"It's Shepard."

I gasp. *If something is wrong with his dad, Miles won't be okay.*

"Come with us."

The entire drive to the emergency department, I picture Miles in an isolated, sterile room, crumpled in a ball at his dad's bedside. He's dying inside over a dozen different tubes tethered to his dad's body, and it's enough to make me jump out of the moving car the second we reach the parking lot. My parents scream, but I don't care. All I can think about is getting to him.

I'm still barefoot, racing through the entrance of Bear Lake Memorial Emergency Department, when I'm met with an empty receptionist desk. I ding the obnoxious gold bell on the corner thirty-six times before a nurse in a pair of black scrubs approaches the counter.

"Sorry for the wait, ma'am. We're short-staffed today. Can I help you?"

"I'm looking for Shepard Bishop. He was brought in... well, I don't know when he was brought in, but sometime between the hours of midnight and now, and I *need* to find him. Can you tell me anything? Please... I just need to know he's okay." *For Miles*, I think.

"Woah, woah, woah. Slow down," she says, easing her hand out on the countertop. "Are you family?"

"Yes!" I lie without thinking. "His daughter."

I can't possibly tell this woman the complicated truth... *you see, I'm not his daughter. More like his neighbor. Hopefully his son's soon-to-be girlfriend? That's close enough to family, right?* It *has* to be.

"Okay, Ms. Bishop," she assumes. "He's stable, and in room three. You can go right through there."

"Thank you!" I holler behind me, shoving through the double doors and down a drawn-out hallway.

I come to a stop, facing the metal number *three* drilled into the doorway. There's a pane of glass to the right where the curtain is drawn just beyond it. I knock, then push it open and pull back at the curtain. Miles is asleep with his head on the bed, holding his father's hand. He startles awake and lifts his weary eyes to the bright beam of light leaking in from the hallway. He rubs his eyelids with the backs of his hands, sitting a little taller as I slip inside and close the door behind me.

He squints, adjusting his eyes to the now-dim light.

"Teddy?"

His voice sounds raw. Thick red rings rim his eyes.

I run to him, throw my arms around his neck.

"Miles, what happened?"

I watch his throat bob. "I went home this morning to bring you breakfast in bed, and I found him"—he looks up at me and wrings his hands, the words coming out stilted as he rushes to explain—"collapsed on the kitchen floor." His chest heaves. "I shouldn't have left him, Teddy." Then he pushes away from my arms.

His words feel like a slap to the face, and my heart breaks. *I shouldn't have left him for you* is what he means. He's pushing me away again, and I can't stop him.

He starts to cry, and no matter how he does or doesn't feel about me, not even our height difference can keep me from letting him fall into me. I hold on to him while he cries on my shoulder. I stay.

"What's all the fuss about," a voice croaks, and we pull apart just as Shep opens his eyes.

"You're awake," Miles gasps, rushing to his dad's side.

"Course I'm awake. And hungry too. Any chance this place has some bacon?"

"I said the same thing," my dad jokes from the doorway as he and my mom enter the room.

"Well, at least someone here has some sense about them." Shep cackles. "What's with the party?"

Miles touches Shep's arm. "Dad, I found you collapsed this morning. Do you remember falling?"

Shepard pushes on his temple like he'll conjure the memory into existence. I remember so many times when I tried to do the very same thing.

"Can't say I do," he admits, and then groans when he tries to move. "But I feel like it. Must have had one wild night at that Bear Shore party." He chuckles again, deep and hoarse.

"Dad, it's not funny," Miles says, sounding pissed.

I reach out to hold his hand and comfort him.

"You were practically gone when I found you. Your blood sugar was so low you lost consciousness. How could you be so reckless?"

"Okay, everyone. It's time to give the man some space," a nurse says, pushing her way past the lot of us to get to Shepard.

"I like you already," he says to her as she slips a blood pressure cuff on his arm.

I note her black scrubs and French braid. She's the same nurse who let me back here.

"Well, I hope not *too* much, because I don't want to have to see you in here again in the same condition you came in," she scolds. "I'm assuming you're not all who you say you are."

She lifts an eyebrow in my direction as I cling to Miles's hand. "Blood relatives are the only ones allowed in this room right now."

I don't want to leave him here by himself, but it looks like I don't have a choice.

"We'll be waiting in the lobby," I say to Miles, leaning in to kiss his cheek.

He nods and lets go of my hand. As I'm ushered out the door, I watch him scrub a hand down his face and wear track marks in two straight lines on the floor while the nurse tends to his dad. My parents pull me in between them and wrap their arms around my shoulders.

"So, if I was Shepard's brother, that must make you Miles's cousin?" my dad teases.

I cringe. "Sister, actually."

He chuckles. "Yeah, that wouldn't fly in the state of Idaho."

When we push through the double doors, the lobby is no longer empty. There's a corner chair taken, a mess of sandy brown curls resting in a pair of large hands. When he hears the doors shut, he lifts his head and stands. Reed doesn't look in any better shape than Miles did.

"We'll be over here if you need us," my mom says, letting her arm fall away from me.

I nod.

Reed takes in the dress I was wearing when I left him on that balcony last night, but his face doesn't register any form of surprise. So much has changed since I last saw him. So many questions have been answered. But there are gaps in my memory surrounding the accident. What exactly happened, I still don't know.

"How is he?" he croaks.

"Well, he still has his humor intact, that's for sure." I huff out a chuckle. "But I think he's going to be okay."

"Sounds like Shepard." Reed sighs. Then he runs his fingers through his disheveled curls. "Teddy, I—"

"Let me start," I say, turning to face him. I pull at his hands so he'll sit down with me. He can't be standing when I confess what I need to say next.

"I shouldn't have kissed you."

I expect to see the sting in his eyes, but I see nothing but recognition.

"You remembered, didn't you. The first time we..."

I nod, feeling the pain from that movement in the depths of my soul. I don't want to hurt Reed. I've never wanted to hurt anyone in all of this, but I don't want to lie to him anymore either. He deserves so much more than that.

"I should have told you, right then and there. I'm sorry. I wasn't thinking when I ran off."

"Because you love him," he states. "You've always loved him."

My face pinches in anguish. "But, Reed, I want to still be friends," I say, reaching for his hand. But he grips mine and sets it back in my lap.

"Don't you get it, Teddy? I *can't* just be your friend. I told you that. I don't know *how*."

As much as it hurts to hear, I *do* get it. Because I can't just be friends with Miles. I wouldn't know how.

I think back on all the moments Reed and I shared this summer... the boat, the CD, LaBeau's. Whether he realized it or not, he was trying to get me to remember him just as much as everyone else in my life.

"If you can't be friends with me, Reed, please be friends with Miles. The more people helping him in his life right now, the better. He needs you."

He nods. "He's a good guy, Teddy."

Fresh tears prick my vision.

"You know he came to see me at the restaurant at the start of summer?"

A memory of running into Miles flashes in my mind.

"He came to apologize. He told me he wants you to be happy, whether or not it's with him. That if there was one person in this world he trusted to take care of you, it was me."

His voice cracks on the last word. "I've treated him like shit all summer after that apology, because I was still so mad at him for —" He stops himself. "All I did was drive you both away."

He collapses his head in his lap, and I can't let him hurt alone anymore. I wrap my arms around his shoulders, and he leans his head against my legs as he cries silent tears. We stay that way for a long time, knowing that when we let go, it's good-bye. I don't know how I ever forgot Reed. Now I'll know what it's like to never forget him again.

That sketch that I've looked at at least a hundred times this summer finally makes sense. It was inevitable that I'd have to choose one of them. But even after giving my heart to Miles, there will always be a part of it that belongs to Reed Morgan.

The doctor monitored Shepard until his blood sugar levels stabilized for twenty-four hours, then sent him home. My dad had to carry me out of the waiting room after I fell asleep on one of the benches, and I woke up in my own bed feeling empty.

"Are you doing okay, Teddy Bear?" my dad asks as both my parents climb in on either side of me. They drape their arms around me like a support blanket, holding me up both physically and emotionally.

If they would have asked me that question any time in the last year, I would have said yes. Even when I wasn't.

I used to tell them everything, take their advice when they offered it, and follow their example as they set it. But along the way I stopped trusting them altogether. I think I tried to be strong for them, hoping if *I* was their bedrock, they would finally believe I was okay. I was never as good at it as I thought I was, or they wouldn't have spent all summer asking that same question. I've been pretending to have it together for so long now that I've forgotten how to need them. It's grown too heavy, and I can't carry the weight of it anymore. I feel tears prick the corners of my eyes, but I don't let them fall. Not yet.

"At the beginning of the summer, I believed it would take leaving this place, leaving you, to find myself again. I believed I would spend a lifetime disappointing you if I didn't."

"Oh, Theodora. We are more proud of you than we've ever been. We've watched you work to heal from a very difficult thing, and we can't imagine what that has been like for you. It's a lot. We didn't care if you never remembered sweetheart; we just want you to be happy. *That's* the part of you we've been missing and were fighting to get back. I'm sorry we've made you feel this way all this time."

For the first time since the accident, I feel seen by the two people who love me the most. My happiness *is* what I've been missing, and I think I found it.

I have to talk to Miles.

I monitor the trailer until a rust-colored truck I don't recognize rumbles down the driveway and into the usual parking tracks. A disgruntled Shepard rides in the passenger seat and an all salt, no pepper version of him drives the old two-toned Ford Ranger. They share the same long sloping nose, but this other man sports a jovial expression to go with it.

Shep spots me before I can retreat into the bunkhouse. I've been longing to climb into those sheets in hopes they still smell like Miles.

"Coming to check on me again?" Shep calls through a rolled-down window.

"Oh, hey, Shep. Not exactly," I blurt without thinking.

He pushes open the door and meanders out onto the grass. "Finally! Someone not worried about me for a change.

"No, I am," I backtrack. "I hope you're feeling better?"

Had I been Miles, he wouldn't have appreciated the worry, but he smiles and says, "Thanks darlin'. This is my father, Artemis Shepard."

The man tips his cowboy hat toward me and lifts his chin, revealing a handlebar mustache.

I wave. "It's nice to meet you."

"I take it you're looking for a certain moody broody sort?" Artemis asks with a hearty grin. "He took off after his dad here was discharged. Can't say I know where he went though."

I nod, disappointed. "Thanks. Good to see you upright again, Shep."

I turn and start back toward the cabin.

"Teddy," Shep calls. "My boy is lucky to have you. Don't give up on him, okay?"

He doesn't wait for me to agree. He follows his dad up the trailer steps and shuts the door.

Every muscle in my body groans in protest as I traverse my own cabin steps. I'd like to just collapse on them, but I want to be alone. When I fall back on my bed, my arm smacks into a hardbound cover. Reaching across my body, I pull it from beneath me and hold it in the air like an accordion over my face. I flip it open to the first page... the moment that inspired me to a put pencil to paper and sketch again. The pages, once empty—a perfect portrayal of my life at the start of the summer—now burst with color. I fan them to the last empty one and sketch until my fingers cramp. Until I know where to find him.

⁓ ꭢ~

I've never been to Bloomington Lake in the evening as the sun sets. Instead of a blanket of warm amber light across the water, cotton candy clouds blot the horizon over a swirl of creamsicle hues. He's wedged between two knobby tree roots, bunched in a tight ball next to the rope swing. Even from several dozen feet away, I see a glistening trail streak his cheek.

I cut across the floating log, through the tall grass, and down toward the water. While he doesn't acknowledge any change around him, he must know I'm here. I can't escape his periphery from this position, and I don't want to. The grass has grown taller, and I smooth it down with my hand before sitting on top of it.

"I thought I'd find you here," I say.

It's minutes before he says something, but I'm not prepared for it when he does.

"It was me," he whispers through choked tears.

"The person who left me all alone in bed this morning? I know," I tease, but Miles doesn't find my joke funny.

He starts thrashing his head back and forth. "You don't remember that part, do you?"

"Remember what part?" I question, but I can feel my throat closing off. It's getting harder to breathe every time I inhale because there's only one part of my life I still can't remember.

"I caused the accident," he says.

I blink, staring at him, stunned.

"It was me," Miles whimpers.

He was right. I didn't remember that part.

The sun bleats through the opening in the ceiling of our tent, waking me around six. There's a dull ache behind the puffy rims of my eyes. I've never felt more conflicted than I do right now. My heart waited years to hear Miles say that he loves me, and of course, it had to come the day after I agreed to be in a relationship with Reed.

Cozy yawns and stretches her arms above her sleeping bag. "Best five bucks I ever spent."

"Remind me never to let you enter another bet again," I gripe.

She props herself up on her elbows. "Why?! I think I did well for myself, thank you very much."

"Okay, touché to the sleeping bags. They are way cozier, no pun intended, than the ground would have ever been."

Cozy flashes me a pleased smile.

"You're only here a few short weeks, what else do you want to experience while in Bear Lake?"

She smirks at me. "I want to know what you were doing with a certain guy after curfew last night."

My eyebrows touch my hairline. "I don't know what you're talking about."

I jerk my gaze to my unfurled sleeping bag, then begin rolling it up like a marshmallow so it will fit in the cocoon-sized bag it came in. It's a struggle that takes my entire body weight.

"That is the guiltiest thing you could have said. Spill it, woman!"

"Shh, keep your voice down!" I look over my shoulder through a shadow-transparent tent as if I'll see the outline of the very people I don't want listening in on this conversation.

I punch the sleeping bag with each roll, gripping it tighter and tighter. Just as I'm about to reach the end, I pounce on top of it as it all unravels. I grunt and toss it aside, slapping my hands on my knees.

"That good, huh?" Cozy jokes.

"Miles told me he loves me."

"What?! Wow, I did not see that coming."

"I know. It's been three years since that kiss."

"Just because the guy hasn't touched you in forever doesn't discount the way he looks at you. I don't know how Reed is oblivious to it, but I sure see it. How do you feel?"

"There's something else," I admit.

"There's more?! Why the hell did you not wake me up last night?!"

"I wanted you to get your money's worth." I wink at her. "And because Reed asked me to be his girlfriend at the caves the other day, and I didn't know what to do, so I said yes." I cringe.

"How is it that you only come here three months out of the year, and you have not *one*, but *two* hot guys hanging around waiting for your return?"

"Ugh, it's the worst," I groan.

"Yeah, poor you. Such a pity," she mocks, rolling her

sleeping bag with ease and tucking it in a succinct roll back in the carrying bag like it never left.

I take a deep breath and attempt round two of martial arts on my own sleeping bag.

"Let me help you with that," she offers.

I toss the damn thing in her lap. "Be my guest."

"What are you going to do?" She curls the sleeping bag in four swift strokes and shimmies it into the bag.

I gape at her. "You're wildly gifted at that."

She shrugs. "Hey, don't change the subject."

I sigh. "I'm going to do what I said I would do... see where things go with Reed and forget that Miles said anything."

At least, that's what I should do.

The problem is, I can't forget. Not even a little bit.

~

Cozy's last four days distract me enough that it's at least not on the forefront of my every thought. Reed, Miles, and I teach her how to fish, show her the best view for sunsets (at the top of the oak tree), get raspberry milkshakes from LaBeau's, and have a *Who can stay on the pineapple floatie the longest* contest.

Cozy and her contests.

It's the hardest goodbye I've ever had with her when it's time for her to leave.

"I can't believe I couldn't convince you to come with me," she whines. "I'm going to miss you." She circles her arms around my neck and clings tighter with every shake of frustration she takes out on my shoulders.

I squeeze her. "Me too, but I'll follow along on all of your adventures."

I open the newly downloaded Instagram app on my iPhone, showing off my first post of the two of us.

Her face lights up and then she seizes the phone from my hand and tags herself in the GIF before handing it back to me.

"See, it'll be like I'm right there with you," I say.

She rolls her eyes. "Do you *know* the time difference between here and London?"

"Well no, but—"

"Seven hours."

"So..."

"So when you get done with classes for the day, I'll be *asleep*," she whines.

"So I'll call before my classes," I volley back.

She wheezes. "When I'm live streaming the Buckingham Palace?!"

"I *can* watch it now." I wink at her.

Her eyebrows rocket up her forehead. "Teddy! That's it! You can more than watch it, you can *join*!"

"Okay, that might be a little—"

She grips me by the shoulders. "Fine. You're new to social media. We'll start small. How about a fall bucket list. We post pictures of all the things we're doing and tag each other in them."

I nod, sending my ponytail in a bounce. "Only if I can draw mine. I refuse to sketch stuffy subjects even if my art professors want me to," I say.

"You know I love a good Teddy original," she whimpers.

My own eyes well with tears. "It's just for a year. It's my way of figuring out what comes next. It might not stick," I convince her.

"Teddy Fletcher, following her parents' advice. Oh, it will stick, all right."

I laugh. She's right. Even when I told Reed and Miles I

planned to attend Idaho State in the fall, they weren't surprised. For a brief moment, I considered gallivanting around the world with my best friend and doing art along the way.

Who doesn't want to see twenty countries in Europe?

It would be the greatest post-senior trip of all time. But I trust my parents' judgement, and it can't hurt taking freshman generals just to see if there's anything else out there that I might want to do with my life. Art is all I've ever known.

I jump back into work at the fly shop when she's gone, making the most of my last summer at my favorite small-town job with my favorite people. Things don't have a shot of being weird with Miles when Shep's always around. I never did tell Reed about my conversations with Miles or Cozy. It feels better to just keep the relationship to ourselves.

Whenever Reed and I are alone, we watch a lot of movies cuddled close and holding hands. We swim and flirt late at night, but it never goes much further than that. I don't know if we're both scared or if it's just not meant to be, but I haven't overanalyzed it. Neither has he. Not until now, anyway.

It's a Friday night and the first week of August. Any other day, we'd be hanging out at his house, but tonight we're sitting on the edge of my dock. My back presses against his chest, one of his arms resting behind him and the other floating on his bent knee. A quilt of shadows dances around us from a looming grey cloud cover. I have to brush my hair out of my face every few seconds, pulling out a spindle woven in the strands from the shedding oak tree in the wind. The lake slaps against the dock in defiance against the current, and flashes of bright yellow light streak through the clouds. From a distance, they look like they're touching the water's surface on the south shore.

"This is nice, isn't it?" Reed says, resting his chin on the crown of my head.

I nuzzle my face against the downy fabric of his shirt. "Yeah, it is."

I love coming out here right before a storm, watching the lake come alive.

"I could do this for the rest of my life."

The way he whispers it, I know he's not talking about sitting on the end of this dock and watching a storm roll in.

"I want to go to school with you in the fall," Reed blurts.

I twist in his arms to see his face. "What?"

"I applied earlier this summer to Idaho State and got in."

He can't be serious.

"But your dream! I thought you wanted to fight fires in the mountains and jump out of planes, not sit at a desk in a bunch of college classes that you could care less about?"

"I want to be near you more," he says, furling me in tighter to his body, but I push from his hold.

"Reed, no. I can't let you make a decision like that. This is your future."

"I know, and it's a future I want you in." he confesses.

I suck in a breath. I was not expecting him to say that. We just started this thing between us. I haven't thought that far ahead, and I don't want to hurt him, but I think he's making a big mistake.

"We *just* started dating. We haven't even kissed! How do you possibly..."

The touch of his hands grazing past my knees stops the rest of that sentence from floating out of my mouth. His hands ghost up my thighs as he leans in closer, his mouth inches from mine. Then he lifts his right hand and brushes his thumb over my bottom lip, studying it as if he needs to make sure this moment is real, that I'm real, before he comes any closer. The pressure of his thumb makes my lips part, and my eyes fall shut with it.

Then I feel his hand sweep behind my neck and his mouth close over mine.

A crack strikes in the distance as his gentle lips stroke over mine. The juxtaposition makes me dizzy.

Rain floods from the sky, drenching the front of his shirt. I grip it with my fist and pull him closer, but the sound of gravel grinding under a shoe stops me. I gasp as we pull apart.

My eyes blink through the droplets of water spilling off my eyelashes before looking behind me. Miles stands there stunned, getting soaked by the rain. A pair of devastated eyes tear my heart in half before he takes off in a sprint.

I can't keep doing this—holding on to one and chasing the other. I need to choose.

Calculating his speed versus my stumpy legs, I know I have no prayer of catching him. But my heart begs me to try.

I choose to run.

Rain pelts from the sky all around us, and the farther into the storm he gets, the more my lungs fight to catch up.

"Miles, wait!" I scream, but the thunder is so loud it washes away the sound before it has a chance to travel through the air.

When he gets to the truck and rips at the handle, I become manic in my attempts to stop him. "Miles, the storm. It's too much. Please don't drive in it!"

His hands shake, but he hops in the driver's seat anyway and fumbles with the key until he gets it in the slot. I make it to the passenger side of the car with enough time to reach for the handle and jump inside before he has the chance to lock me out.

"What are you doing!" he shouts over the marble-sized raindrops beating like a fist into the windshield.

"You can't drive in this! Please, let's go talk."

Miles shakes his head. "Get out of the car, Teddy."

"NO! I'm not letting you go out there alone," I scream.

"Teddy, I'm begging you. Get. Out. Of. The. Car."

"Miles, it was just a kiss—" I start to explain, but he slams on the gas pedal and peels out of the gravel driveway, leaving deep grooved tracks behind in the mud.

The speedometer climbs until he's going ten over the speed limit.

Then fifteen.

Then twenty.

"Miles, please just tell me what's wrong. We can talk about this."

The rain falls in a constant sheet now, the visibility so poor that the white and yellow lines on the road disappear altogether. Miles leans to the left, focusing on the only spot on the windshield clear enough to make out the center line. A car honks when he hugs it, and he swerves to correct. My heart races faster than the truck moves, barreling along in fear.

"Miles, watch out!" I scream as the center line becomes blocked by a mass of grey. He yanks the steering wheel away from the oncoming semi-truck, but it's too fast. Too hard. Not enough time to correct it.

He careens the passenger side into the trunk of a tree.

The side I'm sitting on.

The side that is now a hunk of shrouded metal, trapping me beneath the dashboard and smashing my head through glass.

Then everything goes black.

CHAPTER THIRTY-ONE

I blink a handful of times, digging up my memories with a figurative shovel.

The day I met Miles. The love that I felt for him. The kiss with Reed. But that moment...

"What are you talking about *it was you?*" I study him, unseeing, unable to believe what he's saying.

He's Miles. My best friend. The one who I've loved since the summer I was ten. He would never...

"There was so much rain that night," he says, shaking his head like he's sifting through moments he wishes he didn't remember. "And I—"

"You what?" I press, not even giving him the chance to finish his sentence. I lean toward him, as if closer proximity will help me hear it faster. No one would tell me this part of my past. They've filled in every other gap but this one.

You were in Bear Lake when it happened, they told me. *You hit your head. You were lucky to walk away with your life.*

He swallows and drops his gaze to where his hands clasp around his knees, squeezing them into a vise.

"I saw you with Reed."

Wait, I thought he just said this was his fault? Somehow, it's sounding like mine.

"You kissed him, and I couldn't stand it... the thought of you with anyone but me."

A strangled noise vibrates from his throat. His face pinches in torment, and he starts to shake. Instinct wants me to wrap my arms around him but I... can't.

Confusion swims in my head. "I'm sorry?"

"No, it's me who's sorry! I was so mad at myself for waiting too long back then to tell you how every waking moment I thought of you!"

That should make me feel good, right? To know all those years, he was thinking of me. Instead, it stirs up dread for whatever is about to come next.

"I begged you to get out of the car. I knew it wasn't safe to be driving. But after seeing you with him, I snapped. I just wanted you with me. I wanted to take us as far away from here as possible so we could live free of every distraction that ever stood in our way."

But he didn't. Otherwise, we would be at that place right now. Happy, and with all my memories intact.

Bile rises in my throat.

"But the rain was so thick I couldn't see anything."

He's sobbing now, and I'm not stroking his arms and whispering in hushed tones to soothe his devastation. As much as I'm trying to make sense of this memory, it's not working. The Miles I knew wouldn't do this to someone he loved. He would never be so careless and selfish. Maybe what I remembered is all wrong, and I don't know him at all.

Then it hits—blasts through my brain like the steel doorframe of Miles's 1965 truck did. Fragmented images piece together the scene I've been missing. A shattered window sending shards of glass across my face. A lurch of the truck from slamming on the brakes. The whip of the tires as the wheels locked and the back spun toward the oncoming tree. No airbag deployed. Little chance of...

"When the oncoming semi hugged the median..."

I hold up my hand to stop him, and the anguish settles into the pinched lines that frame his eyes.

He knows I know.

And I don't want to hear any more. I don't *need* to.

He reaches for my hand, but I pull it away before he can make contact.

"Teddy, you have to believe me. I hated myself for what I did to you," he continues. "I made a promise that I would live anywhere but where you were, so you could be safe from me."

"Then why didn't you!" I scream, surprising myself at the volume that comes out of my mouth.

I'm angry at him for coming back. For making me fall...

"I *had* to come back. For my dad. But when I saw you that first day on the rope swing... the tortured look in your eyes? I saw a part of myself I've been fighting to ignore... someone running from their past."

A comment like that stokes my insecurity.

"I'm not running from my past!"

He swallows. "Yeah? Then why have you stopped wanting to remember it?"

I grunt and crush the toe of my tennis shoe into the dirt in frustration.

Who does he think he is, using my own words against me?

"I just said I was leaving. I'm not running from anything. And besides, I don't NEED your approval!" I shout. "I already disappoint enough people in my life."

"You're right. You don't need my approval. If moving away is what you want..."

I want *you*, my heart yearns to yell, but my head fights

against it. Resentment leads my emotional control center, and it would rather point its fire-throwing finger at him than face the inferno inside of me.

"What I want? You know what Miles, you're the coward who doesn't know what he wants." I stomp back toward the trail and away from him.

Blame, blame, blame, my head chants, causing me to whip back around and face him.

"You tell me how much you want to leave this place like your mom did, but then you don't have the actual courage to do it."

Miles sighs and runs a hand through his rumpled hair. "Maybe you're right, Teddy. Maybe you can leave this place and forget all the people in it. But I meant it when I told you I can't. Because whether I was forced to leave last year or not, there isn't anywhere in this world I could go where you wouldn't always be with me."

My tears burn paths down my cheeks. "I..."

I'm desperate to finish that sentence. I was so sure that leaving this place would make everyone happy, including me. But instead, it's starting to feel like a way of punishing myself. I want to punch against his chest and tell him all the reasons why he's wrong. Tell him that the only thing he's actually *right* about is this being all his fault. But I've burned myself to the ground. There's no fight left in me.

When he doesn't chase after me down the trail, I know that's it. I'm leaving and he's staying. There isn't anything left for me here.

Today is my last day in Bear Lake.

CHAPTER THIRTY-TWO

NOW

I wasn't expecting it to hurt when I saw the place I worked all summer for the very last time. I linger in the parking lot, taking in the soft lights that string across the patio. What I would give to go back two weeks ago when my one purpose was to serve the guests that dined beneath them. Before I hurt Reed, and Miles hurt me.

A single car I don't recognize sits in the parking lot next to the closed garage doors.

I hope I'm not too late.

The right thing to do would be to waltz in there and give a formal two weeks' notice. Instead, I'm slinking in after-hours and dumping the news on Mr. Morgan's lap.

When I round the building, a faint glow from the kitchen drifts through the back door that's propped open by a rolling garbage can. The thought of finding Reed through that door and having to tell him Miles didn't choose me has me wanting to run away.

The restaurant takes at least an hour to clean up and close which, whether he's here or not, means I still have enough time to do the right thing.

I push through the back door to an immaculate kitchen, the stainless steel glinting against the fluorescent lighting. The doors to the stock room push open and a mop of curls six inches taller than me bops his shoulders back and forth in a jarring rhythm. He yanks a pair of Beats headphones from his ears and rests them on his neck.

"Wow, Teddy, is that you?"

Ronny Morgan. He hasn't changed all that much from the memories I have of Reed's goofy younger brother.

"Hey, Ron."

He closes in and hugs me, smelling an awful lot like a garbage disposal.

"I heard you were working here this summer. I just didn't think I'd see you after..."

"Oh, yeah," I say, backing away from him and stuffing my hands in my front pockets. I rock back on the heels of my sneakers.

"Are you looking for Reed?" he asks. "Because he's not here."

I sigh in relief. "No. I was looking for your dad."

"Ah." He scrubs the back of his neck beneath his curls in an awkward sort of fashion. "He's not here either. They hopped a plane yesterday. Reed got a mid-season spot on a handcrew."

A smile splits across my face, and Ronny cringes. I'm sure he doesn't love to see me happy at the news that his brother left town after I broke his heart, but I can't help it. Reed's doing it. He's living out his dream just like I always hoped he would.

"You did a good thing by letting him go," Ronny admits.

Tears spring to my eyes but don't tip beyond my lashes. "Yeah," I manage. "It would seem that's my thing. Letting people go."

"I heard you're getting ready to leave soon yourself. Your

parents mentioned it to my mom and me when we got back from boating yesterday."

"They did?"

"Yeah. I can tell they're proud of you."

The tears crest my lash line, tumbling down my cheeks. If I were around anyone else, I'd be more embarrassed. But Ronny has a tender-hearted aura about him that makes me feel comfortable to let my emotions surface.

I swallow. "That's why I'm here. I'm sorry I'm not giving more notice, but I was wondering if you could inform your dad that I'm leaving sooner than I thought. Tomorrow."

"I'm sorry, I didn't mean to upset you. But no problem. I can cover your shifts until I leave for school in the fall. I think it's awesome by the way... you heading off on your own. I just got back from backpacking across Europe after senior year."

On your own, I think to myself.

"Sounds like a dream," I squeak.

If it's such a dream, then why does it feel like my lungs are caving in?

"Yeah, there's nothing better than seeing the world," he muses, staring off into the distance.

I dry my eyes with my shirtsleeve. "I guess I'll find out."

"Well, it was good seeing you again, Teddy. I never blamed my brother for falling in love with you." He blushes.

I lean in and kiss him on the cheek. "Thanks, Ron. Take care."

He waves and slides his headphones back in place, then dances down the hall and into the dining room with a mop as his tango partner.

One goodbye down, one more to go.

Through the cabin window, I see my parents sprawled out on the living room floor in front of the fire, playing a round of Uno. My mom bounces on her knees with glee as she places a wild draw-four on top of the pile. My dad groans, adding at least twenty cards to his hand. No matter how much of it is a game of chance, the odds have always been stacked in her favor.

The sight of the two of them doing something I've seen them do my entire childhood brings a fresh round of tears welling in my eyes. I push open the door after a long day and put a smile on, even though I'm not feeling very happy on the inside. I thought I was done doing that, pretending with them, but one more time won't hurt.

In his haste to avoid the game, my dad whips around first. "Hey, Teddy Bear! How'd your day go?"

I roll back my shoulders. "It was a big one. I just quit my job."

They both drop their hand of cards.

"Oh. Wow. That must mean…"

I nod. "Yep. It's time."

They fight half-hearted smiles.

"I promise I'll call every day and I'll buy healthy food and I'll remember to exercise each morning and I'll be safe. I'll be back before you know it. I won't stay away forever," I say. It sounds like I'm trying to convince myself more than them, but they start nodding in the most understanding way, and I rush toward them.

They wrap me in their arms.

"We love you so much, Theadora. You can come back anytime you want. We'll always be here for you," my mom says.

There's no brush tunneling through my hair this time, but she's running her hands up and down my back, and it's just as soothing as it was that night before I left home for my first day of kindergarten.

"And you can take my *I Arted* shirt with you to remember me by," my dad blubbers into my hair.

I start to giggle, and my mom swats his arm. "Arch, she doesn't want that disgusting shirt."

"Then she can take one of your hats. One of us should part with a prized possession for our one and only daughter."

My mom pulls away from our hug and rolls her eyes at him.

I squeeze them even tighter. "I'm going to miss you guys so much."

"Oh, baby, we're going to miss you too," she says. Then she pulls back with a start again. "But what about Miles?"

My shoulders sink, and I want to tell them *Miles didn't choose me. We just weren't meant to be*. But I can't say it out loud and make it true, so I say, "Miles decided he needs to be here for his dad."

My mom tilts her head to the side, analyzing the feelings swirling across my features like a kaleidoscope. I know she won't tell me *I told you so*, even if I deserve it.

"I'm sorry, sweetheart."

I start to cry. "Why didn't you guys just tell me about him?" *And Reed and Cozy and what happened that night of the accident*, I think too.

"Because Dr. Spalding..." my mom starts to say but stops herself.

She looks at my dad and grabs on to his hand for support.

"Because we were scared. Miles got a misdemeanor for what he did, and while he served his time, it didn't change the fact that he almost took you from us. But we should have told you," she says.

"So, tell me *now*. Everything that happened after the accident, and please don't leave anything out."

They both nod and start from the beginning. I learn that Miles left Bear Lake and moved to Montpelier to stay with his grandfather—a decision he made of his own accord. He waited for his court hearing where he plead guilty to reckless driving and was sentenced to ninety days in the Bear Lake County Jail in Paris. When he was released, he worked to pay off his five hundred–dollar fine at a Maverick a half-mile from home where he could walk to his job. His license was suspended for six months.

Even in my parents' version of events, Miles really didn't plan to come back to Bear Lake until he found out his dad would be left to work the store alone for the summer. It's why, even they, were surprised to see him.

"I hope you'll understand that it's hard enough letting go of your only child after they're all grown up, but even more difficult trusting the person they give their heart to next. We were scared of losing you."

I can't pretend to know their same fear, but I do understand. I saw what it was like when they thought I was gone. The peace I see in them now is such a stark contrast that I believe them, and I forgive them. I can't pinpoint when it happened exactly, but we reached a place where we can finally be honest with each other again. I just wish it hadn't taken until the night before I leave town to get here.

"I know it may not mean much now," my dad cuts in, "but we've forgiven Miles. I'd like to believe that even if our worst fears had come true and we lost you that day, that we'd still get to this place. The accident doesn't define his character, Teddy. He's a good person. Just someone who made a terrible mistake."

I'm hearing, *listening* to everything that they're saying, but their words are sifting through this filter in my head that's hanging on to all the reminders of why I should protect myself from Miles. I'm still at war over the fact that his *mistake* took nearly every one of my memories for *months*. That as I've gotten to know him all over again, he hid this monumental moment from me knowing it would change things between us.

As if they can hear my thoughts, my parents look at me with sympathy.

"I hope one day you can forgive him too, sweetheart. Because you've never looked at anyone the way you look at Miles."

My mom gives me a weak smile, and I start to cry. I cry for the sad, lonely girl inside of me who mourns what could have been had I known. Maybe I'd feel the same level of peace they feel now. Maybe it wouldn't change anything at all. But at least I'd be leaving tomorrow having had months to reach a place of closure.

It's past ten o'clock when we start packing. We spend three hours combining all my belongs into a couple of suitcases. My mom fixes me a sandwich for the road, and my dad adds a few tools to my luggage "in case they come in handy."

I fight sleep as muddled thoughts of my argument with Miles compete inside my head. *You're running*, I hear him say. I can't quiet them no matter how hard I fight, so I stop trying altogether. Instead, I reach for the old sketchbook in my vanity drawer with the intent to flip through the pages one last time. Try to make peace with what I'm leaving behind. I'm only a couple pages in when a core memory surfaces.

I'm ten years old in the backseat of our family hatchback, sulking over the fact that I had to leave behind my best friend for the summer. Even back then, I always drew what I was feeling, and this particular sketch is no different. It's a game of capture the flag. There's only one other person in the drawing besides me, and I'm desperately running to capture her hand but it's too far away. She was always the one person I'd confide in the most when things got rocky. Like they are right...

I reach for my phone. With unsteady fingers, I open my contacts and touch her name. It rings just once before a trembling breath vibrates through the static on the other end.

"Cozy?" I ask.

Will I recognize the sound of her voice? Am I doing the right thing? Will she be happy to hear from me?

"You remembered me," she whispers.

My eyes mist from the warm tone. It's the same one that used to accompany a smile whenever she looked at me.

"How could I not," I say through the emotion that's making my voice tremble.

"Are you okay?" she asks, and I find myself shaking my head. She can't see it, but somehow, like a best friend would, she just knows.

"Tell me everything," she says, and by the time I get to the part that I'm living now, I'm bawling in the fetal position.

"It's okay," she hushes.

"I don't know how to forgive him for what he did," I tell her.

She huffs out a laugh. "Well, Miles has made a lot of dumbass moves over the years."

I choke on my laugh.

I *missed* having a best friend. To talk to. To listen.

"But there is one thing he's always gotten right."

I swallow. "What's that?"

"That guy has never stopped loving you."

I smile for the first time in twenty-four hours. It's something I didn't know I needed to hear until she said it out loud. Even when Miles crashed that truck that changed my world, it was a mistake he made in a moment where his love for me was all-consuming. A mistake that deserves to be forgiven.

Cozy and I talk for hours after that. Mostly about her European travels. She fills me in on all the things that her Instagram account missed—which wasn't all that much—but I find out the campaign has been such a success that they've extended her contract an additional ten countries. She asks about the last nine months for me, and for the first time, I get to tell someone a true and honest version of it. One where I'm not pretending that the past doesn't matter to me.

I watch the sun rise from the end of the dock the next morning, my packed bags beside me. It's the worst day to be traveling with how little sleep I got.

"Hey there, kid. Taking off somewhere?" Shep says, sitting down beside me. He dunks his usual wader-covered legs into the water.

"Trying to stop me?" I ask on a sigh.

I can't take anyone trying to stop me anymore.

"Nah, you won't see me asking you to stay. I already made that mistake with one woman in my life. I'm just here to keep my son from making the same one as me."

"That's not your job. He made his choice."

"Yeah, you're right. He did. I watched him make it a long time ago on this very dock. He just needs a little help seeing it too. You know, some people jump all on their own, while others need a gentle push. Miles thinks he fights for what he wants, but he does it from ten feet in the air without ever leaping."

"That's very philosophical of you, but it doesn't matter anymore. I'm leaving town today. Right now, actually," I say.

"Uh-huh." His eyes flick from where I remain planted on the dock to my waiting suitcases.

"No, I am," I insist. "Just taking a minute to say my goodbyes."

"Yeah, no, I see that," he comments. His stare is still trained on my packed bags that I've ignored for the last hour. Who knows how long he's been watching me for.

"I'm going," I huff, forcing myself to stand, when he grabs my hand.

"I think it speaks volumes that you're still here," he says, and I stiffen.

I've been planning to leave all summer but... I don't *want* to leave. At least I don't without...

"Shep, I gotta go!"

I lean down and kiss his cheek before abandoning my luggage on the dock. I've said my goodbyes to everyone but one person. The one I've said *enough* goodbyes to in one lifetime. The one I never want to say goodbye to again.

I'm done running.

I zip through town and wind my way up the canyon to get to Bloomington Lake in a race against the rising sun.

I can't miss him, I can't.

My eyes scan the brush for any sign of him running back down the canyon, and my heart gallops in my chest the closer I make it to the parking lot without spotting him. I kick up a cloud of dust beneath my tires as I skid into the nearest parking spot and take off up the trail. I get to the top of the first slope and bend in half, panting to catch my breath.

I shouldn't have abandoned that elliptical machine this summer. I take three deep breaths with my hands planted on my bent knees when two feet skid to a stop.

"Teddy?"

"Miles," I pant, grabbing his hand. "No time." I gasp for another breath. "Run"—*gasp*—"with me."

"Teddy, what's going on? Are you all right? You look like you're about to pass out."

He's shirtless, of course, and has sweat running down his midsection, but breathes in an even rhythm.

"Okay, mister hotshot. Carry me then!" I demand, clambering up his back.

He lifts me by the undersides of my thighs.

"That way! Hurry!" I boss him, and he starts jogging with me on his back up the trail. He ambles across the rickety log and propels us forward until we're standing in front of the jute rope that dangles in the very spot our summer began.

His eyebrows meet his hairline as I rip off my clothes, each layer feeling like the shedding of a chrysalis. I'm thankful I've gotten in the habit of putting on a bathing suit every time I leave the house, even when I planned to leave today. My eyes flit to the horizon, and I rush to say everything I need to get out before the sun crests.

"Miles, you were right. I was running. I thought that's what I needed to feel like myself again, for me to be happy. But then I spent this summer with you, and while you held me at arm's length because you were afraid of hurting me, what you were really doing was allowing me the space I needed to find myself again. You never once expected me to remember anything, and I got to fall in love with you as this messy version of myself. I know you're afraid to leave here and for what that might mean for your dad. I am too."

The words I need him to hear are spilling out of me, and even if they don't change a thing, I can't stop them.

"I may not have a lot figured out yet, but I do know I'm someone who feels the most *me* when I'm with you. Someone who believes that the trials of your past only serve to shape the stronger version of the you *now*. It's why, for me, there is nothing to forgive about the accident. It forced me to grow. In your quiet, steady way, you taught me to be patient for the things I want. And I know now that all I want is *you*. I can't leave here without you. I don't know what comes next for us, but I think there's beauty in that, you know? We get to write whatever we want. All it takes is a leap of faith... a jump from a rope swing ten feet in the air."

I hold out my hand. "Jump with me?"

My heart threatens to stop in the seconds he stalls, but then he laces his fingers together and holds them out like a step stool for me to climb onto. I use his hands to leverage me part of the way up the rope. With each additional pull, I feel myself wiggle free of everything I was. I let go of what I thought I had to be, until I'm at the very top, staring out over a glassy mirror that shows exactly who I am. A girl who feels more like herself plunging into an icy crater with the boy she loves than she ever would be surrounded by strangers in a state across the country.

Miles climbs the rope behind me until his body surrounds mine. I know as soon as our feet touch that water, it will crack it wide open, and we'll emerge two new people with a whole world to see. One that can change us for the better if we let it.

And with that thought, we jump.

EPILOGUE

"I've given this a lot of thought..." Miles starts to say as he strokes his hand up and down my bare arm.

I hold my breath, wondering what to expect, as I reflect on all the time we've shared together.

It's been nine months since Shepard gifted the truck and trailer to Miles and me. He moved back to Montpelier where he and his dad could watch over each other. I think he knew that it was the only decision that would make Miles feel comfortable leaving with me.

At the end of the summer, we pulled the trailer out of Bear Lake and hit the road to see the States. We started on the Pacific coast, making our way from Port Angeles, Washington through Long Beach, Oregon, and along the coast of California. *It turns out, you don't need to go clear across the country to feel like you're starting over.*

I had to buy a brand-new sketchbook by the time we reached San Diego. I've learned that even the detailed strokes of a pencil aren't enough to capture the magnitude of beauty there is to see in the world. Only memories can do that.

I send my parents weekly texts with pictures—a modern-day

postcard—so they know I'm okay. That, and we promised to come home for the summer. They sold our home in Boise and reside full time at the cabin now. It feels more like home for me too, anyway.

"Kiss, marry, kill," Miles continues, interrupting my thoughts. A wicked grin creeps across his face. "Ryan Reynolds, Brad Pitt, Ryan Gosling."

I laugh. I can't believe this is the guy who once thought that game was absurd.

I wrap my leg even tighter around his, burrowing into the crook of his arm. "Hmmm, now that's a hard one. I'm going to say... kiss Ryan Gosling, marry Ryan Reynolds, and kill Brad Pitt."

The stroke of his hand comes to an abrupt stop. "You would *kill* Brad Pitt?!" he shouts, a look of horror tattooed on his face. But when I pull away, I see that he's stifling a grin.

"Okay. I see what you're doing. You're just making it a big deal because I did."

"No, no. What girl would *kill* Brad Pitt? He's Brad Pitt! The single biggest sex icon there ever was!"

"Miles." I nudge him.

He pulls me in closer and whispers, "Kiss me," as his lips close over mine. They feather over my skin in the intimate way that I've come to know as my home. As he kisses me, he traces circles on my ring finger, sliding something onto the end.

"Marry me," he whispers next, and my eyes drop to my hand.

I gasp at the sight of a dainty gold band wrapping the base of my finger, the petals of a wildflower etched in the center of it. It's simple, but the most beautiful thing I've ever seen. Tears well in my eyes as they flit from Miles to the ring and back to Miles again.

"You're *killing* me," he groans, dipping his head into my shoulder to hide his face. "Don't make me Brad Pitt."

I giggle, gripping the sides of his face to get him to look at me. "Yes!"

His eyes widen. "You will?"

"Of course I will," I say, kissing him senseless. Then I gape in wonder again at the shiny gold band. It's hard not to stare at it.

He rests his head on my shoulder. "Do you like it?"

I nod, having trouble coming up with the words to express just how much. I wasn't one of those girls who dreamed up what she wanted her future ring to look like. He could have given me a plastic ring with a gaudy red gem superglued to the top of it from a twenty-five-cent machine at the mall and I still would have loved it. But this...

"It was your mom's," he says, brushing his fingers over the wildflower and then down my knuckles.

"What?" I gasp, lifting my eyes to his.

"She said your dad gave it to her the day you were born." He looks down at the spot where it's engraved, and laces our fingers together. "She was sad when she no longer got to carry you inside her."

A giggle-hiccup escapes my lips. That sounds like my mom.

"So, he snuck down to the gift shop while you both were asleep and bought her this ring," he continues, spinning it on my finger. "He told her that as long as she wore it, she'd always have a part of you with her."

You're a wildflower in a field of daisies, Teddy Fletcher. You stand out all on your own.

I clutch the ring to my chest, feeling close to her.

My eyebrows furrow. "But I never saw her wear it."

He chuckles. "It was too small."

"After all that, she couldn't even wear it?"

"She carried it with her in the pocket of her apron instead. She gave it to me the day we left Bear Lake," he says.

My chest shudders with emotion. *That's why she never took it off.*

His eyes fill with tears too.

"I think it meant she forgave me."

I lunge at him, wrapping my arms around his neck. "It means she loves you."

We stay that way for a long time, holding each other close. When he pulls back, he says, "That's my favorite game."

Looking down at my hand once more, I say, "I don't know that we'll ever top it."

Miles lifts my tank top, tracing a circle on my ribs. As difficult as it is to focus with him doing that, I know it's the moment I've been waiting for.

"Wait here."

I shoot out of bed for the tiny, stacked storage compartments next to the stove. The top one is our mini pantry, just large enough to hold the college dropout staples—a few soup cans and some top ramen. The bottom houses shoes and a small duffle bag of belongings I couldn't part with the day we left. I haven't had the need to pull it out until now.

Sliding back the zipper on the canvas tote, I dig to the bottom for the hardbound sketchbook. I cradle it under my arm and shove the duffle bag back in with the shoes.

Miles stretches out on the bed, tucking one arm behind his head so he can see me past his feet. "What are you doing?"

"I have something for you," I say, feeling more exposed now than the night he dropped my dress to the floor for the first time.

He props himself up in bed as I lay the book in his lap.

"What's this?" he asks, his eyes dancing in that way they do sometimes when he hopes what he thinks is about to come true does.

"Just open it," I say.

He cocks an eyebrow and folds back the cover. Then he grips the edges of the pages in his right hand and starts fanning them like butterfly wings.

One thing remains true on every page... the sketch of a girl, her pouty lips and rounded chin, the edges of her bob framing her face, her delicate fingers holding open a heart-shaped locket on her chest.

The only thing that changes is what's inside the locket... an open palm, a sunrise at Bloomington Lake, a truck taking the long way home, a second first kiss in a hot spring, a sleepover in a bunkhouse... every memory we've shared post-accident that led us to right now.

I grip his hands between mine. "Miles, if I never remembered anything at all, it still wouldn't change that you're the one for me."

With that heartwarming, crooked smile of his that I've grown to cherish, Miles picks up the book to press it against his chest, and an envelope drops into his lap. It's addressed to the both of us in handwriting I've only seen one other time scrawled across a Bear Shore napkin.

Miles slides his pointer finger through the opening at the top, ripping it in two. He pulls out a torn-out piece of notebook paper. In a shaky hand, he holds the letter out in front of us as I read it aloud.

Dear Miles and Teddy,

I hope when the two of you find this one day, you're stupid happy. The kind that makes getting out of bed in the morning the best part of your day, knowing you get to spend it with your favorite person.

For as many summers as I can remember, you both were that for me. I gave this letter to your parents, Teddy, and told them to tuck it someplace meaningful, so that when you found it, it would feel more like coming home than saying goodbye.

The truth is, as much as I joked that Miles wasn't any good at them, I've never been great at goodbyes either. The thought of never seeing either one of you again hurts too much. It was easier just to pack my bags early and move forward with what comes next.

I hope you are off on wild adventures together. You deserve it. But if you happen to decide a lakeside town is more your speed... maybe years from now, we'll find ourselves with families of our own, sharing cabin properties next door, our kids the best of friends... because we'll always have Bear Lake.

See them both happy, check.

-Reed

By the time I reach the end of the letter, Miles and I are both weeping. I reach over to the foldout nightstand behind me, snagging two Kleenexes from the box on top of it.

"You're a mess, Miles Bishop," I say, handing him one of the tissues.

"I'm a mess?! I think you dribbled on the paper," he says, holding up the note to show speckled dots splattered across the words.

We both laugh, and then we hug. We say goodbye to our friend long after he's already gone.

"I'm stupid happy," Miles says first.

"The happiest," I agree.

"You think maybe after our wild adventures, we might settle back there one day, like he said?" he asks.

This is the first mention of what Miles wants his future to look like, and somewhere deep inside my heart, I hoped we'd always call that place home.

"You want to?" I ask.

He nods. "Because we'll always have Bear Lake."

The End

ALSO BY MEAGAN WILLIAMSON

Reed's story – coming soon!

ACKNOWLEDGMENTS

When I set out to write this book, I had no idea the village it would take to bring my words into a tangible thing I could hold in the palms of my hands.

The truth is, asking for help has never been my strong suit. Writing this book may have been an endeavor done in the solitary confinement of my bedroom, but turning it into something more than just words on a page is a feat that had a lot of people supporting it, and I couldn't be more grateful for the team I learned to lean on to bring this dream to life.

Britt, this book would not be where it is today without your detailed and thoughtful edits. The way you encouraged me to dig deep into some of the elements of the story made it the best version that it could be.

Nysha, your talent is unmatched. When I came to you with my vision for the cover, you worked your magic and made it into a summer dream.

Alli, our shared love for the book world has always been one of my favorite parts about our friendship. There wasn't a doubt in my mind that you were meant to beta read, and your feedback was just another confirmation that you were the perfect choice. Thank you so much! I adore you!

Mickenzie, I don't know what I did to deserve a friend like you who loves and supports me no matter what, but I'm sure grateful we found each other.

Mom, you taught me that you can be an amazing mother

and have a flourishing career at the same time. Your example in my life has always been something I've admired and cherished.

Dad and Edie, thank you for supporting this dream from the moment I told you about it and for stepping up with my littlest while I edited in the library.

To my in-laws—thank you for raising the kind of man women like me write love stories about... and for sharing Bear Lake.

To my children who've had to sacrifice a part of me and our time together while I wrote this—I hope I can share with you the value of hard work and devotion to something that sets your soul on fire. When you find that thing in your own lives, you better believe I'll be the one cheering you on every step of the way.

Nic, there aren't enough words in the English language to describe what you mean to me. A dream was born that day six years ago when you worked overtime to surprise me with an Apple laptop. You said, at the time, that I'd do amazing things with it one day, and I think I was always meant to do this. You've believed in every creative venture I've ever pursued and championed this dream in more ways than I can count. I love you!

To the readers who have taken a chance on my story... I can't thank you enough. I hope you can escape into the small town of Bear Lake with Teddy, Miles, and Reed and find heart in the young love they share.

ABOUT THE AUTHOR

Photo by Ali Johnson Photography

MEAGAN WILLIAMSON lives in Meridian, Idaho with her husband and three children. After the birth of her last baby, she spent nap times writing and dreaming of sharing the kind of love stories that stay with you long after the last page. She loves spending time outside, celebrating holidays, and country music turned way up. *If I Never Remember* is her debut novel.

Please Visit:
authormeaganwilliamonson.com

Made in the USA
Middletown, DE
11 August 2024

58517799R00187